Stress Test

Alan Gold

Fifth Leg Publishing
www.fifthleg.com

For Sally

Chapter 1

The Safety Belt

The state killed Uncle Roscoe.

Cousin Johnny laid it out plain and simple for Saury.

A palm slapped the tabletop, but the fly escaped into the kitchen with Sandy.

"State killed my daddy dead," Johnny said, with the candor of a child who knows the truth about the Easter Bunny.

Not that it was any big revelation. The whole family knew the story behind Roscoe's execution. Sandy never doubted that the tradition would be passed on to Saury one day. But the kid was only five—too young to remember Roscoe. Way too young to come to grips with this.

A steak knife slipped out of Sandy's hand and hid in the suds like a shy, poisonous fish.

If only Roscoe had been a serial killer, or a monster who forced drugs down pre-schoolers' throats, or a shameless, thieving television evangelist, he might be alive today.

Unfortunately, he was none of those things. Roscoe provided for his family. He budgeted for charity. He loved Oscar, the dimwitted, one-eyed beagle that never even learned to fetch the paper. He only cheated at solitaire once in his life— just to see what it felt like. Fact is, Roscoe was probably the pinnacle Skinner, the very best the bloodline had to offer. He was a world better than the one Sandy wound up with, Stephen X Skinner.

And so, according to the legend, the state went and killed him off early.

As she felt for the knife in the murky water, Sandy thought how much better her own life would have been if Stephen X, not Roscoe, had been the state's victim.

Sandy lifted her hand from the water and rubbed the back

of her wrist against a sudden itch in her left eyebrow. Something like that would have really messed her make-up in the old days. She wore only a trace anymore, ever since she figured the make-up was one thing that attracted Stephen X to her. Long after it mattered, she realized that her mother had been right. The bright paint and soft powders made her look like a tramp. Not that her mother had really given a shit—when Sandy wore too little make up, it emphasized her pasty complexion; when she put on a conservative dress, she looked frumpy; a halter top turned her into a whore. She stuffed herself; she pecked at her food; she slouched and mumbled and her room was a mess.

She was perfect for Stephen X.

Johnny and Saury raised their voices in a wordless song and circled a pile of toys in the living room.

"Don't be so loud, Saury," she shouted. After a moment she realized that Linda was out back with the men, so she added, "You, too, Johnny. I can't think for all the noise."

Not that she really wanted to think where her mind took her. She remembered how they learned that Roscoe was dead. Stephen X had been with him not more than an hour and a half earlier. They'd been to a parts shop looking for some gadget or potion that would make Sandy's car stop burning oil, without the expense of a ring job. Stephen X always had an eye out for a shortcut.

She knew that Roscoe hated him as much as she did, but they were brothers so he had to put up with him. Roscoe knew a little about cars, so Stephen X could talk like he knew something, too. Roscoe also knew a little about people, but Stephen X could never pull off that sham.

Their mother had died before Stephen X could stagger more than three or four paces without falling. It was probably merciful that the woman never knew what she had inflicted on the world. Sandy pictured Mother Skinner struggling to rise a few inches from her deathbed, forcing Roscoe to take some regrettable oath about looking out for his kid brother.

Stephen X had only had time to down two tall boys before the phone rang. "Who the hell is that?" he muttered as he swung the fridge door shut and walked to the phone.

"I don't know," Sandy said, embarrassed at first that she couldn't answer the question, and then embarrassed because she had believed it was a question.

Stephen X cleared his throat the way he always did when the real world closed in, with two short hacks followed by a longer, harsher one. "Skinners," he said into the phone, and then he was silent for a long time.

Sandy was folding clothes with her back to the phone when she realized that Stephen X wasn't saying anything. She turned, thinking—she didn't know what—maybe he had disappeared, leaving behind a tidy heap of ashes, with the phone swinging like a pendulum at the end of its cord. Instead she saw that he had been staring at the back of her head. And now he stared at the front of her head. Or right through it. It didn't matter. She never connected with him anyway.

At last Stephen X grunted and hung up the phone. He cleared his throat again, with the same three-beat cough, and said, "Roscoe's dead."

Sandy flinched. Her hands flew to her face, smudging her peach-dust foundation. She wanted to say that she didn't do anything, that she didn't even know about it until just this minute. She had no idea what her husband would do next. Stephen X had never had a brother die on him before, and he never adapted gracefully to new situations.

Of course, that was before they knew that the state killed him. Linda was still unconscious. Days would pass before she could tell anybody what happened.

"I was just with him," Stephen X said, looking back to the phone, "and now he's dead.

"The phone stinks, Sandy," he went on after a moment. "What the hell did you do to it?"

3

She panicked. She wanted to give him the right answer, but she had never been with Stephen X Skinner when a brother died and she didn't know what to say. Her mind raced. "I was chopping onions this afternoon when the photo studio called. I must have forgotten to wash my hand before I picked up the phone."

"What did they want?"

"Who?"

"The photo studio."

"What do you mean?"

"Wake up! You just said the photo studio called."

"Baby pictures. They wanted to do a portrait of Saury."

"How'd they know we have a baby?"

She stared at him a moment, fear widening her eyes against their mascara rims. "The newspaper! They must have seen the birth announcement in the paper."

"Which paper?"

"I don't know."

"Didn't they tell you?"

"No. I don't even know if it was the paper."

"You just said it was."

"Maybe they call everyone."

"Which is it? You can't have it both ways. You can't change things just to suit yourself all the time. Which is it?"

"I don't know."

"We can't afford pictures. The goddamn kid costs too much already without paying someone to take pictures of it."

"That's what I told them."

"What's wrong with my camera? I can take pictures, too, you know."

"That's what I told them."

"Then what did they want?"

"I don't know. I don't know. Do you want me to call them back?"

"Don't play games with me."

Sandy could put up with that. She felt relieved that he'd forgotten to blame her for Roscoe's death. Stephen X treated it like some terrible, nameless injustice that had been visited upon him. By the time he got around to assigning blame, the story came out and she was safe.

It seemed incredible that a bureaucracy whose governor confused the names of every town beginning with the letter "S," whose lawmakers made headlines more often for indiscretion than legislation, and whose top lobbyists changed allegiance on the whim of a dollar, could have plotted the intricate death of Roscoe Skinner.

The mandatory seat belt law did it.

Roscoe was a sensible man. His only apparent genetic link to Stephen X was a stubborn bent. Even then, principle guided him more than pride.

"I know that seat belts are a good thing, that they save lives," he told Sandy. "I've been wearing one since I was sixteen.

"But by telling me I have to wear one, they've stolen my virtue," he went on, adjusting his rimless glasses. "Something I did because it was right and made sense I now *have* to do out of fear of being punished. People should have the chance to make the right decisions. They shouldn't be bullied into avoiding bad decisions. I feel like I've been raped."

"You don't have the faintest idea what you're talking about," Sandy snapped, feeling angry at Roscoe for the first time in her life. It soon passed and she never felt that way again.

To spite the authorities, Roscoe began leaving his seat belt unlatched. He continued to drive safely and without incident. One night, a burnt-out tail light on his Cutlass Supreme attracted a motorcycle cop. He got off with a warning for the light, but had to pay a small fine for not having his belt on.

Six weeks later, with the city facing a budget crisis, the mayor placed the police force on full revenue-enhancement alert. No violation was too small for their attention. The courts clogged up, but the money rolled in. Roscoe got pulled over and fined again.

Not ten days after that, Roscoe received his third ticket.

It was the next day that Roscoe dropped off Stephen X after their trip to the parts store, and picked up Linda. They pulled into Thrift Aisles for groceries on their way home. Linda said Roscoe was just turning onto Westmore Avenue and gunning the Cutlass to merge with the swift, merciless traffic when he saw the squad car waiting for the light to change.

Pragmatic to the end, Roscoe drew a sharp breath and fumbled for the seat belt under his butt. As he rose from the vinyl, his foot came down hard on the accelerator. With one hand on the wheel, he lost his tracking and sent the car scuttering crablike into the line of oncoming traffic.

They had to cut him out with a torch.

Now the kids shrieked again in the living room just as Sandy's finger found the sharp end of the knife. She gasped and pulled her hand from the greasy water. As she moved closer to the light and studied the slash in her puckered flesh, she wondered why there was no blood.

And she wondered how she would explain that to Stephen X.

Chapter 2

The Spool

Billey Elwood leaned against the black post of the railroad trestle and panted without taking in any air. Sweat collected like dew drops on the patchy, fine stubble that covered his jaw. He peered into the darkness up and down the creek and wondered where Uly had gone.

His right hand still tingled, as if he'd slept on his arm, cutting off the blood. It didn't hurt, but the feeling made him want to cry. He thought he'd worked the crying out of his system when he was a kid.

Billey had grown up with the notion that his mother was a horse.

He'd never actually met the woman, so for all he knew, the taunts he'd heard as he knelt in the playground sand were the gospel truth. It would explain a lot of things: the shallow slope of his forehead beneath the coarse tangle of hair; the bulging, whiteless eyes; the twisted stubs of teeth that lined his jaw like so many tumbling dominoes. It would explain the strength beyond his years that clogged his muscles, his atrocious table manners, his father's pride in being a horse's ass.

It would leave open the question of why his hearing was so bad.

"Yer mother's a whore," the kids cried. That was years before Billey knew what a whore was, so in his mind she became a horse. It wasn't a matter of not paying attention, or not wanting to understand. Billey made up in curiosity what he lacked in brilliance. He was dying to find out how he fell into this world without a human mother.

From what he could make of other kids' lives, his situation was unique. Boy and girl, straight hair and curly, they filled nooks in a private matriarchy that took pains to hide its soft secrets from him.

One day, just a week before Tommy Lagocki's mother barred Billey forever from their home, Billey stood mesmerized as she created their lunch. He was barely conscious of faces in those days—looking at them put a crick in his neck and he didn't know how to interpret what he saw anyway. Most of his lessons in life had been taught by hands, so that was the part of Mrs. Lagocki that his eyes homed in on.

The nails' deep red polish contrasted with the luminous smoothness of her skin. The hands moved quickly and deliberately—separating bread, carving cheese, breaking a head of lettuce—in patterns that mystified Billey. They assembled the first sandwich, and pressed it down with fingers that looked even softer, whiter than the bread itself.

The hands danced like puppets before him as they picked up the gleaming knife, trimmed the crust in four neat, efficient strokes, then rotated the plate to cut a diagonal through the sandwich.

"Let me!" Billey cried, lunging for the knife as it made its first slice in the second sandwich. "Let me! Let me! Let me!"

Billey didn't know how long everything remained motionless around him. Finally, he raised his eyes to see Mrs. Lagocki looking back at him with eyes just as wide as his.

So Tommy ate alone and Billey was left to wonder about these women in the other kids' lives. Somehow, they never grew coarse whiskers or had dirt under their nails or vowed to beat the tar out of anyone. Where did they come from? Where did they go? What did they do when Billey wasn't there?

"Where's my mama?" Billey asked one day while his father grunted against the weight of an enormous cable spool that he'd lashed to the bed of the truck.

To a boy like Billey, his father cut an awesome figure. He could pass a cigarette from one leathery corner of his mouth to the other without ever interrupting the stream of profanity.

He wore sweat and oil stains on his plaid shirt like smelly badges of manhood. He rolled back sleeves that were too short to hide the snakes that twined his forearms. His pants were baggy and buttless and they sagged over his boots like an accordion duet. He was a man who answered life with a slouch and a scowl, who saw no use in answering a shit-brained kid.

"Quit yer whining and fetch me them wire cutters."

Billey knew better than to open his mouth again before he brought the tool.

Elwood set to work with the cutters, grunting and mumbling as his elbows moved up and down.

"Yer mama was a five-buck horse," the man said, making mud from the dirt of his sleeve and the sweat of his brow.

Billey's heart skipped a beat—he'd heard the truth.

"She smelled like wet plaster," Elwood grunted. "Looked like it, too. Had a voice like a crowbar workin' a rusty nail. Had a scar as long as your arm across her belly. And she had you."

Billey watched his father try to snip through the last wire, which was a heavier gauge than the others. Elwood swore. He chucked the cutters in the dirt and wedged himself between the spool and the back of the cab, pushing with both legs.

"Unh, unh . . . you . . . *Mothah!*" he cried until the line snapped.

Billey barely realized that he was about to be crushed, that his daddy's great, wooden wheel was about to squeeze his guts through his nose, like a grape pinched out of its skin.

The spool, as big as a hundred Billeys, slammed down the tailgate, thudded into the dust with a giant's footfall, and sped across the dusty stretch of gravel and dog-licked tin cans that made up their front yard.

Some reflex—even faster and more basic than fear—sent Billey scrambling to an inch's safety. The spool crushed

Billey's plastic eighteen-wheeler before hitting the dead catalpa. It rolled eight feet up the tree trunk, and then barreled back down toward Billey.

Too dazed to move, Billey watched the terrible spool race over him, blotting out the sun as he survived, unscathed, between its two rims. All he felt was the catch in his breath as the thing bounced over an old tractor wheel, shattered the screen door and wobbled like a coin losing its spin on the front porch.

"I got ya, ya *Mothah!*" old man Elwood cried as he leaped from the back of the truck. He ran to the spool, squatted and did a duckwalk around it, muttering obscenities through his cigarette. He stood and kicked the wood, shouting *"Mothah! I got ya!"*

Then he turned to the kid and spat. "What you lookin' at?"

Billey wondered the same thing.

Chapter 3

The Plate

Maybe some kind of ancient, magic writing hid in the serving platter's blue willow pattern. Something gave it the power to defy gravity. Once the soapy plate slipped from Sandy's fingertips, it hung in the air while her hands hovered around it like a pair of nervous hummingbirds.

Sometimes things moved this slowly in the nightmares, where Sandy studied the horrible, majestic path of a bullet as it parted a curtain of flesh and gristle. The things you dreaded seemed never to end. The good things flew by so quickly. Time stood over Sandy like some bearded, teasing god, even as her panic sent her diving for the plate. Her frantic movements became caught up in the object's suffocating slowness, like a butterfly in a fold of gauze.

Sandy never dwelled on the unfair things that erupted in her life. There were so many, she couldn't have found the time if she wanted.

At the most tender age, she knew she would marry Bob Strunk. One afternoon in the sixth grade, the boys got to stay in the classroom to talk about baseball. The girls were herded off to the gym where they learned about feminine things. Then they were sworn to secrecy, as if the teachers didn't realize that young boys had older brothers to guide them through the mystery. Sandy knew she and Bob shared true love because all the other cute boys tormented the girls about the secret hygiene class after that. Bob pretended he didn't even know or care where they had been.

During the most vulnerable junior high years, Bob would walk her home from school. One afternoon in spring, the world reached a perfect balance. The sky vaulted over them like a brilliant, painted shell. The ground had finally thawed and the first, shy flowers perfumed the air. Sandy had survived her period. It was still too soon for mosquitos to be a problem. They walked together and owned the world.

Without warning, Bob grabbed her purse and bounded a safe distance away. "What's this?" he asked, crinkling his nose so that his freckles seemed to pour into a funnel. Then he pulled out whatever his hand had found: a comb or a photograph.

"Stop, Bob," Sandy pleaded. "Give it back." Her voice became more desperate when she suddenly remembered what else hid in her purse that day. "I mean it, Bob. Please."

Bob's hand dipped in again, and his eyes stared far off into space, like a blind man reading Braille. Sandy knew her life would absolutely end when they saw, together, what was in Bob's hand. She froze in one of those helpless moments where the suspense dragged into eternity, where she would have sacrificed his life, and then her own, just to end it.

But Bob's animation drained out. His hand came up empty. He moved back to her. "Here's your purse," he said. "I was just fooling around."

Boys had it so easy.

They were just kids when she saw Bob and his buddy slice their thumbs, press the wounds together and call themselves blood brothers. It was something special for them, something they could choose to share until the end of time.

Sandy found out that girls were bound by blood in a different way, but there was nothing special about it, nothing you would want to share. And, of course, there was no choice. Even in those days, time toyed with her. It upset a schedule that should have been as predictable as the moon, leaving her bloated, miserable and ugly whenever she seemed poised for happiness.

So, even though Sandy's bond of sisterhood renewed itself month upon month, she never seemed to connect with the other girls.

She liked Kathy Smith. Kathy knew all the bands and all the words to their songs. She tantalized Sandy with hints of sophistication. Sandy ran into Kathy and Suzanne Nicols in the courtyard between classes in the spring of her seventeenth year. Kathy's eyes looked radioactive, they were so red and puffy. She'd just broken up with Jeff.

"I'm sorry," Sandy said, touching Kathy's elbow.

"Why?" The girl looked away from her. "You didn't do anything."

"I mean I'm sorry for what happened. I'm sorry he treated you like that."

"Who told you how he treated me?" Kathy's breath fell out in a few ragged chunks. "What do you know about anything?"

"I'm sorry," Sandy's heel moved onto a rock, and she stumbled in a little curtsy. "All I said was I'm sorry."

"You are not. How could it mean anything to you? You're pretty." Kathy's voice rose as the unfairness of it all struck her. "You don't know anything about hurt," she screamed. "You're just like all the other pretty bitches, god damn you."

Her classmates envied her. They thought she had everything, and in an unfortunate way she knew they were right. The brainy girls came to her for advice about make up. The cheerleaders wanted help with their homework. Either way, she felt marked, set apart from those around her.

So, by the time she was eighteen—years after first kindling the romance with Bob Strunk—she had a tough time convincing herself that she was better off when he dumped her.

It was all because she did too well on the Probability and Statistics final. Mr. Dalton of Prunes graded on the curve, so when Sandy outscored Bob, he missed out on being valedictorian. All he had left were cute dimples and a perfect attendance record. He couldn't stand the sight of her anymore.

Sandy had learned to bury that kind of hurt. And the man-made woes of womanhood were too common for her to feel any personal resentment. Sometimes it seemed like each pain prepared her for the next and enabled her to get through it. In just twenty-five years, she'd learned to deal with so much . . .

For all she knew, every cold, brutal father could ply his vice and then switch at an instant to a doting, public facade. And if she had stopped to think about it, she would have figured that everyone was tormented by a private version of Stephen X—sort of a fallen guardian angel.

The one thing that Sandy couldn't cope with was the way time itself had singled her out. She knew that it didn't present itself to other people the way it did to her. Nobody else moved in the fits and spurts that colored her life. Nobody else seemed to be caught up in these cycles—of events, of emotions—that dragged Sandy by the hair out of one day and threw her into another.

Sandy Skinner understood that time was like plumbing, something essential and universal and dependable that the rest of the world could take for granted. But Sandy's pipes were always freezing up, or filthy clots were oozing from her faucets. She might even find the flow suddenly reversed, sucking her back into the things she'd so desperately wanted to forget.

Once she felt the floor tile pressing her cheek before she knew what day it was. As consciousness seeped back in— slowly at first—her head roared with pain, like her brain had been twisted sideways in its casing.

She opened her eyes half a slit, not for fear of what she would see, but because that was all she had the strength to do. At first she thought the redness was a great light intruding upon her eyelids. At some point, she realized that it was not that at all, but a tiny, uncharted ocean of blood that swept her away on its tide.

She didn't feel fear when she heard the voice. Not fear in the sense that something bad would happen to her. She wasn't afraid that something would kick her injuries into a whole new category, the way crash victims move from serious condition to critical.

The terror she felt was on a much higher level when the voice boomed out, like thunder through the valley.

"Sandra." Her eyelids quivered when she heard her name. A sense of identity began to fill the aching vacuum of her being. She knew she had to protect someone at all cost, but she couldn't picture that person's face yet.

"Sandra!" The voice's peal reminded her so much of her father.

As a child, she had wanted to shrink back into the pew whenever her father took up a hymnal. His deep, confident bass, which lurked a full octave beneath his speaking voice, could drown out the entire congregation. It was as if he thought all the world's spiritual composers lived in grottos and wrote their music with giant frogs in mind.

One especially humiliating Sunday morning, Sandy prayed for invisibility as they shuffled through the line to the church's door. She could already smell the promise of safety on the breath of lilacs outside when she glanced behind her. She saw Mrs. Swenson pinch the shoulders of her pink, lacy dress, straighten her pearls and cut through the crowd in four quick, determined strides. The woman touched Sandy's father on the arm and said, "I've been meaning to tell you how beautiful your singing is, Jack."

The woman peered into his eyes for a moment, then looked quickly down at Sandy. "You must be terribly proud of your father, young lady."

Before Sandy could say anything—which was just as well because she had no idea what she was expected to say—the woman looked at her father again in a way that she had never seen her mother look at him.

A long time had passed since that day on the church steps. Sandy tried to gather her thoughts, to remember what point her life had reached. Was it her baby sister she had to save?

Or did she have a child of her own to protect? Through the clouds of pain, she couldn't even remember what dangers they faced.

She'd lost track of everything, but she knew this place and this situation very well. Sandy seemed to bounce between two parallel lives. One involved eating, sleeping, routine chores. The alternate consisted of blinding pain, terror, confusion. Whichever realm she lived in at the moment, she remained aware of the other, but unaffected by it, like the description of someone else's dream.

"Sandra!" The voice boomed out once more. "Sandra, get up, God damn it!"

For the rest of her life, Sandy would remember that moment as the first time she noticed how much Stephen X sounded like her father.

And now the plate, which had remained motionless for so long, suddenly shattered in a million blue and white pieces on the kitchen floor.

"Johnny F. Skinner, what the hell are you doing in there?" Sandy heard Linda's voice through the screen door, but for a moment she couldn't remember exactly who Linda was, or whose house they were in.

"Answer me, Johnny F., or someone's going to tan your hide."

The door screeched open, and then the spring slammed it shut behind Linda. Sandy looked up, with tears welling, and held out a few of the plate's biggest shards.

"Oh," Linda said, "It was you."

Johnny ran into the kitchen with Saury in tow.

"We didn't do nuthin', mom."

Linda headed for the dustpan. "Don't worry about it, honey," she said to Sandy. "It was chipped anyway."

Chapter 4

Dinner

Billey's daddy could cuss the ash right off his cigarette. Most evenings, before the mosquitos got thick, he and Billey would sit by the spool and polish off a pot pie or a can of beans.

Elwood didn't have much use for pride. Fact is, he didn't have much use for anything except the spool. His little shack had weathered down to the wood. Time and gravity had worn away its right angles, leaving an impression of a house rendered in a few quick, gray brush strokes.

Inside, the air hung heavy with the mildew of furniture rescued from the rain. A slant of sunlight smudged itself on the window panes. A grease-caked Coleman stove stood next to the galvanized washtub in the kitchen.

Billey slept in a fiberglass camper that had been moved from a pickup bed onto a set of cinder blocks near the driveway. Rusty piston rods and hub cabs poked through the weeds in the back yard.

But the spool touched something buried inside Elwood. He'd often seen these things near construction sites. They came in many sizes—all of them big. They symbolized power and industry to a man without either.

"Could lay wire clean to Colorado with six of these," he told Billey as he wrestled the spool into position on the porch. "They got machines to wrap it on tight."

Elwood sat on the spool, planted his feet against the porch rail and pushed hard to scoot it into place. The rail creaked and sagged.

"Always wanted me a round table," he said, wagging his cigarette like a conductor's baton with each syllable. "Ain't nobody gonna take it away from me. Ain't no lawyer gonna take what's mine."

Elwood, usually so agitated and aggravated with Billey, became almost serene when the nicotine kicked in after a meal. He was as still as his folding chair while he stared across the way at something Billey couldn't see.

These were Billey's favorite times, when his belly was full of food instead of gas. He loved to watch the ash grow off the end of his father's cigarette. It looked like a snake slowly twisting out of its skin. Billey stared, usually with his mouth open, hoping that this time the ash would creep all the way up to the filter before it tumbled off.

Billey felt safe as long as the cigarette burned. He couldn't imagine anything better than being ignored by his father.

But it never lasted. An instant before Elwood broke his silence, he clicked his tongue, unloading a spoonful of hot ashes. He patted his shirt or pants—wherever the stuff fell—with the flats of his hands rubbing the dust into his clothes.

"Gah-DAM, what you lookin' at?" Elwood's feet dropped off the table and the chair legs crashed down to the porch. "Give me the shits the way you look at me all the time."

Billey shifted his weight, getting ready to hightail if need be. "I wasn't lookin' at nuthin'."

"You was. I saw you."

"Honest, I wasn't lookin'. I was just thinkin'."

"I'll give you somethin' to think about."

Before Billey could jump, Elwood's hand shot across the table and pinned Billey's wrist to the wood. The man untucked the cigarette from his mouth, blew the ash away and held the glowing end over the boy's forearm.

"You don't have to tell me the truth right now, Billey. Only thing is, I'm fixin' to burn me a hole in your arm while I'm waitin'."

Billey's lips squirmed back from his teeth as he looked up and saw terrifying things in his daddy's eyes. The eyes smoldered with an intensity he never saw in the kids at school even when they were yelling about his mama. Those eyes were just like the cigarettes, always burning without ever breaking into flame. At the same time, the eyes were distant, not looking at Billey at all, like those on the staring crust of a squirrel he'd found by the road last week.

"It's up to you, Billey. You can lie your stinky little ass off if you want. I'm just gonna burn me a hole clean through your arm is all."

Billey tried to wrench himself free, but struggling only brought his arm closer to the cigarette. He felt the awful little cone of heat.

"I wasn't lookin'." Billey's tears rolled off his cheeks and down his arm as if they might douse the coal. "I promise I wasn't lookin'."

Elwood had nothing if not time. He rested his head sideways on the table to get a better look at how close the cigarette came to his son's flesh.

"Are you gonna make me burn you, Billey?"

The man lowered his toy ever so slowly, measuring its heat by the contortions that transformed Billey's face. Anticipation drove Billey through hysteria to resignation. When Elwood sensed the game was over, he said, "You can't lie to me, boy." He jabbed the cigarette into Billey's arm.

Billey shrieked. But the ash had gone cold. His father laughed and tipped his chair back against the house.

"You sure do give me the shits," Elwood said, as Billey rubbed the gray tattoo of ashes from his arm.

Of course, it didn't do Billey any good to try to *leave* after dinner, either.

One summer night, after he'd scooped up the last bean, he set his tin bowl on the porch to let Black Wolf, a low-slung dog of colorful heritage, have a lick.

"What the hell you doin'?" Elwood roared. "I never paid no man for that dog and I'll be double damned if I'm gonna feed it. Bad enough I gotta feed you, always eatin' like beans grow on trees. And you never brung me a nickel."

Billey shot halfway around the side of the shack before his daddy's ass left the chair. He darted into his camper, snapped its feeble latch and covered himself with his once-green blanket. An instant later, he heard the fist pounding on the wall.

"Never brung me a nickel, did ya?"

Billey felt his sanctuary tilt and rock and come crashing down on the cinder blocks, as if he had been caught in an earthquake.

"Yer just like a gah-dam dog, Billey. Only a dog don't stink as bad as you."

Chapter 5

Westmore Avenue

When Sandy held steady at forty-five miles per hour down Westmore Avenue, she could make all seven green lights between America Thinks, Inc. and Kid'n'Kaboodle. Cars on either side flew by. Those on her tail downshifted, gave their engines a throaty roar and swung into the passing lane. She pulled even with them at each light as they punched it again from a standstill.

It wasn't so much that she was a level-headed driver, but that Stephen X had never gotten around to fixing the Impala. Between the engine's knock and rattle and the slip in the transmission, she could have used an hourglass to check her zero-to-sixty performance. Once she built up a head of steam, she was loathe to slow down.

Depending on what point in the light cycle she merged with the Westmore traffic, things could get pretty scary. Forty-five would carry her through, but if she came up on the first light just as it turned green, she would be in for a bad time. Each succeeding light would change on cue, but she would arrive at it before the last clutch of traffic had cleared.

The drivers who cursed her an eighth of a mile earlier took one shocked glance in the rear view mirror and then tromped on the gas when they saw her patchwork grille bearing down on them.

Sandy worried about it even more than they did because they had no idea how bad her brakes were. But she hoped that if some guy had just dropped thirty grand on a gleaming, over-powered phallic symbol with personalized plates, he'd make sure he got out of her way in time.

She drove Westmore Avenue ten times a week; once each way, Monday through Friday. She hardly even noticed anything but the color of the lights. Block after block of convenience stores, gas stations, pawn shops and car lots faded into oblivion. Billboards changed as slowly as the seasons. Even the pedestrians seemed the same, day after day, week after week, always waiting on the same corners, always wearing the same clothes.

She thought how much her life was like the drive down Westmore. Surrounded by frenzied people, she remained totally isolated. She geared every thought and action toward moving so smoothly that she would not cause the slightest disturbance to anyone else's plans—she'd even pray to become invisible if that would help. Her route was straight and unvarying. Only a construction gang or a pile up could move her from her lane.

Every inch of the way, her stomach knotted around the certainty that she would get a ticket or that the Impala would finally die in a cloud of smoke and a pool of stinking oil, tying up traffic for hours.

So Sandy battled her nerves as each light turned into a life-or-death crisis. Her knuckles turned white on the wheel. She thought about unrelenting stress and what it can do, what it did to her grandmother.

As Sandy was growing up, Mama Gore lived in a tiny Airstream trailer in back of their house. She had tacked skirting around its base and built a couple of wooden steps rising to the door. A green-and-white striped canvas awning shaded the south side of the trailer and the single painted chair beneath the window. A pale yellow picket fence set the Airstream's tidy little lawn off from the long, narrow garden where she planted tomatoes, beans, onions and corn.

Every morning, Mama Gore wore a floppy straw hat and one of her faded floral dresses as she worked the garden. She stooped there for hours, loosening the soil's dark, rich aroma, or uprooting the first green hint of a weed.

The old woman gave Sandy the only comfort she ever found in her family. Sandy would wipe the crumbs of dirt from her knees and sit next to Mama Gore's chair. Sometimes while she listened to the stories, she would pluck a blade of grass and shred it to make a tiny spray of green fibers. Sometimes, she would prop Jennifer up and translate Mama Gore's stories into the special, lilting language that only the Gore sisters understood.

Mama Gore was nearly deaf, so she knew nothing about Jennifer's secret language. And the girls' parents refused to hear of it. Sandy always remembered the time she'd hurried to tell her father about her baby sister's invention.

"Jennifer made up a language," Sandy panted as she rushed over to Jack Gore's recliner one Saturday morning.

"Jennifer's only two." Gore held up his newspaper. He brought his hands slowly together to turn the page, and then shook out the crease. "She doesn't even know English yet."

"We learned in school about kids who know what day of the week any date will come on in any year until the end of time. Maybe Jennifer's like that. Maybe she could be on TV. Come and listen."

"Not now, princess."

"Come on, daddy, you've got to hear it."

Her father leaped to his feet, dumping the family, sports and business sections of the paper out of his lap. "I don't have to do anything, you little bitch."

He wrapped the world news around her head and rubbed it back and forth over her ears.

"You're just like your mother. All of you kids are just like your God damned mother."

Through the paper, Sandy felt a hand shove her to the floor. She heard her father storm up the stairs.

Sandy could hardly believe that her father was Mama Gore's son. His temper and abruptness, the whiff of gin, the way he laughed like it was something he'd learned from a book—all of the things that made him her father—were absent in Mama Gore.

Mama Gore, with skin like pink lace, must have known her days were numbered. Yet she had infinite patience, while Jack Gore had none. The old woman's hearing and sight were just about gone, as if years of use had depleted them. Meanwhile, Sandy's father could spot a crumb in a carpet pile or hear a giggle from the far end of the house, but the keenness of his senses did nobody any good.

Sandy built her life on certainties. She found a strange comfort in the knowledge that punishment would always be as swift as it was capricious. As surely as the sun would rise, she knew she would be guilty of some crime that day. Her mother would rant over some detail in her appearance. Her father would speak of her as if she weren't even there. And Mama Gore would tell her wonderful stories from a time before Sandy's parents were born.

Mama Gore worked for the railroad when she was a willowy, beautiful young woman. She told Sandy how she used to stay up all night so that she could throw the switch that moved the track after the 3:17 came through.

She could never see the engineer in the dark. The freight crept through the yards as a powerful hulking shadow that seemed to have nothing to do with the puny concerns of men or this earth. The rails rose and fell with its passage. The metal groaned as a young woman huddled by the stove in the switchman's shack.

Sandy's grandmother supported herself at a time when young women were not expected to do that. But the job cost her daylight. Late in life, she took up gardening and tried to collect on the sun's long-standing debt to her. It was at a time when old women were not expected to do that.

With her failing eyesight, Mama Gore fell prey to Mick Long and a couple of his slick-headed pals. Every morning through the summer, or any day when they were ditching school, they would hide behind the back hedge and toss pebbles into her garden. She would see the stones, or hear them, or sometimes even feel them rain down on her, but she could never tell where they came from. It wasn't so much the mystery or even the potential for injury that bothered her. It was just so much work to pick them out of her neat rows of dirt. The garden lost its pleasure for her.

Sandy caught the teenagers in the act one day. She tried to tell her grandmother what had been happening, but she couldn't make herself understood. Mama Gore slumped into her chair and fanned herself until she fell asleep. The next day, her tormentors were back.

Long got himself suspended from school that spring for carrying a switchblade. That gave him plenty of time to toss stones over the bushes. Mama Gore's cheeriness began to fade. She developed a twitch in her left eyelid that had nothing to do with age.

When Sandy heard the hail begin on the day of the tornado, she looked out the back window in time to see Mama Gore stumble out the Airstream's little door. The woman's straw hat took flight. The long silver hair that she sometimes let Sandy braid whipped across her face.

"Take me, if you want me so bad," Mama Gore shouted. The wind carried her voice to Sandy in the house as if she were standing at her side. The old woman waved her fist against the black sky. "Just take me, if that's what it is."

A sheet of lightning framed her just as the wind shattered the glass in Jennifer's bedroom. Sandy ran to answer her sister's cries, with no idea that she would never see her grandmother again.

Chapter 6

The Can Opener

Billey might never have learned to use the can opener, if not for the cops.

Sometimes he would be alone for days after they came to see his daddy. He could sleep as late as he liked and forget about school. He and Black Wolf could root around the yard without fear. Only trouble was, they sure got hungry when they were on their own.

Elwood brought home all kinds of things besides the spool. One day, it was strange, gleaming pieces of machinery. Other times, it was a stack of railroad ties or fence posts. Once he showed Billey a crate full of hammers. The only pattern Billey saw was that whatever his daddy brought home was heavy. It involved a great deal of cussing and sweating. And Billey could count on a whupping as soon as the stuff came off the truck.

Nothing was ever there for long. Things sat next to the house for three, four days. Then Billey got up one morning and saw nothing but footprints and an outline in the dust. He figured that was why his daddy kept finding new stuff. Whenever he had something, somebody—maybe those cops—came by in the middle of the night and took it all away. Maybe those cops had clean clothes and shiny cars because they were always stealing his daddy's stuff. Maybe that was why his daddy hated cops even more than he hated Billey.

Billey didn't get to ride in the pickup too much, but every time he did, Elwood found a chance to run down his enemies.

"Smell that stinkin' pork, Billey?" he said, tipping his head back and squeezing his nose when they passed a squad car. "Like to gag on all that bacon fat."

Then his expression sent Billey to the far edge of the seat.

"Why ain't you laughin' with me? You gonna be a stinkin' cop when you grow up?"

They came to a place where all the cars seemed to have just parked in the middle of the road.

"Betcha hunnert dollar bill there's a cop at the other end of this mess," Elwood said.

The truck jerked along in the traffic jam a few feet at a time. Elwood swore and stuck his head out the window. After awhile, he cussed and pounded one of the gauges on the dashboard.

"GAH-dam, Billey, them cops are gonna burn up my motor if we don't get movin'." He switched the engine off and hopped out of the truck. Billey saw him craning his neck as he walked and skipped along the dotted line in the center of the road.

As soon as Elwood disappeared, the cars began to move in front of Billey. Behind him, horns sounded, sporadically at first, but then one blare joined another and another until a great jeering wall of sound threatened to topple on Billey.

Just when he thought the noise would bust his head open, Billey felt the truck tilt. He opened his eyes to see his daddy climbing back into the driver's seat.

Elwood stuck his head out the window, looked behind and laid on the horn. Somehow he was able to stick out his tongue without losing the cigarette. "How d'ya like that, ya stupid jackass?" he shouted, pumping a slow rhythm out of the horn. As he gunned the engine, he muttered, "Stupid jackasses. Shouldn't be 'lowed to drive."

They soon caught up with the creeping line of traffic. Billey looked out the window and saw a truck on its side like an enormous dog that had run until it dropped. A little further, he saw what was left of a big, red car. It looked like a beer can after his daddy had belched and crushed it in his fist. Billey saw part of a man hanging halfway through the windshield. Blood spread out from his head and across the hood.

It ran over the fender like long, thin fingers looking for the gravel.

Police cars and fire trucks waited at crazy angles with their lights flashing between the truck and the car.

"What'd I say, Billey?"

"I dunno." Billey couldn't remember anything at that moment.

"Like I tell you, every time there's a mess, you see a bunch of pork asses acting like big shots."

Billey got to ride in the pickup that day because his daddy needed his help. They drove along a lonely road until near dark. They pulled up to a wide, flat-topped building with a big, gravel parking lot.

"I'm gonna see me a man, Billey. If a car comes in here or anyone comes pokin' around, you honk on the horn, understand? You just honk your little ass off."

Billey rested his hand on the horn for a long time and didn't see anything. He felt his head nod as if it were as heavy as his eyelids. He thought of Black Wolf back home, how they could run together all the way to the grassy spot before they collapsed, with their sides heaving.

Suddenly he heard a great commotion at the back of the truck. Even before he swung around to see the two shadowy figures, he pounded the horn. He pressed it hard, as if cramming it down the steering column would boost the volume.

An instant later, the driver's door swung open and Billey flew through the air. The rocks scraped his arms and legs raw in a dozen places when he landed.

"What the hell you think yer doin', you little shitbrain?" Elwood's voice boomed out of the darkness. "You wanna get us all shot?"

Elwood threw the kid back into the truck and sprayed gravel in a tight arc. "Damn stupidest kid I ever seen."

Billey woke the next morning to find a wondrous mountain of copper tubes next to his camper. The wind played a haunting piper's melody for him. The metal tasted clean and tangy on his tongue.

It wasn't yet noon when his daddy spotted the cops coming around the bend.

"Get in the room right quick, Billey," he yelled. The house had three rooms, but Billey knew he meant the bedroom, the only one with a curtain. "Keep your mouth shut and don't come out 'til I tell you."

Billey wanted to find out more about these awful cops, but the drill always prevented that. He and Black Wolf had to flatten themselves against the wall beneath the window and keep still as death while his daddy talked to the intruders. When they were that close, Black Wolf couldn't help but lick Billey's face with his big, sloppy tongue, but Billey knew it would cause a ruckus if he tried to make the dog stop.

When the cops finally left, they would either take his daddy with them, or they would leave him behind to give Billey a whupping. He always hoped they would take his daddy, but—even if they were cops—he couldn't blame them for not wanting to be with him.

He strained his ears, but couldn't make out much of what was said.

"Somebody musta dumped it here," he heard his daddy say. "Never saw a thing."

Billey heard footsteps clomping back and forth on the porch, saw the shadows cast on the curtain over his head. He finally heard the police car start up and drive away. Then everything remained still for a very long time. The cops must have taken his daddy. But still Billey waited, silent as the house itself, until the room grew dark.

At his bladder's final warning, Billey eased himself up from the floor and poked his nose over the window sill. He couldn't see anything outside, so he tip-toed through the door and watered the trunk of the catalpa. Black Wolf sprang over to see what was going on. After being still so long, he bounced up and down with excitement and hunger like a shaggy black ball.

Billey had watched his daddy use the can opener enough to understand it in principle, but the fine points of its use would take some practice.

The first time hunger drove him to experiment, he could only make the can opener take one tiny bite of the metal at a time. After perforating the entire rim, he used the wooden-handled knife to pry the top of the can open just enough to spoon the beans out. His daddy had taught him what words to say each time he nicked his hands in the process.

Billey and Black Wolf each ate a can of beans and licked the spoon. They snuggled together in the camper and dreamt of running to the grassy spot.

The sun was high the next day as Billey sat on the copper mountain and listened to the music the wind made. Before he could look to see what made Black Wolf bark, the boot sent Billey sprawling.

"Thought I told you to git in the room 'til I told you to git out." Elwood's shadow fell across his son. "Gonna have to teach you a few things now."

Chapter 7

Artie

When she picked up Saury on fingerpaint day, Sandy found the tall lady with the bows in her hair bending over him.

Miss Busse looked like one of the kid's creations. She adored bright, simple colors. She tossed them on her lips and nails and around her eyes. She pared her wardrobe down to the essential bands of the rainbow. Even her laughter splashed against the walls like tempera paint. She could make a five-year-old long for subtlety.

"Show your mother what a wonderful picture you made today, Saury," Miss Busse gushed, resting a hand on the boy's shoulder. "Saury was so busy, he was a little angel all day."

"See, mom?" Saury looked over a sheet of paper covered with blue and green shapes.

"It's absolutely the best barn in the whole class," Miss Busse confided in Sandy.

"It's a house," Sandy said.

"I told her it's a house," said Saury, too young to bother hiding his annoyance.

"Saury always paints houses."

"But we did farm pictures today." Miss Busse's face flushed ever so slightly, complementing her yellow blouse and bow. She seemed to forget who she was talking to. Her voice jumped back and forth between the sing-song she used with the children and the even, professional tone that worked on their parents. She pointed to a brown smear on the paper. "I thought you said that was a horse."

"Robin did that," Saury sighed. "I couldn't stop her. My dad doesn't let horses in our house."

"That's a good idea," Miss Busse laughed and stood to her

full height so that her bow waved like a lonely sunflower. "That's a very good idea." Her color deepened when she saw that Mrs. Skinner was not smiling.

Sandy couldn't afford a better day care center on what she made at America Thinks, Inc. At least this one didn't let the kids drink the paint.

She tried not to think about the irony of her daily shuttle between Kid'n'Kaboodle and ATI. Both places used self-expression as a tool for manipulation.

She started at ATI as an over-qualified data entry clerk. She worked with the raw surveys, transforming the atoms of opinion into monolithic trends that inspired multi-million dollar gambles.

Sandy settled for the job because a small part of her already knew that her self-esteem would always be inversely proportional to Stephen X's influence.

She didn't work harder than Caroline and Cindy to impress anyone, but because she feared she would be exposed as lazy or incompetent. Her co-workers resented the way she never left her station for coffee or a smoke. They figured she was screwing Wally Conner, the Vice President of Information. Meanwhile, she plowed through record numbers of surveys.

The statistics she extracted rarely surprised, or even interested, her. What fascinated her was the way adult Americans—just like the ones you see every day—would dutifully color in little boxes to describe their most complex or personal feelings.

The surveys were anonymous, but Sandy could read volumes in the pencil's stroke and weight. Most people were so eager to bare their souls about dog food, dish soap or bowel movements that they attacked the surveys' hot boxes.

The question might be, "Does your dog weigh: under 20 pounds, 20-40 pounds, 40-60 pounds, over 60 pounds?" People who had marked the previous boxes with a light hand suddenly engraved the page when they recognized the goofy, lop-eared mongrel that had won the family heart.

Sandy saw how respondents bared secrets they hid from their spouses, beer buddies or shrinks. But the forms always trampled the respondents' sense of pride or individuality. By the time people had portioned their souls in the line of dark boxes, they had fallen into a pattern identical to a hundred or a thousand others. Whichever pattern prevailed dictated the diet of all America's dogs.

After her promotion to assistant data manager, Sandy immersed herself in bell curves and standard deviations to chart public opinion. She didn't really need to see the papers at all anymore. But she made a point of thumbing through a stack of surveys at least once a week, just to keep in touch with America's feelings, as well as thoughts.

That's how Thursday morning turned sour when she found the form Stephen X had completed.

The age, sex, marital, education and region boxes could have fit fifty thousand decent citizens. But Sandy could tell this was her husband by the way each box had been blackened by a dangerously sharp pencil tracing a series of ever-tighter squares. Crowding the margins were the same pointed beaks and wings that Stephen X always left on the message pad by the telephone.

It was the standard 1320 Survey Form on Marital Infidelity. Sandy followed the pattern of boxes: "What percentage of Americans have had extramarital sex: less than 10%; 10-25%; 25-50%, 50-75%, more than 75%?" "I have had an extramarital affair: never; with 1 individual; with 2-5 individuals; with more than 5 individuals?"

Stephen X had filled in, and then tried to erase, the 2-5 box. He blackened the "more than 5" box, and then circled those words to make sure that his correction would not be misinterpreted.

The discovery shocked Sandy, but only for an instant.

Then she felt relief and hope that maybe some of the attention he gave her would be siphoned off to other women.

Unfortunately, whether he cheated or not, Stephen X had always been obsessed with her, just like Artie Sandoval. It seemed that men—boys—were always obsessed with women. Funny, she never knew a woman to be so caught up by a man. Of course, when she thought about it, that made perfect sense. God knows men had no mysteries. None that would attract you, anyway.

She couldn't see women as mysterious, either, but there it was. She thought of how Linda had gotten those phone calls. They hit at all hours, day and night. The guy said he knew everything about her. The police wouldn't do a thing. Linda wound up moving, getting an unlisted number.

And there were too many guys like Artie on the loose, even if their acts of love lacked the shocking finality of his.

Artie smashed the shell Sandy lived in after Bob Strunk dumped her halfway through senior year. She'd lived in a shell before Bob dumped her, too, but that was different. She reckoned her life in terms of BD—Before the Dump, and AD—After the Dump.

She and Bob used to sit next to each other at the front of the class in Probability and Statistics. The rest of the students existed as a field of uniform faces, a gray backdrop for Bob and Sandy. Artie Sandoval hid under that blanket of oblivion until Day Three, AD.

Sandy had seen Artie's striped shirt, but she could not have described his face to save her soul. She was so distraught over Bob that she hardly knew what Artie was saying when he cornered her after class that Thursday.

"I know you probably don't want to, but maybe we could go to a movie or something tomorrow?"

Sandy drew back half a step and tried to remember this boy's name, where she had seen him before. In her confusion, the silence stretched to one moment, then two.

"I didn't think so," Artie said, his face burning as he turned quickly and escaped down the hall.

Thinking back, it seemed like Artie became famous the next day, but in reality, a full week passed. Sandy sat at home that Saturday night, like she planned to do every Saturday night for the rest of her life. She watched some stupid television show and then sat like a zombie through the lead news stories. They dealt with a small war, the discovery that a minor-league politician had lied, the extinction of some slimy kind of invertebrate—things that had nothing to do with her life.

Artie led the local news as the broadcast cut away to the live camera crew beneath the Oak Street water tower. The structure erupted from a sea of ranch homes and light industrial buildings. It looked over the neighborhood like a bulletin board of lust and school pride.

Someone had painted "LIONS FOREVER" in fat letters around the enormous tank. Other messages shouted to the world that "Susie has the big ones," and "Dalton of Prunes Eats It." No sooner were the words whitewashed than the kids refreshed their messages. No matter how hard the city tried to cover them, obscene things seemed to bleed through the paint.

The giant, wild graffiti provided a curtain for Artie's one-act play. The cameras pointed up at his shadowy figure while his Yearbook picture appeared in a cutaway in the corner of the television screen. The newsman told how the kid had put his intentions in a suicide note delivered to the TV station. Just as the psychologist came on to explain how Artie's apparent desire to publicize his death showed that he did not really intend to die, Artie's body crashed audibly into the unforgiving earth.

The first camera missed the action, but a producer with keen reflexes quickly showed a replay of the fall from the second unit camera.

Sandy felt a knot of vomit rise in her throat as she watched how the jerky lens tried to track the falling body. "I know that kid," she thought, but she had no idea how well Artie knew her.

The next day, the police came around to "clear up a few routine questions."

Both officers were big. Sandy noticed the man's sparse, uneven moustache and the gold studs in the woman's ears. Together, they crowded the entryway until Sandy's father realized the business would take a little while.

The police sat on the over-stuffed sofa that no one ever used. Mr. Gore settled into his recliner and Mrs. Gore brought in a chair from the kitchen. Sandy took the seat opposite her father and noticed how stiff and lumpy it was. While the policeman talked, all Sandy could think about was how nobody but her father ever used the living room. All the seats were so uncomfortable because they'd never been broken in.

She suddenly realized that the room had become quiet. Everyone watched her.

"I'm sorry," she said, rising a bit at the sound of her own voice. "What?"

"Did you know Artie Sandoval?" the policeman asked.

"No."

"Oh, come on, young lady." Mr. Gore slapped the arm of his chair. "This is very serious. You said last night that you knew him."

"I meant I've *seen* him. I didn't *know* him."

"Then how in God's name did you know it was him?" Mr. Gore looked to the officers for sympathy. "She's always like this. I wonder if she ever listens to the things that come out of her mouth."

The policewoman explained that Artie had built a shrine to Sandy from a candid photo, a strand of hair and stacks of self-addressed letters in his dark, airless bedroom. His final note said her change of heart doomed him. The officers said they understood, they'd seen these things before. She could tell they were lying.

For weeks, Sandy's parents talked about "the Liability Question" and dropped their voices when she came in the room. One way or another, everyone at school found out that Sandy had given birth to Artie's fantasy life. She might as well have walked the halls with blood on her face. She wanted to die herself, as if it were some disease he'd passed to her in Probability that day.

Years later, Sandy understood that the horrible thing that transformed boys as they embarked on their teens killed Artie before he had a chance to grow out of it. Sandy wished he had taken his burden of guilt to hell with him instead of shifting it to her. There were a thousand prettier girls in school. Some of them had probably even talked to him. Why did he pick her?

She figured that Artie's suicide would be the worst day of her life.

But that was before she met Stephen X.

Chapter 8

Black Wolf

Black Wolf was so ugly and he stunk so bad he couldn't belong to anyone but Billey.

At first sight, Billey thought the dog was a chunk of tread that some old truck had thrown into the bushes.

But when it barked at him, Billey smashed his head against a low branch. Not much bigger than a can of beans on Sunday, the starving, mange-gripped pup reared and yapped at him.

"Here, boy," Billey said, patting the ground. "Here, Black Wolf."

A couple hanks of hair that even the mange wouldn't mess with poked out of the dog's wrinkled, dirty pink hide. Angry sores spotted his body. His belly swelled from the taut spring of his ribs like a brown berry about to rot. His brief legs bowed and ended in abrupt, floppy paws. His face looked flat as a penny on the railroad tracks.

At first, Billey tried to hide him in the camper, but he could hardly breathe for the smell. Before he could reckon what to do, Elwood spotted him.

"What the hell you got there?" Elwood asked, turning his head to the side and wiping his nose with his fist the way he did when he was figuring whether or not to whup Billey. "Where'd you get that?"

"I dunno."

"Don't tell me you don't know when you know. You think I'm as dumb as you are, Billey Elwood? Well, I ain't."

"He just came here."

"Ain't nothin' comes *here* without a damn good reason. I oughta shoot that son of a bitch." Elwood glanced at the truck. "Oughta shoot you, too, for all the good you are."

Billey tried to get rid of Black Wolf for the dog's own good. He walked half a mile from the road with the fast cars and told Black Wolf to stay. Soon as Billey took a step, the puppy bounded after him, its pink and black tongue poking in and out in synch with its stride.

He laid a plank across the creek, carried Black Wolf to the far side, then sprinted back and kicked the board away. The dog yelped and splashed through the water.

Wherever Billey went, Black Wolf was sure to follow.

"That dog's got the mange, Billey." Elwood spat in the dust. "What's the matter with your nose you can't smell it?"

"I dunno."

"That's right, you don't know a damn thing. That's why I'm tellin' you. You go touchin' that damn dog anymore and your weenie's gonna swell up and drop off on the ground. Then how ya gonna pee, Billey? Tell me that."

"I dunno."

"Boy that can't pee ain't no good to nobody." Elwood shook his head. "Might as well be shot. Fetch me that can of kerosene 'round back and we'll fix this doggie's mange up good."

Billey ran around the shack, with Black Wolf in hot pursuit, grabbed a can and brought it back to his daddy.

"Not *gaso*line. *Kero*sene!" Elwood threw his cigarette down and ground it under his heel. "Come around here."

He led Billey to the jumble of cans and bottles behind the shack. "Gasoline. Kerosene. Turpentine." He swung each one in Billey's face. "Got that now? Fetch me that bucket."

Billey brought the tin bucket and watched Elwood empty the can into it. The stuff smelled bad, but not as bad as Black Wolf.

"Dunk him in there, Billey." Elwood waved at Black Wolf. "Just like your pork pig friends dunk their donuts."

Billey cupped Black Wolf in his hands and lowered him gently into the bucket. The dog howled and his leg stubs swam in four wild directions as the kerosene bit into his sores.

"Don't let go. Push him down in there real good," Elwood barked. "Sometimes it hurts to make things right."

Billey couldn't stand the wailing and squirming for long. He relaxed his grip and Black Wolf shot to the ground. The dog coughed and shook. It looked up at him like a wet, scalped rat. Elwood scooped him up and plunged him back in the bucket.

"Don't worry about the eyes, Billey. He'll close 'em real tight when he gets under there. Now you do it." Elwood grabbed his son's hand and wrapped it around the struggling animal. He rubbed dirt over his hands to blot up the kerosene and then reached for a cigarette and matches.

"You just listen to me," he said. "I know how to fix that dog's mange real good."

Billey looked up to see his daddy waving the match over him. Black Wolf thrashed free and sent the boy tumbling backwards just before the flame leaped from the mouth of the bucket.

•

Black Wolf filled out on bugs and bones and stolen beans. He assumed the shape of a mature animal, but one designed by consensus. He had the tooth and jaw of a killer, but the temper and leg of a lapdog. The broad pads of his feet propped up a body stout as a hydrant, shaggy as a goat. He defended Billey with a proud, defiant voice.

Billey's world ran from the creek to the highway and over to the hill that had been half scooped away. His daddy said the rock miners gouged out the hill, but Billey always figured some big, old brown dinosaur came by and got so hungry he decided to eat himself some dirt. Eating dirt made some sense to Billey.

Billey's world existed in the simplest possible terms. If you needed rocks, it had abundant rocks. If you needed dirt,

dirt was cheap and plentiful. If you needed loneliness, it could provide that, too, because Elwood hardly ever came looking for Billey; he probably would have been just as happy if the kid wandered off for good. Anyway, Billey could always be counted on to come back in time to eat. "Little bastard plays deaf," Elwood always muttered, "but he can hear the Coleman fire up a mile away."

Billey shinnied up the tree that leaned over the creek bank. He stripped off his shirt and dangled it over Black Wolf who danced on his hind legs and barked like a fool. The tree trunk left a rough pattern on Billey's chest and gray flecks of it clung to his skin as he pulled away.

They found tadpoles, minnows and a little green snake that never blinked. Billey sat on the patch of grass and chucked stones in the water while Black Wolf watched with his long, pink and black tongue hanging out. The damp grass bled through his pants and made his skin feel cool and clean. When he leaned back, he could feel how the clear, blue sky came right down into his lungs and swelled his chest. Black Wolf felt it, too.

Chapter 9

Stegosaurus X

Sandy and Saury made regular appearances on the pet shop circuit. They were never in much of a hurry to get home, so they stopped a couple times a week after Kid'n'Kaboodle, plus most Saturday mornings. Sandy liked the birds and fish, Saury the turtles, rodents and lizards.

"How are you?" asked Osgood, the burly, green parrot with a beak that looked like it had been carved from a cake of soap.

"Okay, I guess." Saury shrugged. "How are you?"

"How are you?" The bird cocked its head and rolled its orange eyes.

"I'm okay. How are you?"

"How are you?"

They laughed together while the bird echoed itself after they turned away.

Sandy lifted Saury so he could watch, with eyes bigger than sea shells, as the fish fell into formation. They looked bright as one of Miss Busse's blouses, one shimmering color to a tank, swimming free of boredom, hour to hour, end to end.

The sweet boy who had been a tiny baby just a day or a week ago, felt so heavy, propped against Sandy's hip, with his legs dangling along hers. But she could hold him there forever without growing tired. She finally understood that the female pelvis was designed not to make shopping for jeans tough, but to ease the burden of carrying a child.

Sandy thought the day's frantic sequence of crises should have drained her. Instead, exhilaration flooded her. She drew strength and energy from the simple act of holding her son. It was one of the special things about motherhood that her own mother had neglected to tell her. She never would have dreamed that a five-year-old could be her best friend.

Saury fell in love with a baby beagle. "Will he grow up to be like my cousin Johnny's dog?" he asked.

The pup looked so pitiful and awkward that Sandy wondered what inspired Mother Nature to create such vulnerable things. If not for pet shops, how could a creature like that hope to survive?

She thought about Stephen X, who believed the only difference between a puppy and a baby was that one came with a tax break. Either way, you paid too much, brought the thing home, found someone to take care of it.

"You're fat," Stephen X had said one evening, dropping his briefcase on the dining room table.

She'd laced her hands beneath her swollen tummy and turned to give him a side view. "I'm pregnant," she said, still in wonder.

"You're disgusting," he said. She saw his face transformed into the awful, black-eyed mask that meant the devil had come to collect another debt. "You look ridiculous."

She felt relief when Stephen X practically disappeared for the last half of her pregnancy. If nothing else, that gave her a few months in which she didn't have to go along with him to see the latest monster movie, or squirm through the video of some classic at home.

Sandy used to think it odd that Stephen X, whose imagination fell off the bottom end of the scale, could be so enthralled by movies about the most fantastic bone-crushing, disemboweling creatures Hollywood could muster. She finally realized that the utter predictability of the plots appealed to him. No matter if the title role went to a cunning, alien race or a primordial destructive force, Sandy could tell the fate of each human member of the cast from the character's first appearance. There was never any room for chance.

On Sandy's last birthday before they married, Stephen X

gave her a tape of *Plague of the Time Warp*, an obscure film about hundred-foot tall dinosaurs that crawl out of the past and head for Los Angeles. One creature looked like an over-fed salamander with slabs of papier mache lashed to its back.

"What is that supposed to be?" Sandy asked, trying to take her mind off the hurt.

"It's a stegosaurus," Stephen X said through a mouthful of popcorn.

"It looks ridiculous."

"You wouldn't say that if you saw a real one."

"What? A real lizard that's been dressed up by third-graders? What are we watching this for?"

"I paid seventy-five bucks for this." Stephen X knocked the popcorn bowl from his lap. "You can't just get this at the video store. I had to special-order it for your birthday."

He slammed the door as he stormed out, but he was back the next day with roses and a story about how much stress he'd been under at work.

Sandy figured it was easier to put up with the movies than to make a big deal about them. But not having to watch them turned out to be one of the nicest parts of her pregnancy. Stephen X always seemed to be working late, grabbing a bite at the office, flying to Pittsburgh for a few days. Looking back on it, she realized he'd been messing around.

In any case, she remembered those precious, solitary months as the happiest of her life. She allowed herself the fantasy of being a single mother-to-be. Strangers spoke to her as if she were someone worth knowing. They shared intimate details of their own lives. After a time, she even accepted the way they fussed over her, holding doors, waving her to the front of grocery lines.

Never reckless, but never especially cautious, Sandy watched her diet, avoided disease. It never crossed her mind that she took better care of this restless thing inside her than she'd ever done for herself.

A baby girl would have been nice, but she somehow felt more secure with this emerging boy. He would mean fewer heartaches in the long run. How would she ever be able to explain the world to a daughter? With a son, her biggest problem would be picking a name. There were no men in the child's family whose name you would want to borrow, except maybe Roscoe. But "Roscoe" sounded so dated; it had probably been dated even before Roscoe was born.

Primitive people had the right idea. Wait for the child. See what it was like. Pick a name to fit.

Late one morning, Sandy took a bagel, an apple and a slab of peanut brittle to the park for lunch. She'd just finished the candy and was about to start on the apple when an old, old woman sat next to her on the bench.

"Won't be much longer now," the woman said.

"Just three more weeks," Sandy said, not feeling any shyness with this stranger.

"It's like waiting for Christmas and a trip to the dentist all in one," the woman said through ill-fitting dentures. "So wonderful, but so much pain."

"There's no pain," said Sandy, surprised and puzzled.

"It's your first, then." The woman eyed her knowingly. "It's all right. I had three of them myself. That's what God meant for us."

Sandy's breath faltered. The trust she'd placed in this stranger had been betrayed. After the woman left, Sandy shredded her bagel and tossed the crumbs to the pigeons.

She had never been able to depend on her body's cycles, but she went into labor on the day—probably at the precise moment—the doctor had predicted. She put in a call to Stephen X at the office.

"He's in a meeting, Mrs. Skinner," Lucille said.

"But I'm having a baby," said Sandy, startled by the urgency in her voice despite the depth of her breathing.

"It's a very important meeting." Lucille seemed not to

understand Sandy. Or maybe she understood Stephen X very well. After a pause, she said, "You mean it's Mr. Skinner's baby?"

"Of course it's---"

"I'm sorry. I guess I can send him a message."

Linda and Roscoe drove Sandy to the hospital in their big, blue Cutlass Supreme. Roscoe even ran a couple of red lights, although Sandy kept telling him there was plenty of time. They stayed with her and everything happened more quickly than she expected.

Another male—weak, but relentless—left her exhausted, bleeding, and relieved that it was over, but not the way Stephen X always did. Stephen X was the farthest thing from her mind as she cradled this wondrous, new creature. She felt happy beyond all comprehension, as if the very molecules of her skin had mingled with the air. She hummed and brushed her lips against his soft, flushed skin.

"So, I have a son," Stephen X said when he finally arrived, late that evening.

"Where were you?" Sandy's ordeal had made her forget certain basic rules of their relationship.

"I couldn't get away." The man sniffed and let his gaze wander the corners of the room. "It would have looked bad."

"We wouldn't want that."

Stephen X's eyes locked onto hers. "Who have you been talking to?"

"Nobody. That's the point."

"I'm not going to let you take advantage---"

A nurse knocked, poked her head in the door, and looked bewildered by what she found. "Skinners? Some paper-work," she said. "We need a name, just a few details . . ."

"My wife needs some rest," Stephen X said, taking the nurse's clipboard and leading her back into the hall. "I came to handle these things."

Chance had no place in Stephen X's world. In all matters,

he would not rest until the tiniest detail had been resolved, clarified, executed. Yet he'd shown no interest in naming his son, beyond the fact that he wouldn't stand for "Roscoe."

"It's been 'Roscoe says,' and 'Roscoe does' all my life. I'm not going to listen to any more of that," he'd announced one morning in mid-term. Then he added, without any enthusiasm, "Maybe Stephen X Jr."

"A boy should at least have his own name," Sandy said. "I feel very strongly about that."

"Fine." Stephen X went back to his newspaper. "Then why do you keep bothering me about it?"

The question of a name was still up in the air when Sandy went into the hospital. Now she looked at the flowers that Linda and Roscoe had left by the window and decided "Roscoe" had a nice ring to it. It was a name people would never forget.

She'd dozed off by the time Stephen X came back.

"You think you're pretty smart, don't you?"

"What?" The lights were brighter in the hall than the room and it took her eyes a moment to focus on his silhouette.

"You and your girlfriends got it all figured out, don't you?" She knew something was wrong by the way Stephen X bounced around on the balls of his feet. "We'll see how smart you are."

Another nurse carried the baby in. She looked around and turned the lights up. "Mrs. Skinner? We've got a visitor for you," she said in a voice that rose and fell like music. "Little Ste . . ." She frowned and turned the baby's wrist band to get a better look at it. "Ste . . . Stego . . ."

The father practically rose off the hard floor. "See, Sandy?" he said. "Your little Stegosaurus X is here. Just like his daddy."

Chapter 10

Tommy Lagocki

Tommy Lagocki called Billey his good buddy. Billey wasn't sure what that meant, but he liked it. He liked the way Tommy's green eyes lit up beneath his straight, blond hair when he talked to Billey. The other kids' eyes flashed with a different light when they looked at him.

Billey liked the way Tommy walked, straight up, but bouncy on his feet, like any second he might break loose and race Billey to the next tree. When they played Shirts and Skins at recess, Tommy's skin looked smooth, all one shade of cream. His shoulder blades stood out in neat, efficient little triangles; his belly button formed a pocket just big enough for the end of his pinky.

Billey hated his own body. Deep purple patches mottled his skin. His raw bones met at awkward angles. The kids teased him for having an "outie." If he hadn't been such a good blocker, they never would have let him in the game.

"'Attaway, good buddy," Tommy said. "Brewster can't get by you, Billey."

The kids caught their breath as they linked arms in the huddle. Tommy squatted and traced lines in the dirt. "Sanger and Barton, go long. Billey, you do a buttonhook," Tommy said, dipping his head for gulps of air. "On seventeen."

Billey went to the line and heard Tommy calling out random numbers before he realized he didn't know what a buttonhook was. He wasn't even wearing any buttons because they were the Skins this time. Dankowski snapped the ball and players on either side charged against each other. Caught up in the game's momentum, Billey lunged forward three steps. He stopped, spun around and waved his arms at Tommy, hoping to get a sign. The football hit him like a bullet.

The Shirts never covered Billey because they figured if he caught the ball, he wouldn't know what to do with it anyway. They were right, but somehow Billey picked Tommy's instructions out of the shouting that engulfed him.

"Turn and run," Tommy yelled. "Go, Billey!"

What Billey lacked in speed and finesse, he made up in size and determination. Four of the Shirts hung off his arms and legs by the time he staggered into the end zone.

The Skins danced wildly. They slapped each other's hands. Some of them even called Billey by a grown-up name.

"Way to go, Elwood," they cried. "You shithead."

"One thing about Elwood," Billey heard Dankowski tell Barton, "his mother must have been a *big* old horse."

Billey tried to bask in these strange, new feelings of friendship while they lasted.

"You want to come over to my folks' house after school?" Tommy asked when the bell interrupted the Skins' celebrations.

"I dunno," said Billey, who had never been invited anywhere before.

"Come on. We'll have fun."

The anticipation helped Billey make it through the last hour of school without falling asleep or getting in trouble.

Tommy got good grades, but he was the first one through the door when the bell sounded. "Go, Skins!" he shouted, clicking his heels and throwing a fist high in the air.

Billey lumbered outside in time to see Tommy surrounded by his classmates. Some of them had been Skins today, but some he wasn't sure about. The teams changed every day and Billey couldn't tell who had been a Shirt and who a Skin because they all wore shirts now. He lingered by the stark brick school building as the crowd hoisted Tommy overhead. They chanted, "Who's gonna win? Skins! Who's gonna win? Skins!" But the sound grew fainter as they left him behind on their march to the street.

None of that mattered to Black Wolf, who worshipped Billey as much as any dog could.

Black Wolf had grown into a dog's dog. His snout had lengthened to accommodate perfect teeth in a powerful jaw. He had the sharp bark of crude joy. His keen nose could catch Billey's scent from clear over the scooped-out hill. Whether Billey had bean juice or dirt or even boogers all over his face never made any difference to Black Wolf when he licked it.

One thing Billey learned in school was that only Black Wolf would never betray him.

•

Elwood let Billey in the house only under three conditions. If the cops came, the boy had to hide in the bedroom. If rain fell at dinner time, or it was too cold to eat on the porch, he could have his beans by the greasy Coleman. And if Billey had to take a crap, he could use the bathroom.

"Go pee outside," Elwood always said. "Pee's gonna wash away, but I sure as shit don't wanna be steppin' on your turds in the driveway."

Black Wolf always tagged along with Billey, but Elwood only let him in the house when the cops showed up.

"Don't need that stinkin' bastard barkin' at me when I'm doin' business," he muttered.

So Black Wolf didn't have any better concept of indoors and outdoors than Billey. The dog would have followed him right into the school house if the teacher had allowed it.

The kids snickered that Billey should be a patrol boy because traffic always stopped when he and Black Wolf walked along the road. Tommy Lagocki poked his head out the window of one of the cars.

"Billey! Where were you yesterday?" he said. "I thought you were coming over."

Billey tried to see how many shapes his shoe could make in the dirt.

"Is that your dog? Where'd you get it?"

"I dunno," Billey said. It seemed now like he'd had Black Wolf forever. "He was the only one there."

Tommy convinced Billey to come home with him that afternoon. Black Wolf waited in the schoolyard all day long with nothing to do but chase a couple of birds or see what kind of holes he could dig by the fence.

Tommy lived in a real house with windows you could see through, chairs, carpets, the works. He had his own room with a bed and a chest of drawers.

"Tommy, why don't you show Billey some of your toys?" said Mrs. Lagocki. She held out a bulldozer, its yellow paint striking a bright contrast to the deep red of her long, smooth nails.

Toys were nothing new to Tommy, but Black Wolf was. He rolled the dog onto its back and tickled its tummy as its stubby legs paddled the air and its tongue drooped down to the carpet.

"Fetch, Black Wolf!" Tommy lobbed a tennis ball across the room and the fur ball bounced after it. "Bring it here."

Black Wolf stood in the middle of the living room, shaking his head back and forth with the ball between his jaws. He peered up from the tops of his eyes as Mrs. Lagocki brought in a tray of milk and cookies for the boys.

Mrs. Lagocki cocked her ear at some noise she couldn't identify. She looked at Black Wolf, so low to the carpet it was hard to tell what he was doing down there. Suddenly, she skidded the tray across the coffee table and lunged for the dog. "Billey, he has to potty!"

She grunted as she lifted the animal—he was heavier than he looked. Some of the dog's thick, black hair pasted itself onto her white dress before she stumbled out the door under his weight.

Black Wolf found himself barred from the Lagocki household after that, but Billey still got to come in sometimes.

In her charitable way, Mrs. Lagocki understood that Billey

lacked some things beyond his obvious shortcomings. And Tommy was too young to pick out the things that made his good buddy different. After a few visits, Billey even quit jerking his head around to see what lurked behind him.

One morning when Billey didn't have to go to school, he put his ear under Elwood's window and heard the steady snoring that signaled safety. He'd dreamt about Tommy, so he walked over to Tommy's house, thinking it only natural that his friend would be thinking about the same things.

Before he got to the door, he heard voices around back. Billey poked his head around the corner and saw a clutch of women wearing gloves and pastel dresses. The gloves looked like lights that waved through the air, pulling his eyes out of their sockets and his tongue out of his mouth.

Billey had been in such a hurry to see Tommy that he hadn't taken the time to complete his morning routine. He unzipped his pants and watered a rose bush, unable to see past the gloves to the women's shocked faces.

Billey never got to go over to Tommy's house again. He was nine years old and he wouldn't have another friend in his life, until he met Uly Bondarbon.

Chapter 11

The Book of Miles

Sandy slipped the car into park and turned off the engine. She took the red spiral notebook from the glove compartment and logged the date and odometer reading. She broke down the day's miles into those traveled to work and to the day care center. The trip to the pet shop fell under entertainment.

The black pen ran dry before she finished. She scribbled an invisible tornado on a scrap of paper, but the thing was dead. She found another pen in her purse and completed the entry before she noticed its ink was blue. She stared at the abrupt color change in the middle of the line and wondered if that mattered, if she would have to copy the whole damn book over in blue ink.

"Can we go in, mom?" Saury asked.

"In a minute." She frowned, then shook her head. "I'm sorry. Just a minute, Saury."

Stephen X took a hard line on keeping proper records. Once she'd mistaken a seven for a two in her checkbook and wound up with five dollars more than she expected at the end of the month. That made him furious. He'd ripped open her purse and pulled out ten dollars.

"Five makes it even," he said, rubbing the first bill against her nose until she turned her head as if the money stank, "and five for a penalty. Just you remember, most lessons don't come that cheap."

He made a living in some murky realm of finance or accounting but she was never able to figure out exactly what he did. It seemed to involve long hours with businessmen and bourbon. She couldn't imagine what qualifications he had, unless the job description called for humorless self-importance. Yet somehow he made money—lots of it—although the first sign she saw of it was on the sheaf of tax papers he slid across the table at breakfast one day in April.

"It's just a formality," he said, his eyes daring her to look through the papers. "The IRS says you have to sign it, too."

She couldn't help but see the staggering figures on the top form. Where had all that money come from? Where had it gone?

A tiny fraction had gone for a car phone for Stephen X. "Friend of mine gave me a great deal," he said, fingering the handset. "With the tax deduction, I'll be getting it for a quarter of market."

At least when he was happy, he was only insufferable. It was almost safe to ignore him.

Saturday morning, Stephen X sprang from bed and began flashing the lights on and off. "Rise and shine!" he bellowed. "Wake up, sleepyhead! Grab that kid of yours and let's go for a ride!"

"Where?" Sandy rubbed her knuckles into her eyes.

"Who cares where? Let's just pack up and go."

They drove for mile after aimless mile, as Sandy tried to contain Saury in her arms and Stephen X hooked his wrist over the spoke of the steering wheel. He let his other hand dance across the phone.

"Look at that!" he cried. Sandy looked out the window and immediately felt foolish for thinking there was something to see. "I can call the weather number while I'm out in the weather! Is this a great country or what?"

He rang TrafficWatch, Dial-a-Smile, GardenTips, movie listings and the ScoreLine while they cruised the city streets.

He raved on, but his noise faded into the background, like the sound of jets to someone who lives by the airport. For the first time, Sandy saw what Westmore Avenue really looked like. "No wonder I blot this out every day," she thought, as the tackiness and commercial squalor closed in on her. She saw vicious, snarling dogs herd used cars behind cyclone fences. The sun had not yet cleared the tattered billboards that hawked cigarettes and sex, cheap booze and good deals. A breeze lifted yesterday's newspapers from the pavement and wrapped them around telephone poles and stop signs. She pulled Saury tight against her bosom and prayed that he would go back to sleep. She wondered where this world ever came from. Who had asked for it to be like this?

"The time is six fifty-one," Stephen X parroted. "The temperature is sixty-three degrees."

"Why don't you call a human being?" Sandy asked.

"It's Saturday morning," he shrugged. "Nobody's up yet."

He dumped a deck of business cards in her lap, trying not to veer into the curb. "You should have brought the phone book. For my birthday, you can get me one of those little Rolodexes that fits right on the console."

Before the scream could leave Sandy's throat, Stephen X heard the dull thud, like someone had used his car as a bass drum. He smashed the brake pedal to the floorboard and looked around.

"You almost hit that kid," Sandy said as soon as her breath worked again.

Stephen X saw the boy, in shorts and a sweat-stained tee shirt, jogging along the curb, scowling over his own shoulder. He saw a challenge in the kid's twisted, red face. He threw the car in reverse, jolted to a stop, and rolled down the window on Sandy's side.

"You got a problem?" Stephen X asked, leaning over so that his head crowded Saury in Sandy's lap.

"Why don't you watch the hell where you're going, man?" The boy gulped more air than his running required.

"Did you hit my car?"

"Why not? It just about hit me."

"Do your parents know where you are?"

"What?"

"What's their number? We can clear this up right now." Stephen X reached for his new car phone.

Sandy stared far beyond the windshield and shook her head ever so slightly. The boy picked up the cue and began to edge away.

"You're nuts, mister."

"Come back here. I don't appreciate that."

Stephen X puffed his chest and peeled rubber as the boy began to jog again. "See that?" he said. "Little prick even had snot on his face. Thinks he owns the road."

He punched Roscoe's number and waited a long time.

"Hey, what're you doing, big brother?" he said at last. "We're driving around trying out my new car phone. Why don't you and Linda grab little Johnny Cakes and meet us down at Mama M's for breakfast?"

He listened and frowned, making an unpremeditated right turn at the stop sign.

"You know Mama M's on Finley Road. Sure, Mama's open all night." Stephen X didn't like what he was hearing. "It's easy from your place. Just go east on Washington - or Lincoln—whatever it is. Turn left at Jefferson. There's a Shell station on the corner . . ."

He continued to zig-zag down random streets while giving directions to Roscoe.

"Then it's just two, three blocks on the left. Next to the U-Haul place. Okay. See you there." Stephen X replaced the handset and looked around. He slowed down and studied the road. "Sandy?"

"What?"

"Where are we?"

She put one hand beneath her and pushed herself up a little against the seat belt. She craned her neck around to study the landscape. "I don't know, Stephen X," she said, letting her voice sound faintly like his secretary, Lucille. "I didn't notice what that last intersection was."

In the months that followed, she wondered how long it would take him to make a useful call on his new toy. Weeks passed before he got the idea of phoning her from the car. As soon as she lifted the receiver, she heard the static, rising and falling like electronic surf.

"Honey, I'll be home late tonight. Don't worry about me."

The caricature of Stephen X's voice might have drifted down from the moon for all its familiarity and warmth. Even the tinny words were someone else's.

"Where are you calling from?" she asked, but she was really just thinking out loud.

"What?"

"Where are you? I can hardly hear you."

"I'm with a client. We're driving down Delancey. I'll grab a bite on the way home, Honey."

The conversation reminded her of those movies he always dragged her to, where some alien life form invades people's bodies and tries to pass for human—but the way they talk or stare is always a dead give away.

The car phone's only benefit to her was that it meant she didn't have to talk to him much anymore. She played deaf whenever she heard the telltale crackle and hiss of static on the line.   "Hello? Is anybody there?" she shouted. "We must have a bad line. If you can hear me, try again later."

She couldn't imagine that he needed the phone for work, like he said. What client would put up with shouting and straining to hear? It made her wonder more than ever what kind of a job he had.

"I pop bubbles," he had told her, not long after they met, but she sensed even then that the answer had been rehearsed. The following years bore out her suspicion. "I show them where they're wasting good money. They never want to hear it, but I've got the numbers on my side."

Stephen X carved cold, granite numbers to fit his purposes. He pored over spreadsheets, marshaling time and events into stark columns and rows. He took comfort in the razor edge of precision.

Sandy made her living with numbers, too, but hers shimmered in the moonlight of uncertainty. She swept the hopes, dreams, and habits of the common man into grand, parabolic curves. Her figures sprang like quicksilver into a thousand shapes.

For Stephen X, the numbers were predictable, obedient. They pacified him, so she knew better than to quit filling in the miles in the little red book. She kept it up year after year, even after what had happened when she presented the completed log to him on January 1, the first year they were married.

"Here's the mileage record," she said.

He'd looked up from a bologna sandwich and thumbed through the notebook. "What is this?" he asked, studying a page.

"The miles I drove last year. Where I went. How far it was, like you showed me to do."

Stephen X had nodded slowly. "Yes," he said. "Thanks."

"Mom, can we go in now?" Saury asked again.

She looked at the house's dark windows and smiled. "Sure. Let's go."

Chapter 12

Otis

Billey probably wouldn't have noticed he was getting bigger except that he had to squeeze a little bit more to fit in the camper at night. Then again, Black Wolf seemed to be standing lower and lower to the ground, too.

Billey might be growing, but the rest of the world stayed the same. Everything else—eating beans beside the spool, hiding from Elwood's rages, pissing on the gravel, being shunned by his classmates, coaxing Black Wolf to dance on his hind legs—remained constant. These things were the air and water of Billey's life.

His muscles began to bunch up, hard as baseballs beneath the mottled skin when he crooked his arms. When he found himself alone, he crouched against the spool and strained to nudge it a few inches across the porch. Week by week, it became a little easier until finally he could push it like some enormous hockey puck from the side rail to the door and back.

Billey lifted Black Wolf onto the spool. He heaved the massive rim by eighth turns, faster and faster, until it spun like a merry-go-round. The dog raised his head and howled at the stars, his long, pink-and-black tongue trailing great arcs of saliva in the breeze.

The faster he spun the spool, the stronger Billey felt until he had to howl, too. The moment dug down deep in his gut and pulled out an awful string of vowels. Sounds Billey had never imagined gushed up from his belly. They left his lungs feeling cold and clean as the tiny stars on the moon-free night.

When the spool wobbled to a standstill, Black Wolf's eyes bulged from their sockets. The dog tumbled to the porch and rolled around just like Elwood did on the nights when Otis came over.

Except for the cops, Elwood never got many visitors. But now and again Otis would show up in his battered old half a car. The body of Otis' green Ford Fairlane had been cut away behind the driver's seat. It might have been a sedan converted to a pick-up at one time, but now the bed was gone, leaving the chassis, back wheels and gas tank exposed. It reminded Billey of some big, stupid bug with a skinny butt.

Otis had whiskers and tattoos just like Billey's daddy. His cheeks sunk in no matter how hard he pulled on a cigarette or the flat bottle that smelled like kerosene—or was that turpentine? He had the same droopy eye and cratered complexion as Billey's daddy. But Otis' oily, blond hair sprang from his head like a field of corkscrews. He looked bigger, puffier than Elwood, like a bean that had been cooked too long. Each movement and word came slowly, as if he wanted them to be unslurred, although that never made any difference.

"Hey, Billey boy," Otis cried, sweeping his arms for balance as he stumbled out of his bugmobile. "You gonna be old enough to start whackin' off pretty soon here."

"Did you bring that thing we talked about?" Elwood said, leaving his feet propped on the spool. "What the hell took you so long?"

"I's just tellin' Billey he's gonna have a big, old peter 'fore too long. Course he ain't never seen one bigger 'n mine."

"You couldn't keep a flea horse happy with no more peter than that, Otis."

"Shit, don't lie to the boy. You told me to get one o' them organ cards so's they could sew my peter on to you when I die."

"Otis, I guarantee I never knew me a man as dumb as you."

The big man smiled, as if proud to be best at something, and lumbered over to the porch. He sat in Billey's chair by the spool. The two men passed the flask back and forth and spoke in low voices.

Billey knew better than to stick around. Something about Otis always made Elwood walk crooked, whup Billey twice as bad as usual, then sleep on the porch until the sun stood still in the sky.

So Billey took Black Wolf down to the creek. He got hungry, but that seemed like a fair swap for what he'd get if Elwood and Otis found him. As the sky darkened, Black Wolf cocked his ear at the sound of the crickets and the distant roar of the trucks on the big road. Billey leaned against the willow tree's worn trunk and dozed off.

He woke to the chattering of his teeth in the middle of the night. Black Wolf, with all his hair, could sleep forever. Billey hugged himself and hopped around to get warm, but it didn't do much good.

He walked carefully back to the shack, shushing Black Wolf if the dog so much as took a deep breath. For a big, clumsy kid with shoddy hearing, Billey knew how to move lightly over the gravel. Fear cushioned every step.

Billey got close enough to score a touchdown even with all the Shirts in the world hanging from his limbs. But he knew he couldn't make a run for it. He squinted at the camper in the meager starlight and tested the air with his ears.

He lifted his leg high at the knee, wheeling his arms for balance. He eased his foot to the ground, then repeated the procedure with the next leg. The more slowly he moved, the more quickly his heart beat. It might have taken the rest of the night to cross the final forty yards to safety.

Billey heard the crack of the gun at the instant he felt the plug of dirt the bullet kicked up. Elwood and Otis roared at the way he jumped.

"Watch out, Billey boy," Otis laughed. "We thought you was a burglar out there in the dark."

"Man's gotta defend his land," Elwood said as he sighted

along his wobbling arm. "Says so in the Declaration o'Dependence."

He pulled the trigger and staggered backwards with the recoil. Billey thought he felt the bullet graze his leg, but it was only a stone on the ricochet. He fell to the dirt, picked himself up and sprinted for the camper. Black Wolf made the door at the same time, so both their butts waggled in the breeze for a moment before they scrambled through.

Billey wanted to catch his breath, but he didn't want to breathe that deeply because the rasp of air in his lungs made it hard to hear what was going on outside. The men shouted and laughed. Now and again a gunshot rang out. Billey felt too scared to be awake, too excited to sleep. It seemed like the night would never end.

Chapter 13

Home

Rollingwood Park, the enclave where the Skinners lived, had Westmore Avenue's convenience without its down-scale image.

Rollingwood Drive fed directly into Westmore so the residents could make their way quickly to any part of the city. But when they stayed home, they never had to see or think about Westmore and its ugly utility.

While Westmore, straight as a razor, split the city in two equal parts, Rollingwood coiled through the hills like yarn that a cat had played with. Corky Cartwright, the agent who attached himself to Stephen X and Sandy when they were buying their house, claimed linear streets were relics of the past.

As the little man under the bouffant hair drove them around in his white convertible, he gushed and waved his arms. "This is the modern thing," he said. "People like you folks have been to college. You know Einstein said, `Space is curves.'"

"The space I like is all curves," Stephen X said. "Isn't that right, Sandy?"

The stranger brayed. He blinked and paused for an instant when he saw in the rear view mirror that Sandy wasn't smiling. Then he looked at Stephen X and laughed harder than ever.

"That's right, Mr. Skinner," he shouted as if he were far away. "You and Einstein."

After awhile, Sandy leaned forward to interrupt the men. "Elmwood, Ashwood, Beechwood, Birchwood, Maplewood—all of these streets named after trees go in circles. There aren't even any trees on them. How do you find your way around?"

"That's why they call it Rollingwood Park," Corky said, trying to keep a straight face as he glanced over his shoulder. "They rolled all the wood away to make room for it.

"But seriously, folks, the community's layout is one of its best security features. You can get lost here for hours. Burglars can't stand it. They want to go somewhere they can get in, get out, be gone. That's why you get your high crime rate down on these straight roads like Westmore. They may be crooks, but they're no fools."

The scrubbed, pink brick and slightly pretentious facade of the typical Rollingwood home appealed to Stephen X. He loved the idea of a planned community that prized central shopping, concealed power lines and bump-free streets over sidewalks or vitality. Corky closed the deal and told Stephen X he was going to buy himself a fat cigar and a bottle of sipping whiskey.

Sandy allowed herself the luxury of thinking that other things would change with the move—things more important than bricks and beams; things she never even dared to pull up to the conscious levels of her mind. Maybe life didn't have to be the way it had always been.

It seemed like they had barely unpacked the last box when she learned she was pregnant with Saury.

"How did that happen?" Stephen X snapped, looking up from the wingtips he'd been tying.

She bit her tongue but couldn't keep her expression from saying, "Didn't they teach you that in school?"

He sprang across the room, trailing one lace. "I said, 'How could you let that happen?'"

This time she couldn't help it. "I think you were there, too," she said, lifting her eyes to him.

Stephen X didn't stand much taller, but he had a good forty pounds on her. He had a way of staring hard into her eyes. If she flinched and looked away, they both knew that he had won some victory as significant as it was bizarre. If she held his gaze, she won—as far as that went—but she also lost track of his hands, and that was always dangerous.

"So you think I was there?" he sang it like a nursery rhyme gone sour.

Sandy's head snapped back as he tugged a fist full of hair from behind. She swung around to try to grab his wrist.

"You *think* I was there, do you?" He gave up the hair and crushed her hand, twisting her arm behind her back at an awful angle. "So who do you think the little bastard's father is?" He wrenched her arm to the limit. "Huh, Sandy? Who is it?"

Doubled over beneath his weight, she felt as if she had only a straw to breathe through. "What are you doing?"

"I'll show you what I'm doing." He released her so she straightened up like a spring. He sprouted a thousand hands in a grabbing, slapping, poking frenzy that drove her backwards across the bedroom.

Instinct kept Sandy rolling when she hit the floor, but his feet struck faster than fear or reflex. The hard edge of his wingtip gouged her back, her thigh, her ribs, her breast and skull before she lost track of the blows.

•

Sandy never knew how old she would be when she opened her eyes. Time swept her up and threw her back down in the strangest places, like the tornado that nails a straw in a tree. Her life unfolded in such chaos that feelings of pain and injustice at least provided a thread of continuity. But she never knew when she opened her eyes if she would find herself as a child or adult, pregnant or mother, alive or dead.

Her father had hardly ever knocked her unconscious. When he did, she found herself in her mother's arms. That woman pressed Sandy's head to her breast and rocked her. She hummed to soothe her, then dabbed the wounds with cotton and antiseptic.

Sandy thought of the kind of parallel universe she saw when Stephen X dragged her to the horror movies. It was a world governed by its own science, its own math, its own etiquette of pain. It voided clocks and calendars so that no matter how long she was away, it remained unchanged when she returned to it.

She could never visit that other land by herself. A Jack Gore or a Stephen X Skinner had to take her there. When she was in the brighter world, she might even forget that place existed, but it always lurked there, like a bloated, blue-green tumor just beneath the skin. In the dazed moments when she crossed between the two dimensions, she couldn't tell which was the host and which the cancer.

The only constant was the desperate need to protect someone who was helpless against this world that she had somehow created. Maybe it would be her baby sister, Jennifer. Maybe her own baby, Saury. She clawed at the slippery face of consciousness, afraid that the child would be gone when she woke.

In the end, there was nothing she could have done for Jennifer, and that made her all the more desperate to save Saury.

The early signs of womanhood had flared through Sandy's body by the time Uncle Josh got out of the army. Looking back on it, she supposed that meant she was already too old for him.

Funny how in the twelve years, eight months and twenty-four days of her life, she'd never met Uncle Josh before, never heard mention of him. He looked like a younger, pudgier, stupider version of her own father. She couldn't imagine how silly he must have looked in uniform, and nobody seemed to have any photographs to satisfy her curiosity.

"Sandy, Jenny, say hello to your uncle Josh." Jack Gore herded his daughters forward. "He's been in the army a long time."

Even at first sight, Jennifer had tried to duck behind her big sister, pulling Sandy's skirt like a veil across her face.

"Hello, ladies," said Josh through a mouth that never quite closed. Sandy thought maybe gravity had dragged his brains down into his face. That would explain his vacant expression and why his fat, pimpled cheeks promised to burst with the pressure.

Josh lived with them a month—maybe six weeks—washing potato chips and cupcakes down with grape soda. When her father wasn't around, Josh would pretend to be struggling to suppress a belch, then suddenly unleash a mighty, gaseous roar that filled the house. Sandy figured all that carbonation must have collected in his brain.

He didn't bug Sandy much, but Jennifer told her how he always rubbed against her back when he squeezed behind her chair at the dinner table, how he invited her into his room to play or to see his stuff.

"How could you play with him?" Sandy said. "He's even too dumb to have fun."

Jennifer tossed her hair back, strutted and made faces outside his closed door while Sandy tried to contain her laughter. Josh was a joke with a thousand punchlines. All of their father's disgusting and ridiculous traits had been distilled into this fat, lead-brained caricature of him.

Hysteria replaced the laughter when Jennifer burst in and told Sandy how Josh had touched her. Their mother pounded the door.

"Sandy! Jennifer! What on earth is going on in there?"

Sandy opened the door a crack and pulled the woman in by the sleeve. She told her what had happened.

"Why us, mom?" Sandy fought for control of her voice. "What did we ever do?"

"Be quiet. Don't tell anyone about this."

"What do you mean, don't tell anyone? Didn't you hear what I just said?" Sandy's tears came in spurts, like blood from an artery. "How can you let him live here?"

"Shh, shh. He'll hear you." The woman, this stranger, clapped her hand over Sandy's mouth. "Okay, okay. I'll talk to your father."

Mrs. Gore may have talked to Mr. Gore about the incident, but nothing ever came of it. Josh ranged freely about the house, and the girls did their best to avoid him.

"Pass the butter, Jenny," Josh said, breaking the silence at Sunday dinner.

Jennifer stared at her plate. She'd become bone thin, her sunken eyes rimmed in red. Sandy ached to see her smile and laugh again.

"Josh asked you for the butter, darling," Jack Gore said, as if they were all just waiting for some detail to be clarified. "Did you hear me, Jenny?"

Sandy tried to be somewhere else by counting her heartbeats. She pressed her fork into her thigh to keep from screaming.

"Damn it, Jenny, give Josh the butter."

They all knew Mount Gore was about to erupt. Jennifer picked up the butter dish, but her hand shook so badly that when she held it over to her uncle, the margarine slid off. Josh swatted his hand out to catch it. In a single, clumsy sweep, he squeezed the soft stick and batted his greasy hand to his chest. Before he realized what he was doing, he wiped the margarine into his shirt.

"Oh, that's going to stain for sure," Mrs. Gore said.

"Look what you've done, Jenny." Jack Gore couldn't believe that he had spawned such irritating girls. "What gets into you? Tell Josh you're sorry."

Jennifer threw her plate against the wall. "It's not fair," she cried. "I hate him."

She sent her chair crashing to the linoleum and burst out the front door.

Gore had time only to say "What in God's name is wrong

with that little—" when they heard the noise from outside.

The important things always happen too fast. But even through the flash of confusion that followed, Sandy would always remember that the horn sounded *after* the squeal of the tires.

After it was too late.

Chapter 14

The Tank

Billey didn't remember going to sleep, but daylight streamed through the cracks in the camper when he opened his eyes. Black Wolf panted and dabbed his tongue on Billey's neck, eager to get going. But Billey wasn't so sure he wanted to know what the world looked like today.

He cracked the door an inch and sucked a sharp breath of air when the hinge squeaked. He didn't get himself killed—or even whupped—so he nudged the door little by little until he could fit his head through it.

The sky came down in brilliant blue sheets, giving the shack a tinge of rustic nobility. The sun set it apart from the gravel and scrub with such clarity that it looked like a model of a shack that Tommy Lagocki might keep in his toy chest. A big old crow spread his wings near the top of the dead catalpa and looked around for food.

Billey crawled out of the camper and eased himself to the ground. He walked in a half-crouch, holding Black Wolf in check by the long hair on his neck, and sneaked around to the front of the shack. He saw Elwood's legs sticking out from behind the spool. Even with bad ears and a good distance, he could hear the ragged snoring that signaled safety. Billey's own breath came more freely.

Black Wolf expressed his relief in a different way. He shifted his weight to his haunches and barked as clear as a school bell.

"Ssshhh!" Billey tugged on the dog's thick hair. "Down, boy," he whispered in a voice suddenly hoarse with fear.

Elwood's legs jerked, smashing one knee against the spool. The heels of his boots clattered on the porch as he sat up.

"What the hell's that racket?" Billey saw one leathery hand grab the rim of the spool for balance. "Billey! 'Sat you, Billey?"

Billey dashed around to the back of the house with Black Wolf yapping at his heels. The camper wouldn't be safe now, and there was too much open space to break for the creek. He pressed his shoulder blades against the building and turned his head to the sky. The sun washed over his face, drawing fine drops of sweat from his temples.

For a moment, the panic fell away and Billey saw the depth of the sky. He wondered how something as fat as a crow could fly without beating its wings, how dust formed a fragile blanket over the world. Black Wolf looked to Billey for the next move and Billey felt like the gear that pulled the can opener around the rim. For a moment, he felt unafraid.

Elwood's shadow crossed the boy's face, snapping him out of his dream.

"Shut your mouth 'fore you swaller a fly, Billey." Elwood snorted, but he didn't take a swing at Billey. "I got me some work for you today."

Elwood made him pull up nearly every big weed in two acres. As Billey tugged at them and shook the dirt from their roots, Black Wolf scampered around on his stubby little legs. Billey heaped up the weeds about as far from the shack as you could get without going into the creek. A horse could have hidden behind the pile and nobody at the road would have been any wiser. But even Billey knew the weeds would bake down to nothing in a couple of days. Then you wouldn't be able to hide shit back there.

"Gonna get us a big one tonight," Elwood said, slapping small clouds of dust out of his jeans. "Fetch yourself some beans so you'll be ready for some real work."

Otis came over late that afternoon and the two men drove off in the pickup. Soon as they were out of sight, Billey sat on the porch and shook his head. He knew nothing of philosophy. He couldn't have defined the word, spelled it, or even repeated it three times without getting his tongue in a jumble. Avoiding Elwood and waiting for beans crowded his attention most of the time, so he never much looked at how the world fit together. But now it seemed like he spent his whole life either working or getting whupped. It seemed like there ought to be something in between the two things. Or maybe there ought to be a reason for either one of them.

Black Wolf didn't care. He didn't know the difference between working and fooling around. He was so fast and so low to the ground that Elwood didn't even bother trying to kick him anymore, much less whup him.

Billey lifted the dog onto the spool and spun it a couple of turns, but he felt too tired after pulling weeds all day. He sat in his daddy's chair with his feet on the spool, and with Black Wolf panting softly at his side. They watched the darkness come down from the top of the sky and listened to the crickets all around. Now and then, Billey's head fell forward, until he caught it with a start.

He bolted upright and Black Wolf set to barking when the pickup roared up the drive. The horn blared and Billey could see the shadow of Otis leaning out the window, pounding on his door. Lashed to the back of the truck was a giant yellow plastic tank. The truck looked like an ant hauling a big old grub back to the hill.

Billey ran around the shack and watched the truck speed over the rough field to the heap of weeds down by the creek. The headlights circled the spot three times, then came back toward him without stopping.

The truck—top-heavy with its cargo—veered so sharply to dodge the potholes, engine blocks and tree stumps that Billey thought it would tip over. Otis and Elwood's chorus of obscenities served as counterpoint to the engine and the horn, unbridled by any need beyond filling the night. The truck jerked to a stop.

Billey stood bewildered in the headlights as the two men staggered out.

"Yer daddy done pretty good," Otis said, waving his flask at the truck, "for a man what ain't got no more peter than he has."

"Otis, yer so full o'shit you'd pop if you ever shut yer mouth for two minutes." Elwood circled around the truck and reached for the bottle.

"Don't listen to him, Billey boy. I heard yer daddy and Pierce sayin' they's gonna draw straws to see who gets my peter when I die."

"Said we was gonna draw a *picture* of a peter so's you'd know it if you ever saw one."

"You gonna make Billey boy grow up to be a liar if you keep talkin' like that." Otis tried to grab the bottle back but he lost balance and wound up on the ground, staring into the sky. "I'm awright. I'm awright," he said, as if anyone cared. Then he broke into laughter that fed on itself until Elwood kicked dirt in his face.

"What do you think this is, Billey?" Elwood asked, drumming the bottom of his fist against the tank.

"I dunno."

"Ain't you never seen a gas tank? Swear I don't know how you got to be so stupid. Sometimes I think Otis musta been yer daddy." He spat and shook his head. "'Cept he ain't got no peter."

Otis wobbled upright and rubbed his eyes. "Shut yer mouth afore I put somethin' in it."

Elwood pounded the tank, nodding at the deep sound he produced. "They bury these mothahs under gas stations, Billey. Fill one up and you got gas for life. Never have to worry 'bout shit again."

He walked around the back of the truck, admiring his prize from every angle. "Ever seen anything like it?"

"I dunno."

"Well, I know for a fact you ain't, so don't get on your high horse with me." Elwood slapped the tank hard. "I seen where you come from, Billey Elwood. I know ever'thing 'bout you. Fact is, I know stuff 'bout you that you don't even know you don't know. So don't you try tellin' me you don't know when I know you ain't. Unnerstand?"

Billey thought a moment. He watched Otis rocking back and forth with the bottle clutched tight to his belly. "I guess so," he lied.

•

Come daybreak, Elwood pounded the camper. "Wake up, Billey. You gotta helluva lotta work to do."

Elwood had rolled the tank off the truck behind the pile of dead weeds during the night. Now he handed Billey a spade. "You know why we gotta bury this, Billey?"

Billey looked at the hard ground and the tank that towered over him and wondered that very thing. When he looked at his daddy, his mind raced behind his searching, fearful eyes. "I guess so."

Elwood's eyes narrowed. "That right, Billey? S'pose you just tell me why then."

Billey thought harder and time seemed to crawl like a snail up a stem. "So if it catches fire, it'll just burn underground," he said at last.

"Fire? Fires don't burn underground. They need air, Billey. We ain't never gonna have no fires here." He shook his head sadly. Then he spread his arms and lifted his voice. "We gotta bury it so's nobody comes and takes it away. Whatever you got, they want. Just you remember that."

"Why?"

"'Cause I'm your daddy, that's why." He scraped the ground with his shovel, moving no more dirt than a bird would. "You start diggin' there and I'll start here. We'll meet in the middle."

Elwood lasted maybe fifteen minutes. "I gotta take care of

some things, Billey. You keep diggin' till I get back." He propped his shovel against the tank and walked back across the field, rubbing his palms together. He looked over his shoulder once and saw Billey watching him. "Don't you wait for me, Billey. Just keep a'diggin'."

Elwood seemed to get smaller and smaller the closer he got to the shack until he looked no bigger than a bug.

Without anyone near it, Elwood's shovel slid to the ground, startling Billey. When he saw what had happened, he started scratching the earth again. The dirt made harsh sounds against his spade. It didn't give way any more than rock would.

Billey's hands already felt a little sore from the work. A tiny river of sweat found its way along his spine, right down to his butt. Pretty soon he wouldn't be able to fit in the shadow of the weeds anymore. Billey kicked a rock out of the way.

It was going to be a long day.

Chapter 15

The Invitation

Every detail of the October afternoon Sandy met Stephen X remained sharp. It was three days before Halloween, although that hadn't seemed so significant to her at the time.

The maples carved fiery shapes in the sky. Sandy feared she might damage the tender corners of her lungs if she breathed in too much of the cool, pure air. Seven high school kids in a convertible cruised past her on Main, blowing a trumpet because the big game was at hand. Someone's sticky shoe had stretched pink threads of bubblegum along the sidewalk.

Sandy wore her blue windbreaker over a thin, white sweater and jeans. Linda zipped her yellow windbreaker to the neck. They stopped at Burger Castle for fries and a Coke on their way home from classes.

They didn't have any reason to notice Stephen X pushing aside his onion rings when they walked in. He was just another upperclassman in a plaid shirt. "Too old for acne," Linda always said. "Too young to die."

They sipped their Cokes and marveled at how different their professors were from their old high school teachers. They seemed to be wiser, timeless versions of the students. A lot of them even dressed nicely.

"What would Dalton of Prunes say to someone like Chappel Crownfield?" Linda spread her fingers wide, as if trying to hold the table down with both hands. "Like, `where do I get a lime cardigan around here?'"

They both laughed so Sandy didn't know how long Stephen X had been twisted their way in his booth. Then she heard his deep, even voice for the first time.

"You've got Crownfield?" he said, like a tourist who'd

caught a snatch of English in a crowded, foreign market. "Isn't he great?"

Sandy nodded, brushing her hand against her mouth to make sure no Coke spotted her lips.

"We thought history was going to be a big, fat nothing," Linda blurted, then blushed ever so slightly at her enthusiasm. Sandy wanted to say something to smooth over her friend's embarrassment, but her mind went blank.

The young man wasn't interested in Linda anyway. He fixed his serious, brown eyes on Sandy. "He's the best," he said. "Only thing I could never figure is why he's teaching here when he could be pulling down the big bucks in the Ivy League."

That question never would have occurred to Sandy. She let the talk drift past her while she wondered what kind of a person would say such a thing. Certainly not anybody she'd ever known, and that lent an aura of mystery to this self-assured man.

"I started as a history major under Chappel," he was saying. "But I switched to business last year. There's no career path in history—unless you're like Chappel.

"I may not be too bright." He pressed his thumb to his forehead. "But give me credit for knowing I'd never be that good."

He wasn't that much older than the boys her age, yet he held nothing in common with them. His unblinking gaze, his confidence, his strange blend of self-effacement and megalomania caught Sandy off guard. She didn't know whether to laugh or accept him at face value or send him on his way.

She was so intrigued by the way he talked that she didn't realize he was asking her to go to a masquerade party Saturday night.

"Some friends of mine," he was saying. "You wouldn't even need a costume." He paused for just an instant then pulled a business card from his pocket. "Of course, it's such short notice," he went on, shrugging. "But here's my number if it turns out you can get away. It'll be a lot of fun."

The card had thick, blue ink on gray stock. "Stephen X Skinner," it said, "Uncommon Accounting."

He slid a couple of coins next to his untouched onion rings, turned and walked away. Sandy and Linda stared at each other with their jaws hanging.

"I think he likes you," Linda dead-panned.

"He doesn't even know me."

"Maybe that's why he likes you."

Sandy rolled her eyes and punched Linda's shoulder. "Well, I hope he has a brother who doesn't know you."

•

Sandy had been too young to understand her grandmother's warning to be careful in all decisions. Even the tiniest things sometimes brought mammoth consequences.

They sat in the shade of the Airstream's awning. Sandy cradled baby Jennifer in her arms while Mama Gore braided Sandy's hair with sure, quick movements.

"I had a brother and four sisters, all younger than me," she said in a voice so strange and distant that Sandy twisted around to look at her face. "I helped my mother all day and worked in the rail yards all night. I was young and impatient. I was tired of waiting for my own life, so I married your grandfather."

She spread a lock of Sandy's hair in her palm and stroked the wave. "He wasn't a good man. He had no warmth," she went on. "He had so many strange ideas and he lived so many years."

"What kind of ideas, grandma?" Sandy held Jennifer a little more tightly.

"About the world." She began twining Sandy's hair again. "About women and men.

"The trains that came into the yard weighed hundreds and hundreds of tons and I weighed a hundred pounds," she laughed. "I was never a big woman—"

"Yes, you are, grandma. You're the biggest woman in the world!"

"Now, listen a bit. Just a hundred pounds and I could make hundred-ton trains go this way and that. It wasn't even hard unless they let the switch run out of grease. But do you know what, Sandy?"

"What?"

"Once I threw the switch, there was no way I could bring that train back, not if I weighed a thousand pounds, a million pounds."

The moral was too abstract for Sandy at that time, but not many years passed before she recognized her father in Mama Gore's image of the runaway train. Whatever track he happened to be on was all that mattered—not where the track led, or who might be crushed along the way.

The Gores entertained small parties of business associates or neighbors on weekends. Jack Gore always banished the girls, which was no hardship to them. They talked about serious or silly or interesting things, until one of them drifted off to sleep. Sometimes loud voices and laughter woke them in the middle of the night. Then they stared into the darkness beneath the ceiling, straining to hear what was going on, but the words they could pick out never made any sense.

Grownups were so weird.

One night, a few minutes after the voices woke them, their father swung open the door, letting in the hall light.

"Sandy, come on down and meet the Wootens," he said.

"I'm asleep, daddy." She thought that was her best shot. Then she added, "I'm not dressed."

"It's alright. They have a girl just like you."

"Here?"

"No, of course not here." His tone changed ever so slightly, ever so significantly. "Get up, Sandy. I've told them all about you."

Sandy clutched her robe tightly to her throat. She found

herself blinking at her parents and two strangers in the living room. The woman smiled, but the bright red lipstick she'd slathered across her face mocked the expression. The man had no expression at all.

"What's seven times nine, Sandy?" Her father hadn't taken his seat yet. He studied her closely.

Sandy's teacher had sent the Gores a note a few days earlier. It told how Sandy had mastered her multiplication tables more quickly than any of her present or past students.

Sandy didn't want her expression to show that her father was a moron, but she was tired and it may have slipped across her face, goading him.

"Sixty-three," she said.

"Isn't she precious?" Mrs. Wooten asked, and Sandy thought the woman's lipstick had hardened, freezing her mouth in that unnatural shape.

"She gets it all from Jack," Mrs. Gore said. "Lord knows I've got no head for numbers."

Gore locked his eyes on his daughter. "Seventeen times twelve," he said.

"Two hundred and four," Sandy answered, glancing at the stairway back to her room.

"Nine times thirteen."

"One hundred and seventeen."

Mrs. Wooten laughed and clapped.

"We're so proud of her," Mrs. Gore lied.

"Twenty-nine times thirty-three." Gore raised his voice over his wife's.

"Nine hundred and fifty-seven."

The numbers rushed higher and wider, like a flock of birds after a gunshot. Mr. Gore clipped the spare syllables. Sandy answered calmly, but never pausing for air. The women stopped chattering.

"Two hundred thirty-seven times three hundred nineteen."

"Seventy-five thousand, six hundred and three."

He broke his rhythm as if he suddenly realized he had no idea whether she'd been giving the correct answers.

"Go back to bed, Sandy," he said, boring into her with cold, steely eyes. "Now."

As she rushed up the stairs, she heard Mr. Wooten say, "Looks like she's got your number, Jack."

"What are you having, Ed? Honey, get Ed another Seven and Seven."

As much as practical, Sandy tried to conceal her interests and achievements—anything that mattered—from her father so he couldn't turn them against her. It wasn't difficult since he was so self-absorbed. But now and then he'd find out about something in Sandy's life, usually by accident, and seize it as a tool of misery.

So when Jack Gore answered the phone at nine-thirty the night before Halloween during Sandy's freshman year in college, she knew there would be trouble.

"Sandy, it's for you," he said, holding the receiver as if it were a rotting fish, "It's a boy."

He stood eighteen inches from her, staring, as she answered.

"Hello, Sandy," the calm, deep voice on the line said. "Was that your father? Sounds like a nice guy.

"But this is Stephen X Skinner. You met me at Burger Castle on Wednesday."

She hadn't given him any thought since that afternoon, and it took a moment to place him. She turned her back to her father and hunched her shoulders to hide her confusion. She felt his gaze like a spider scrabbling over the back of her head.

"Oh, yes, hello." She tried to replay the Burger Castle scene in her mind, but everything was jumbled. "How did you get my number?"

"You'll see that I have my ways, Sandy," he laughed. "Look, I just wanted to check about the party tomorrow night. You're coming, aren't you?"

She couldn't put down the phone until she got her thoughts together. She asked him for details about the party, but she was already hearing what her father would say as soon as she hung up.

"Who was that?" he would demand. "What does he want? Do you know what he wants? I'll tell you what he wants. You've got no business with boys like that."

The voice in her head and the one on the line canceled each other out.

"Sure," she said, turning back to face her father with composure and resolve. "I'll go with you."

Chapter 16

Digging

He could never be sure when it would happen, but some days the men came by to check on Billey's progress.

"That all the further you dug?" Elwood scowled at the hard-won pit, as long and wide as the tank, but no deeper than the boy's knees. "Might as well send you back to school if you can't dig no better than that. How'd ya like that, Billey?"

"Okay, I guess." Billey looked at his arms to see which was cleaner. He couldn't tell the difference, so he wiped the sweat from his forehead with the right one this time. He would try to remember to use the left one next.

Elwood always said he never could figure who was dumber, Otis or his own flesh and blood. Leastwise, Billey had enough sense to keep his mouth shut most of the time. And then the boy went and made a liar out of him.

"I guess you would think that's okay," Elwood said. "That's because you're dumber than a piece of dog shit, Billey. Otherwise you'd be smart enough to know you don't wanna go to school.

"'Sides, I can teach you more in a day here than you're ever gonna learn from them priss-ass teachers of yours. Ain't that right, Otis?"

Otis rubbed the stubble on his chin and said, "Yeah, and he can do his homework on my peter."

"I'm awful thirsty," Billey said. His head throbbed from the heat like it always did when the sun got this high.

"You dig another foot all the way around and we'll get you some water, Billey," Elwood said. "Faster you dig, faster you can drink. Simple as that."

As quick as they came, the men went away, leaving Billey

and Black Wolf panting in the sun. Black Wolf draped himself over a pile of cool, fresh dirt and let his tongue hang out like a wet towel flapping in the breeze. His head shook back and forth in time with his heaving sides, but he never took his eyes off Billey.

Billey felt so bad he would have tried drinking creek water if not for the suds. The long walk back to the shack would mean that much less time he'd have for digging, but he figured he'd drop over dead if he didn't get some water. Then there'd be nobody left to dig Elwood's hole for him. He didn't want to be around if that happened.

Billey let his shovel fall. He staggered back to the shack, a journey that seemed to take hours. He weaved and lost focus. He shook his head, but couldn't clear it. At last, he found himself leaning against the shack's rough, bare wood for balance. He spun the knob on the faucet. The water ran hot after standing in the pipes, but he knelt and let it rush over him. He shook his head back and forth, pulling great gulps straight into his belly. The flood over his eyes made the world look the way it did through the shack's smudgy windows.

He couldn't see Black Wolf for the water, but he could hear him prancing and panting and yelping in the spray that bounced from Billey's head.

As the water cooled by degrees, the earth turned to mud beneath him. But he felt cleaner than he ever had. He screwed his head through the blinding stream and held his mouth to the spout.

If he hadn't been so absorbed in the relief the water brought, he might have been warned by the sudden, sharp change in Black Wolf's pitch. Instead, the hands around his ankles took him by surprise. Elwood and Otis each grabbed a leg and jerked it high in the air.

Billey's head smashed the faucet, his shoulder slammed the wall. The world spun upside down.

The two men stood there with Billey hanging between

them like a wishbone as Black Wolf snapped and snarled at their heels.

"Couldn't wait for your drink, could you, Billey?" Elwood shouted between breaths shortened by the excitement. "Here's all the water you want." He grunted and propped his leg so Billey's head split the downpour from the faucet.

The water rushed up Billey's nose, flushing the air from his mouth until the men dumped him in the mud.

"Just come on up here any time you get thirsty," Elwood said. "We've got plenty of water for you."

By the time they hauled him back down to the pit, the mud had already caked on his skin. His sopping clothes made his movements slow and squishy. He stayed cooler for awhile, but as the fabric dried, the heat crowded down on him again and drew his sweat back into the cloth.

It had only taken the sun a few days to bake that big wall of weeds down to a crisp, little pile. The tank stood out plain as a harvest pumpkin. Elwood got so antsy he nearly took up a shovel.

"Blind man could see that tank," he said, pacing back and forth in front of it. "You 'spect me to stay up all night guardin' it? I 'spect you'd best dig faster if ya know what's good for ya."

The job was bad enough without his daddy's fussing, unbearable with it. Billey fought the earth with his spade from early until half past late, but he could scarcely see a difference from one day to the next. A mighty hole yawned before him in his dreams, so the shallow pit of reality always brought disappointment in the morning.

One dream gave him hope.

Billey hadn't yet started school when the tornado came. Elwood fished his pocket for a cigarette while they sat on the porch watching the storm build up that afternoon long ago. The sky grew dark and the wind came down the way carrying half the road with it. Hard, white beans of hail clattered against the roof.

"Damn, Billey I'm outta smokes," Elwood said, slapping the porch's warm, gray wood. "Run yonder to the truck and see if I got a pack in there."

Billey stuck his hand out just long enough to feel the sharp sting of the hail. He looked up at Elwood like there must be some mistake.

"Go on, ya little bastard." Elwood planted his foot on Billey's butt and pushed him to the edge of the porch. Billey lost his balance and fell into the open at the precise moment the hail stopped.

"Now git on over there." Elwood's voice boomed against the sudden silence so that he seemed to surprise himself with how loud he sounded. He lowered it to a coarse whisper. "Do what I tell ya now."

Billey picked himself up from the mud and ran for the camper. He hadn't scrambled six steps over the slippery hail stones when he saw the dirty, howling finger of God dragging across the earth the way Billey's finger mopped bean juice up from the bottom of the bowl.

He froze in his tracks, which set his daddy to cussing again. Elwood came down from the porch to whup him, and then he saw it, too.

"Look at that muthah!" He cried in a voice Billey didn't recognize. He sprinted for the pickup. "Billey, move your ass," he shouted over his shoulder, "'cause I sure ain't gonna wait for no turd-brain bastard like you."

Billey wasn't quick enough. He wasn't even sure which was worse, his daddy or this terrible new thing. Elwood gunned the pickup and sent gravel flying. When the stones met the wind, they hung in the air like they'd suddenly forgotten where they were going. Billey had dived between the cinder blocks that held the camper by the time the truck fishtailed onto the pavement.

As he watched, he couldn't tell if the sky had torn down into the bowels of the earth, or if the earth and spouted up to the sky. It looked like a fat, wicked bolt of black lightning that never stopped flashing as it jerked closer and closer to the camper.

Billey's fingers clawed the ground. He wanted to bury his face in the dirt, but he couldn't look away from his fate.

The tornado rushed within an inch of the camper when it broke its path and headed up the road Elwood had taken.

A few, terrible moments in Billey's life fed his nightmares for years. So many times, the tornado made his eyes fly open in the middle of the night. He felt his jaw ache, felt his fingers digging into his palms through his once-green blanket, felt he would never be free of the terror.

But since he began digging, the tornado dreams had changed. Now he saw a tool that scooped dirt and rocks in an instant to make way for the tank.

Now he remembered the fear etched across his daddy's face the day Elwood ran for the pickup.

Chapter 17

Let X Be a Number . . .

The wolfman honked his horn at seven o'clock.

Sandy, a makeshift Cinderella, flew out the door before her father could leave his seat.

Stephen X had peeled back the top of his bone white convertible to show off the immaculate red interior.

"You have a Mustang," Sandy said, climbing in without letting the image of her father's face in the window crowd more than the corner of her eye. The beast in the car seemed more appealing.

"I have a Mustang," the driver said. He made a broad, rolling gesture that took in the car and ended with his hand tangled in the ratty hair on his face.

"Nice costume," Sandy said. "You must do this a lot." She paused an instant, then looked directly at him as she buckled her safety belt. "You are Stephen X, aren't you?"

"Not tonight," he said, looking into the rear view mirror as he backed out of the driveway. "But we're late for the ball."

As he straightened the car in the street, he glanced at her and added, "You're beautiful in rags."

They drove to a modest ranch house where the town thinned out in a patchwork of two-acre lots. Cars fanned across the grass in all directions. Music shook the bricks, swelling to a sharp crescendo whenever the door swung open to let a cowboy or gladiator pass. On the porch, a surgeon held two bottles of beer and lit a cigarette for a cave woman.

"You're going to have a great time," Stephen X said, placing his fingertips on the small of Sandy's back to guide her through the crowd inside. "You're going to want to meet everybody.

"Enrico, hey, Enrico," he said, waving to a bullfighter in the far corner, but not raising his voice over the noise. "Come here. You have to meet someone."

Enrico's disinterested eyes panned the room. "I don't think he heard you," Sandy said.

"He never listens. He's not classy enough for you anyway," said Stephen X, his voice muffled by the mask. He surveyed the party, comfortable in his element. "I'll get us a drink. What are you having?"

Everyone in sight held a longneck Budweiser. "A beer, I guess," she said.

"Yeah, but what kind? You want a Bud?"

She nodded. "Sure. Whatever's easy."

A wall of costumes covered Stephen X's retreat.

Sandy never cared much for parties. They always seemed to be too loud to talk, too frantic to enjoy. Last spring, she'd let Linda drag her to one a month after she broke up with Bob Strunk. Everyone talked like Bob was some vital organ torn out of her instead of a patch of dead skin she'd sloughed off. The next morning she woke up with a slight hangover and the certainty that she would never attend another party for the rest of her life.

She convinced herself it might be better with Stephen X. Nobody would know her or judge her for the actions of her boyfriend or her father. She could start at point zero and nurse her life along from there.

But the costumes made it worse. People at Stephen X's party seemed nice enough, but they were all strangers. She couldn't be sure if she were meeting them, or the alter egos they'd chosen for the night.

A few minutes after Stephen X left to hunt for beer, it occurred to her that almost everyone there was a man. A muscular woman in a low-cut top and a high-cut bottom walked by, munching from a plate of crackers and cheese. Sandy stopped her.

"Hi. I'm Cinderella," Sandy said, hoping to fall into the spirit of the evening.

The woman arched an eyebrow. "Hi ya doin'? I haven't seen ya around. Ya workin'?"

"Just part time." Sandy shrugged. "I'm going to school."

Cracker crumbs flew through the air as the woman laughed. "You'll learn plenty here, I'm tellin' ya."

Sandy thought the woman's tight, shiny costume might have been modeled after some comic book heroine. "Who are you supposed to be?" she asked.

"Anyone they want." She laughed again and put her hand on Sandy's shoulder to draw her close. "Maybe we can work together if we find the right job. Let me know." She shifted her weight back and looked past Sandy. "Gotta go."

Stephen X must have gotten lost looking for a beer. Sandy edged back toward the wall and watched the people around her. A few, like her, had tossed together a few things on a theme. Others wore elaborate, detailed costumes. She studied the perfect likeness of a youthful Adolf Hitler and wondered what kind of a person would devote so much energy to that image.

"You're with Stephen X, aren't you?"

She turned to see Babe Ruth hulking at her side.

"Why, yes—" she smiled.

"I knew it! That son of a gun." He propped his bat against his shoulder and walked away.

It seemed like hours passed. Sandy grew bored with watching people when she couldn't even tell who she was looking at. Feeling awkward standing alone, she walked through the kitchen and out the back door.

That's where she found Stephen X sitting on a few oil drums with a mad scientist and a bicycle racer.

"I thought you got lost," she said, hoping he'd tired of her already and would take her home.

"I've been right here." He spread his arms and scooted

over to make room for her.

"We'll catch you later, Stephen X," the guy in the white frock said as both of the others stood up. "Nice to meet you, Sandy."

Hearing her name caught her by surprise. "Nice to meet you," she said. When they were gone she asked, "Who were they?"

"Friends of mine," Stephen X said. "Everybody here is a friend of mine."

"Then why do they all call you Stephen X? It sounds so stiff."

He turned his head toward her and the teeth and hair of the mask suddenly chilled her. "It's my name," he said.

"Would you please take that off while we talk?"

He peeled it from his smooth-skinned face and became harmless again, kind of cute, the self-assured, nerdy guy she'd seen at Burger Castle. He draped the mask over his knee.

"What else would they call me?" he asked.

"I've never met anyone with the initial X. What does it stand for? Xavier?"

"It's not an initial; it's the whole name." Stephen X let a smile spread over his lips. In the years ahead, Sandy would think of smiles oozing across his face like butter stains in cloth. She would see how they served him as camouflage, as automatic as a chameleon. But that night she had no reason to be on guard. "In fact, my brother is Roscoe X Skinner," he said.

"Two X's in one family? Couldn't your parents afford a book of baby names?"

"My dad had his reasons." He let his hand stroke the mask on his leg. "His name was Benjamin Franklin Skinner. They kidded him about that when he was growing up, so he went by B.F. Skinner from the time he got out of grade school."

"B.F. Skinner—" Sandy started, but he waved and turned

on his deep sincerity to keep her quiet.

"I know what you're going to say," he said. "But 'B.F. Skinner' was okay until he moved here. A college town is no place for a name like that. Every fall he got a ton of calls from psych undergrads who needed help.

"Reporters would call and ask him what life with a famous name was like. There used to be a Franklin Roosevelt and a Woody Guthrie living here and they talked about forming a support group, but it was easier for them because they had actually been named for those guys. Dad was B.F. Skinner before B.F. Skinner was."

"You're kidding me, right?"

"No." He shook his head very slowly, as if her doubts were so inconsequential they didn't need a quick rebuttal.

"You know from your math that X is a variable—it can mean anything—when it comes to numbers," he went on. "But for names, it's just the opposite; it identifies you very precisely. He named my brother Roscoe X and me Stephen X because he wanted us to be secure in who we are. He didn't want us to be mistaken for anyone else."

"How did you know that?" Sandy brushed a strand of hair from her forehead.

"He told me."

"I mean that I'm taking math."

"Like I told you, I have my ways, Sandy." He stretched the mask back over his face. "Ask anyone here, I'm very big on research."

Nobody had ever studied Sandy before. Nobody had ever even asked her what she thought about anything. The idea of being researched was so novel and flattering that she overlooked the creepy side of it.

Stephen X straightened his mask and they went back inside to escape the quickening chill of the November morning.

Chapter 18

Water

Only way Billey could be sure of getting water was if he filled a few old coffee cans and headed down to the hole before Elwood woke up.

That wasn't too hard because Elwood never got up early and he had more old coffee cans than he and Otis could count, even if Otis used his peter after he ran out of fingers. Elwood kept screws and bolts and rusty bits of odd hardware in the cans back by the kerosene and the rest of the smelly stuff. Seemed like he had enough junk to screw just about anything in the world to anything else. Trouble was, he didn't have anything worth screwing.

Most of the cans were only half or a third full. As Billey dumped one into another to free some up, he thought it was funny that he could never remember seeing his daddy drink all that coffee.

"I'm a night person," Billey heard Elwood shout from the window one morning while Otis scratched himself in the driveway. "So shut that gah-dam mouth of yours afore I make you say `good night' permanent."

Billey usually wound up baby sitting Otis any time the big man came over before Elwood was up. That wasn't too bad either, because Otis didn't talk about his peter so much when Elwood wasn't around.

"How ya doin', Billey boy?" Otis said as he tramped around the back of the shack.

Billey set down the can of brackets he was holding. "I dunno," he said.

Otis bent over and pulled a six-inch bolt out of one of the big cans. He straightened up and held it at eye level, turning it around and around, squinting. Billey imagined a little can opener working away inside Otis' head, trying to pull out a peter joke.

Finally Otis just snorted and dropped the bolt back into the can with a clatter. "So what are ya doin' here, Billey boy?"

"Nothin'." Billey shook his head. "But I live here. What are you doin', Otis?"

Otis looked around and tapped the can of big bolts with the toe of his ratty gym shoe. "You got that smart mouth from your daddy, didn't you?" he said. "Why don't you go in and fetch your daddy so's I can do my business?"

Billey glanced around the corner of the shack to make sure they were still alone. "He told me never to come in the house 'less he tells me," he said. "'Sides, I don't want him to get up."

"Why not?"

"'Cause he'll whup me for getting him up." Every time Billey figured he knew how dumb the Otis was, the man surprised him. "Why don't *you* go in there, Otis?"

"Oh, I'll just let him sleep a bit, then." Otis shrugged and looked back at the coffee cans. "Ain't you supposed to be diggin' today, Billey boy?"

"I'm gonna. I gotta get ready." Billey wished that Otis would leave so that he could keep the water a secret. He emptied the hardware from some more cans to stall for time.

"Yer daddy said you'd do the diggin'," Otis said, puffing up his chest. "That's how we 'greed. I'd be the brains and you'd be the brawn. I find the tank. I find the gas. You dig the hole. That's how we 'greed."

"So what does my daddy do?"

Otis looked high up in the sky, as if he'd forgotten where the sun was. He rubbed the raspy whiskers under his chin with the back of his hand and said, "Why don't you go in there and fetch him?"

"Don't you remember what you just said?" Billey looked up at Otis like the man was crazy. "You're the one's gonna wake him up. That's how we 'greed."

Otis stood there wheezing a moment before he clapped his hands against his sides. "I swear your daddy should send you to law school," he said, turning to go back to his car. "I don't know why I ever try to be nice to you."

As soon as Billey heard the door shut on Otis' bugmobile, he began filling cans with water. He and Black Wolf made the long walk back and forth to the hole, carrying cans until he figured he had enough to drink all day long.

He hid the cans over the slope of the creek bank in case Elwood came by. He hadn't even started working when he realized if he drank that many cans of water, he would have to sweat and pee that much by the end of the day. He felt a little better when he realized he would sweat and pee that much whether he drank or not.

Billey had known thirst and he didn't like it. So he finished off one can before he started to work. He killed another and then another before he swung the kinks out of his arms. He lifted the shovel, hopped into the hole and jabbed the hard earth in the tank's shadow.

The blade balked and scraped, but Billey pushed harder. The ground fought back, jerking the shovel in his hands. Billey couldn't tell who was winning, him or the dirt. He looked over at the hill that had been half scooped away by the miners or the dinosaurs or whatever it was. It seemed like the dirt had been there a lot longer than Billey. He propped the shovel against the edge of the hole and scurried over the creek bank for another drink of water.

By the time Billey got down to some serious digging, the tank didn't have any shade left. Elwood still hadn't shown up, so Billey figured he must have driven off to see Otis.

Black Wolf waited down by the water cans while Billey soaked his shirt with sweat.

Billey never used to worry much about where he peed. But having been so thirsty so near the creek, he didn't want to make that water any worse than it already was. He thought about peeing in the hole to soften the ground a little, but he figured he'd probably wind up stepping in it. Since he'd pulled up every weed in sight, there was no place left around the hole that wouldn't just leave a big old messy puddle. But he sure had to go somewhere.

Elwood and Otis had staked a couple of old ropes over the tank so that it wouldn't blow away if a big wind came up. Billey was awful tired of working the shovel, so he grabbed one of the ropes and tried to walk up the side of the tank. He got about half way before he found himself on the ground with a sore butt.

Billey spanked the dust out of his britches and tried again. He got a bit further this time, and managed to break his fall with the rope. His feet and hands shot out for safety and pounded a deep, echoing sound from the tank. Each time he tried, he made it a little further up the smooth, round side of the tank. It was hard work, but nowhere near as hard as shoveling.

He learned about strength and balance and determination as he inched higher and higher. Billey finally made it over the hump before his feet lost their hold. He pressed his cheek against the hot surface and tried to gather strength. With feet, knees and hands working the cord, he managed to drag himself to the top of the tank.

Billey sucked in great quantities of air before he felt steady enough to see where he was. He raised his head to take in distant horizons.

The hill the dinosaur had scooped away had become a tiny mound of dirt. Far, far away, he could see trucks no bigger than match boxes on the big road. He could see how the dead catalpa dwarfed Elwood's house.

Billey rose to his knees, then stood cautiously at his full height, spreading his arms out for balance. He looked in every direction and his eyes took in the farthest reaches of the world. He pulled the air deep into his lungs and wanted to throw it back out in a mighty roar.

He crouched down and inched over to the spout that stuck out from the top of the tank. He eased himself back up to his full height and listened to the deep, satisfying resonance of his pee as it filled the tank.

If Otis could see him now!

Chapter 19

Prime Numbers

Prime numbers always fascinated Sandy. They were the simplest numbers, those which could be divided only by one and themselves—two, three, five, seven, eleven—and on up to infinity. Stable as bricks, the foundation of the universe.

They helped her make it through the sleepless nights of her sixteenth spring. That was the year the ghosts came when her head thrashed the pillow. She ran through conversations she should have had with Jennifer or Mama Gore. She even rehearsed what she would say to the little girl who sat on the swing—pumping the air with her legs—who was Sandy's memory of herself. She wondered why she'd been swindled out of so many precious things before she even knew she had them.

She tried a variation on counting sheep. With a pot of warm milk beside her at the kitchen table, she saw how many prime numbers she could pin down before dozing off. She verified each one systematically, without inspiration, the way a computer would. "Can seventeen thousand thirteen hundred thirteen be divided by twenty-seven?" she would ask herself. "By twenty-nine? By thirty-one . . ."

It helped her take her mind off the way her father's forgiveness could be extended or withdrawn at any time without notice.

Every night of Sandy's life, Jack Gore demanded penance over some little crime of omission. Repetition of the charges made the tiniest things significant. He zeroed in on two or three offenses at a time, rolling the list ever so slowly, dropping one off as he introduced a new one. Years passed before Sandy realized she hadn't been hearing about some particular incident; how she left the mayo out to decompose that Friday afternoon, how she went to see a brainless romantic comedy and left every light in her bedroom blazing, how she forgot to give him such an important phone message.

When her father bounced in and out of town, Sandy carefully watched every step. She could almost see herself as a model daughter. Sixteen and sinless.

"How are you?" Gore's voice crackled over the line while she tried to remember which coast he was on. With the distortion, she could almost imagine him as a polite stranger, so she didn't feel the usual urge to throw down the phone in disgust. "How's your mother?" he asked before she could answer the first question.

Sandy was in the kitchen doing her primes one rainy night in the middle of the week when Gore missed his connection and flew home late. The driveway ran closer to the kitchen than the front door, so he pulled the car around to the back porch for the short sprint through the downpour. He had a cat's aversion to water, but he never carried an umbrella. "Too old-schoolish," he always said.

The sound of the engine and the glow of headlights against the curtain didn't break Sandy's concentration on her numbers. Those distractions registered at a lower level so she could reconstruct the scene later, without having been aware of it at the time.

Suddenly, Sandy picked up on the clomp of widely spaced steps coming up the back porch, the rattle of the door. Then the man barreled in on the storm. With one hand shoving the door knob out of his way and the other swinging the shatterproof suitcase, he emitted only one prehistoric syllable before the wind washed him in.

His first step on the linoleum brought its own slick puddle with it. His foot arced to the ceiling, his back to the tile, the case to his solar plexus.

Sandy shot backwards from her chair in horror. The

motion cleared the table, splashing warm milk over the red-faced man who gasped and clawed the floor. It took the sound of his voice to identify him as her father.

"Look what you've done, girl," he bellowed. "Didn't you hear me come in?"

"I saw you." Her half-clenched fist dropped a few inches from her mouth.

"Couldn't you get off your butt a minute to help me?"

"Help? I didn't—"

"What did you do to the floor?"

"Nothing."

"Was it grease? Soap?"

"What?"

Gore heaved the suitcase against the wall and pulled himself up against the counter. "You want to kill me, don't you?" he shouted, closing in on her so she could smell the airline liquor on his breath. "Just like you killed your sister."

•

People blab to strangers secrets they would never dream of confiding to friends. That's how Stephen X learned all about Jack and Mrs. Gore a few years later. In the first months they dated, Sandy used him as a sounding board for all the wrong reasons.

One day she would look back and see that the comforting anonymity she felt with Stephen X grew out of the way he hid the most important parts of himself from her. She'd mistaken his apathy for empathy. She would see that his patience had been that of a spider resting in a fresh web.

One day she would look back and see that he could listen without hearing.

"Don't be so hard on the old man," he said over hot chocolate at Burger Castle on the three-month anniversary of the day they met there. "He can't be all bad if he made you."

She raised her eyes from her hands to his face. "You've got a glob of marshmallow on your lip," she said. "We were accidents. He wanted boys. He got Jennifer a baseball bat on her birthday."

"He doesn't seem so bad," Stephen X protested. "Besides, all women go through that with their fathers. It's just a natural thing."

"Do all women get treated like shit by their fathers? Do we all get ignored when we need attention? Do we all get pulled out of bed to do tricks for strangers? Is that just natural?"

He scooted around to her side of the booth and put his arm around her. "Hey now, Sandy," he said in his deepest, most soothing voice. "You've always got me right here."

She buried her head in his chest and somehow she wasn't even ashamed to be crying in a burger joint. He could handle problems so much better than she could if only she would let her trust flow into him.

She felt safe with Stephen X, but she still couldn't confess the worst parts to him, so she didn't really expect him to understand. Telling anyone the whole truth would let slip her fragile hope that somehow it was all a horrible dream. She thought of how she herself had misunderstood when Mama Gore told the cautionary tale about her own husband.

When Sandy and Suzanne Nicols were in the seventh grade, Suzanne's mother wound up in the hospital after her father threw her down the stairs.

"She's got a punctured lung," Sandy told her parents at the dinner table, struggling for composure as she repeated Suzanne's graphic account. Still, a part of her wondered where the air goes when you puncture a lung.

"Oh, my," Mrs. Gore said. "What did she do to him?"

"She probably tripped," Jack Gore said, setting his glass down hard enough to make little waves in the water's surface. "She drinks, you know."

Sandy thought her parents had somehow misunderstood the situation. It took years for her to see the pattern: whenever a woman told the truth in public, so many excuses surrounded it, like vultures about a carcass.

As they sat in the booth at Burger Castle, Sandy watched Stephen X smear the marshmallow from his lip. He looked back at her, the way boys did, intently, but focused somewhere a little shy of her eyes. She longed to tell someone—even Stephen X—about things her father had done, about what had happened to Jennifer. At the same time, she was afraid to find out the full range of the conspiracy. By keeping quiet, she could nurse the illusion that someone would understand if she broke her silence.

Her thoughts spun as she tried to control them.

"What's the matter?" Stephen X had finally focused on her eyes.

"Nothing," she said too quickly. "Why?"

"You look funny."

"I burned my tongue," she said, holding out the cup.

"You need ice cream. I'll get us a banana split."

The red flags should have gone up when she saw how quickly her father had come to accept Stephen X. She tried to keep them apart, expecting Gore to leap to the worst conclusions if he remained ignorant. Maybe he would fancy Stephen X as a drug-crazed, free-loading Sodomite if he never met him. That would gall him.

But one evening the Mustang pulled into the driveway early, while she was still in her bra and panties. She heard the door slam a moment before the bells chimed. She couldn't remember what she'd planned to wear, where they were going, what she'd been doing an instant before.

She threw some clothes on, thinking, "Hurry, hurry up. It doesn't matter what you wear." The zipper jammed. A button fell before the mad rush of her fingers. She switched to her green blouse, but by the time she got it on she realized it was too dressy for her faded jeans.

Beneath the urgency, she knew that something in her life was about to change forever. She wanted to be ready for the pivotal moment, so that nothing could take her by surprise.

" . . . when the Fed decides to bring down the prime rate," Stephen X's voice said as she took the stairs in threes.

"Here she is now," Jack Gore said, turning half way when she bounded into the room. "We've been waiting for you, Sandy."

Chapter 20

The Big Picture

Each day held everything Billey needed. He stashed water by the river and he peed in the tank. The sun darkened his bare chest. Black Wolf kept him company. Digging gave him all the exercise he could ever want. He looked forward to an extra bowl of beans at the end of the day.

But he ached every night when he crawled into the camper. When he crawled back out in the morning, stiffness had replaced the pain in his muscles. The hardness of the earth he worked by day spread into his body at night. His arms bunched up with new power. He remembered a picture Tommy Lagocki had shown him of a man with arms like tree trunks lifting a pony over his head. Billey wanted to be that strong some day.

He slipped a hand beneath Black Wolf's chest and one beneath his belly. He straightened up and tried to hoist the dog overhead, but Black Wolf kicked and twisted and sent himself flying into the dirt.

One morning before Elwood woke himself up with that loud, uneven snort of his, Billey heard shouting from the road by the shack. There was never much traffic out there, seeing as how it didn't go anywhere, so Billey set down the coffee can he was filling and ran around to see.

Two boys were riding bicycles down the road, zigging and zagging against the backdrop of the sunrise. They were big kids, laughing like no one cared if they laughed. Billey stood on the gravel near the road and watched them, silent as a telephone pole.

"Howdy!" yelled the big kid in the green shirt as he steered through a tight circle in front of Billey.

"Yeah, howdy," shouted the other one who just kept pedaling straight ahead.

The green shirt stood up on his pedals and worked hard to catch his friend. They said some things to each other and then looked over their shoulders.

"Hey, Elwood," they shouted, coasting down the road. "Nyahhhhh!"

It wasn't until Billey's third water break that he realized those guys were Dankowski and Barton. How had they grown so big? It used to take both of them and two more to tackle Billey. Now they looked almost like real men.

When Billey and Black Wolf trudged back to the shack to sneak some lunch, they found a hub cap peeking out of the ground. Billey kicked the gravel away and pried it out of the dirt. He spit on a section and wiped it clean on his pants.

The shiny patch of metal caught the sun and threw it anywhere Billey wanted. Even in the middle of the day, he could light up a tree stump or a rusty engine block just by tilting the hub cap at it. He made the light dance like a fairy across the bleak landscape. Black Wolf barked and chased it.

Billey had to blink or go blind when he turned the hub cap on himself. After it flashed in his eyes, he saw his rippled reflection through the spit streaks and rust spots. The curved metal surface made his arms look huge and hard as tree trunks. He held the shield closer, looking for the face he remembered but he found a dark man with big, useless ears and a rough jaw peering back at him.

Once in awhile, Elwood brought home a paper bag stuffed with old t-shirts and undies, maybe some jeans that weren't quite ragged yet.

"Damn if you ain't bustin' outta yer clothes," he said, running his finger up Billey's sleeve and out through a hole in the shoulder. "These oughta be plenty big for ya."

The underwear had "Jimmy" written along the band with a red laundry marker. Billey thought of Jimmy as someone bigger than himself, even bigger than Elwood from the way the stranger had stretched the elastic. He wanted to meet him some day.

"Don't you go throwin' away that old shirt," Elwood said. "Got me a man pays good money for them things. Trouble with you, Billey, is you don't know how hard it is to raise up a shit head like you. Never will know, neither, 'cause any horse worth her rubber's gonna turn hightail when she sees you comin'."

Most of the time, Elwood only brought home stuff for himself. He never said much about most of it, but the big gun was different.

Billey was sleeping off his exhaustion when thunder split the night. He knew the sound of Elwood's gun well enough, but this was like the difference between a tree toad and a bull frog.

"Gimme that, Otis," Elwood said outside the camper. "I swear you couldn't hit a horse on Westmore Avenue."

The blast came again and Billey tried to make himself flat as his threadbare green blanket. Tommy Lagocki once told him that an A-bomb made the loudest noise in the world. This sounded like a Z-bomb.

As Billey survived deeper into the night, the thunder came less often. Finally, he slipped into a fitful sleep, with his eyes flashing open at the slightest sound.

Come daybreak, he found his daddy and Otis on the porch. Elwood had his feet propped on the spool, with his head lolled back and his mouth wide open. Otis had his big old butt in Billey's chair. His head and arms spilled over the spool, like somebody had plopped a handful of wet clay there.

As he got closer, Billey saw the enormous silver gun lying across his daddy's lap. Elwood's hand crooked lightly around the barrel, moving back and forth slightly each time he snored. Billey thought he'd better not let him wake up just yet.

Billey had been digging a couple of hours when the pick-up came bumping across the field to the hole. The two men waited for the dust they stirred up to pass, then climbed out, squinting against the sunlight.

"Looky here, Billey," Elwood said, holding the shiny gun up to the sky. "You ever seen anythin' like it?"

Billey thought about his answer carefully. "I seen your gun plenty of times."

"You ain't never seen no gun like this," Elwood snapped. "Ain't that right, Otis?"

Otis didn't say anything at first. When Elwood turned to look at him, the big man nodded like a slobbering dog. "Shoot the peter clean off a chinaman with a gun like that," he said.

"That's right." Elwood held the gun at arm's length and swung through an arc of the sky. When his sight reached the willow that stuck up over the river bank, he pulled the trigger.

All three of them jumped at the sound. Black Wolf dashed behind the tank. A branch as thick as Billey's leg flew off the top of the tree, its leaves streaming behind like hair in the wind.

Elwood seemed kind of glassy eyed. He shook his head a couple of times.

Billey's ears were the first to quit ringing. "What are you gonna do with a gun like that?" he asked.

Elwood looked into the hole and shouted. "Trouble with you, Billey, is you can't see the big picture. You know that?"

"I dunno."

"*What?*"

"I dunno."

"Yer just like Otis here. He can't see past the end of his peter."

"Need a telescope, don't you, Otis?" said Billey.

"*Tele*scope?" Otis snorted. "I need a *miker*scope!"

"I got me the gun now," Elwood said. "But I still ain't got my goddam hole, Billey, and whose fault is that?"

Billey kept quiet.

"Gun don't do me no good without a hole, and a hole don't do me no good without a gun," Elwood said. "Is that too much for a shitbrain like you to unnerstan'?"

"I dunno." Billey looked at Otis and could tell that he didn't know either.

"I done my part, Billey." Elwood said, sighting along the barrel again. "Now you best hurry up and dig afore I blow the dirt out of the ground. Me and my one-eyed friend want to get us some gasoline."

Chapter 21

Roscoe

Linda always was luckier than Sandy. When they were kids, Linda was the one who found change along the sidewalk. In high school, she won all the records, tapes and posters she could scoop up in a three-minute frenzy at Chartbuster Music. Linda's parents were nice when they didn't have to be. They talked to you and even looked at you like you were a human being.

Linda got Roscoe; Sandy, Stephen X.

"My brother knows a guy who can get you a good deal on a car," Stephen X said that first winter when Sandy's battery died.

"I got the basic recipe from my brother," he told her the first—and mercifully the last—time he sacrificed spaghetti for her, "but the improvements are all mine."

"Roscoe X is big on the arts," Stephen X said when she paused to look at a Pollock print. "He knows all about that stuff."

Roscoe X grew larger than life. Each week saw a new virtue sprout from him, like a feather in an angel's wing. His hair was blonder, his eyes bluer, his knowledge more complete than any man Sandy had ever known.

"I'd like to meet your brother some day," Sandy said. "He must be one in a million."

"A billion." Stephen X bristled like a cat whose territory has been challenged. "But he's real busy. He doesn't get out much."

For all his talk of Roscoe X's talents, Stephen X didn't seem very eager for Sandy ever to meet the man. The more he bragged on him, the more it seemed he tried to keep their paths apart, as if it occurred to him that his brother could never fill the expectations he'd created. Maybe he thought having a mortal brother would expose him as a liar.

It was only by a chance reading of one of Stephen X's lists that Sandy learned Roscoe X's birthday fell on Valentine's Day.

Stephen X jotted even the most trivial things on note paper that read, "Do this for Stephen X Skinner. Now."

His master list for the day referred to various sublists which he spent weeks compiling. The master list included "get groceries" and "do the laundry." Once, "make lists" even appeared next to a bullet.

The grocery list itself itemized his favorite brands of chili or canned pasta products. The laundry list contained detailed instructions to "wash three loads," "hang shirts right from the dryer," "sort socks."

Sandy and Stephen X stopped at his apartment on the way to a matinee of *Death Behind the Door* on February 10. While he changed his slacks in the bedroom, she brewed coffee and saw the day's agenda hanging on the fridge. "Get Roscoe X's birthday card," it said.

He came back to the kitchenette, inhaling deeply through his nose. "Ah, java!" he said as he tucked his shirt tails in. "I've always said the woman I marry will have to make a good cup of coffee."

"When is Roscoe X's birthday?" Sandy asked.

"It's coming up." Stephen X looked around the room like he'd lost something. "Why?"

"I saw his card on your list of things to do."

"There's lots of stuff on there."

"What day is it?"

He set his coffee on the counter and slipped an arm around her waist. "There's a price for that information," he said, nudging her hair with his nose.

"You're just awful." She pushed him back, but wound up paying the price anyway.

At the card shop later, Stephen X found one that said, "I Thought I'd Give You A Couple Of Serious Bills For Your Birthday . . ." It opened on a picture of Shakespeare holding a plumber's invoice.

He slipped Sandy's card out of her fingers. "Roscoe X hates birthdays," he said. "It's one of those things when you hit thirty."

"I just feel like I know him already. I want to say 'Hi.'"

Stephen X put Sandy's card back on the rack. "Roscoe X really hates attention," he said. "He's just tired of it."

Come Valentine's Day, Stephen X sent flowers after standing her up for a lunch date. It was no big deal. It didn't hurt. In fact even then Sandy sensed that she enjoyed the flowers more than she would have enjoyed his company over burgers. The roses cost more than lunch, and that counted for something in Stephen X's world.

But it did leave her at a loose end. She called Linda and on a whim they found Roscoe X's address in the phone book and headed over there. It seemed like a fun idea.

"Roscoe X?" Sandy said when the tall man with the straight, blond hair opened the door.

"Just Roscoe."

"Roscoe? I'm Sandy and this is Linda. Your brother sent us over here to meet you on your birthday."

He held the door with his right hand and the door frame with his left. "That's nice, but you don't have to do anything," he said. "I won't tell him."

Sandy cocked her head. She knitted her brow at Linda, who never took her eyes off the man. "We didn't come to shine your shoes, buddy," Linda said, resting her hand on the door knob.

He looked down at his stocking feet as his toes curled involuntarily. "I didn't mean anything."

"You're letting all the heat out," she said. "Aren't you going to ask us in?"

He looked over his shoulder—as if trying to remember when he had last tidied the apartment—then shrugged and stood back to give them room to enter.

"Nice place," Linda sniffed, rubbernecking. "I guess your brother's the only neurotic asshole in the family."

He laughed abruptly from deep below his diaphragm. "He's the last of a long line."

"Thank God for that." Linda shook her head and cocked a thumb at Sandy. "I don't know how she can stand him."

"Oh, you don't even know him," Sandy protested.

"No, but Roscoe does and you haven't heard him say anything different, have you?"

Roscoe was a quiet man. From all the stories, Sandy had expected him to be a cross between Confucius and Einstein. In fact, he bore no resemblance to the hero Stephen X had spoken of so highly and so often. As the three of them sat on his sofa, she suddenly felt they had barged into this poor guy's simple, ordered life.

Linda didn't mind. "So, this brother of yours—how long have you known him?" she asked.

"I changed his diapers," Roscoe said. "I kept him out of trouble."

"Well, it was nice meeting you." Sandy put her hands flat on the sofa and straightened her elbows. "We'll all have to get together sometime."

Roscoe and Linda had not broken eye contact since he'd let them in. "Earth to Sandy! Earth to Sandy!" Linda laughed. "We're all together right now. Where are you?"

"I mean with Stephen X—"

"Oh," Roscoe deadpanned. "I thought you wanted to do something fun."

"Roscoe, meet Sandy," Linda nodded. "Sandy, Roscoe."

Like most things that swayed Sandy's life, the romance of Roscoe and Linda didn't seem to have any definite beginning. She talked to Linda one day and realized what was going on, what had been going on for some time.

She should have known even before the first of March when Linda called to say that she and Roscoe had had a wonderful dinner at Pierre's Place.

"Roscoe? How did you go there with Roscoe?"

"It's a long story," Linda said. "First he asked me. Then I said okay. Then we got in his car and he turned on the engine. Then we drove down Westmore—"

"I mean why did he ask you?"

"Beats me. You think I should have told him on the first date that I'm a scheming, credit-card abusing coke head with syphilis and six months to live?"

She didn't have to tell him anything. Information passed between Roscoe and Linda by telepathy or osmosis. Sandy could hardly keep up. By spring, the only time she could see her friend was with Roscoe, so Sandy felt awkward unless she brought Stephen X along.

Of course, she couldn't confide in Linda in those circumstances. It surprised her that she missed sharing her feelings and private thoughts with another woman. She had always imagined herself to be independent, self-sufficient. So many things nobody could ever understand had shaped her. Nobody could ever guess what fears made her heart beat more quickly. She didn't realize until now how much she might miss seeing herself in the mirror of Linda's irreverence.

On a windy Saturday in May, the four of them piled into Roscoe's Cutlass Supreme and went to the park for a picnic. They were barely out of the car before Stephen X had the badminton net up.

"Let's go! Men against the girls." He flipped Roscoe a racquet.

Roscoe, who stood a head taller than his brother, plucked the racquet out of the air. "I'll take Sandy," he said. "You take Linda."

Stephen X put on a headband and bounced around on the

balls of his feet, although they rarely left the ground. He huffed and puffed with every dive and stab, slamming the birdie back over the net, shooting a fist against the sky when he scored.

On the other side of the net, Roscoe's long arms let him return most shots while rooted at center court. Sandy saved the deep ones.

Linda crossed her arms and turned her back to the net. "Hurry, lemonade!" she taunted her teammate. "Hurry, lemonade!"

Stephen X made a showy save to the right and began to celebrate the point, but Roscoe spiked the birdie back into his brother's nose. Stephen X fanned the air furiously. "Do you think you might try to get a few once in awhile, Linda?" he snapped.

When Roscoe tapped the game point into the corner, Stephen X put his hands on his hips and let his lungs heave. He raised his flushed and dripping face to look at Linda. "What's this lemonade crap?"

"Roscoe told me about your lemonade stand," she said.

"What do you mean?"

"How you sold lemonade but you were so afraid you'd miss a sale you wouldn't even go to the bathroom." Linda turned to Sandy. "Didn't he tell you how he stood in the street hopping up and down because he had to go so bad, yelling, 'Hurry, lemonade! Hurry, lemonade!'"

Sandy shook her head, puzzled.

"He wound up peeing in his shorts," Linda went on. "When his first customer finally did come, he was so embarrassed that he accidentally-on-purpose spilled the pitcher on himself so that it would look like it was *all* lemonade."

"I did not!"

"Come on, Steve," Roscoe laughed. "We all saw it."

"I don't remember anything like that," Stephen X said, with color taking over his face. Sandy felt sorry for him for taking himself so seriously. He'd given himself no graceful means of escape.

Linda patted him on the shoulder. "That's okay," she said, enjoying the moment. "You were just a little boy. Wasn't he, Roscoe?"

Chapter 22

Whiskers

The hole was plenty wide and nearly deep enough for the tank. Billey figured if he'd saved all his sweat, it would just about fill the hole to the brim by now.

Each day, it seemed a little harder to straighten his back when he took a break and fetched himself some water. Each day, Black Wolf's tongue seemed to hang a little bit longer; his head rocked a little more quickly as he panted. Each day, the sun seemed a little more determined to cook them up like two beans that had spilled onto the Coleman.

Used to be Billey's skin was smooth, and pretty much the same whatever part of his body he looked at. Now shapes stuck out all over his arms and chest like hub caps under a blanket. He could make a fist harder than the dirt he fought every day.

Billey leaned against the shovel and bowed his head as he caught his breath. Even when he heard the pickup, he didn't move his head more than an inch so that he could see the truck bucking over the field, kicking up plumes of dust.

Elwood climbed out and swung the door shut. "Otis, I swear I can't tell if Billey's holdin' the shovel up or the shovel's holdin' Billey."

"Can't tell by me." Otis hawked and spit. He walked around the pickup with stiff knees, swinging his legs out sideways as he hitched up his oil-stained pants.

"Which is it, Billey?" Elwood hunkered down and squinted at how the shovel's handle touched Billey's forehead. "That shovel proppin' you up?"

"Hell, no, it ain't."

"Hear that, Otis? He says, '*Hell*, no, it ain't.'" The man turned back to his son. "What good's a shovel for, if it ain't proppin' you up and if it ain't diggin' no hole by itself? What kinda good is a shovel like that?"

Billey stared at the ground he'd cut up beneath his feet. He rubbed his forehead back and forth against the smooth, wooden handle. "I dunno," he said.

"I dunno," Elwood sang through his nose. "I'm Billey an' I dunno shit." He circled around the young man. "I bet you don't even know what day it is, Billey."

"Tuesday?"

The men burst out laughing. "Tuesday!" Elwood shouted. "Otis, tell Billey what day it is."

Otis pointed to his crotch. "Mr. Peter says it's Wednesday, Billey boy."

Elwood shook his head. "Otis, I don't know how you ever got to be your age without dyin' 'cause you forgot to breathe. I swear if you was any dumber, you'd rust." He turned a sour look to Billey. "So what the hell you doin' if you ain't diggin' and you ain't holdin' up that shovel. You think that hole's gonna go and dig itself?"

Billey sighed heavily. "I dunno."

"You look at me when yer talkin' to me, Billey Elwood."

Billey raised his head and showed Elwood his eyes, reddened by sweat but defiant. "I said, 'I dunno.'"

Elwood narrowed his eyes for a long moment. Black Wolf padded closer to see what was going on.

"What's that shit on yer face, boy? Looky that, Otis. Is that peach fuzz or dog shit?"

"Yeah, yeah," Billey said. "You're real funny."

"Don't you sass me or I'll whup you good. You think you're a big, tough man all a sudden? That what you think?"

Billey looked at the sky. "What do you want?"

"What do I want?" Elwood thumped his chest with his fist. "What do I want? Tell him what I want, Otis."

"He wants my peter when I'm dead. That's okay. I won't need it no more then."

Elwood didn't even bother to scold Otis. "*I'll* tell you what I want, Billey. I want you to dig me a hole, just like I told you before. Can you hear me this time or you got whiskers growin' inside your ears, too?"

"You want a damn hole so bad, why don't you just dig it yourself?" Billey threw the shovel in the dirt and turned to go down to the river.

The hand on his shoulder spun him around a split second before Elwood's fist thudded into his stomach. Billey doubled over and gasped for air. The fist cracked against his jaw like a rock, sending him through an arc to the gravel.

Far, far away, Black Wolf barked in excitement. The sound came closer and Billey opened his eyes to see Elwood and Otis shimmering like angels in the sky. The tank glowed behind them.

Elwood spat, but missed his mark, even though Billey hadn't moved yet. "Yer a long way from bein' a man, Billey Elwood. You push me again and I'll show you just how long."

Black Wolf snarled and barked at Elwood. He lunged and hopped back, looking for an opening.

Billey propped himself up on his elbows and moved his head from side to side to see how much it hurt. He wobbled up to his feet just as Black Wolf found his chance. The dog darted in and sunk his teeth in Elwood's ankle. He growled and shook like a wild thing.

"Gahdam sonuvabitch!" Elwood tried to kick Black Wolf with his free foot but lost his balance and thudded to the ground. Black Wolf let go of the ankle and scrambled for the eyes with blood on his teeth. Elwood slugged him and Otis kicked the dog in the ribs.

"Leave him alone!" Billey cried out, surprising himself as much as the others. "He's a good dog."

"I'll show you what he's good for," Elwood said, running to the truck with Black Wolf nipping at his heels.

"Black Wolf! Come here." Billey felt sick in his guts.

Elwood reached through the window of the pickup and yanked out the big, silver gun.

"Black Wolf, get out of there!"

Elwood danced around trying to get a clear shot at the dog so he wouldn't blow his own foot off.

"Hold still, you muthah! Otis, come here and hold this dog while I shoot it."

Black Wolf pressed his advantage, darting around Elwood's feet. Billey dived to help. Otis got to the dog first, but fumbled it into Billey's arms.

Maybe Elwood got tired of trying to aim, or maybe the collision of Otis, Billey and Black Wolf jarred the trigger. The gun blasted and they all fell to the ground, ears ringing like church bells.

Black Wolf's tail landed near Billey's face, but he saw the rest of the dog sprint under the pickup and across the open field. Elwood saw it too and jumped back up and took aim through the open passenger's window of the pickup.

Elwood must not have noticed that the driver's window was rolled up. When the gun roared again, glass peppered the field, confusing Elwood long enough for Black Wolf to get out of range.

"Look what you made me do, Billey," Elwood snarled. "How you gonna fix a mess like that?"

"It's your mess, you fix it."

Elwood looked at the gun in his hand. He rubbed the barrel against his cheek. "Maybe I oughta shave them whiskers offa you with a lead razor, Billey."

"Maybe you oughta."

"Hell. Bullets cost money and I can't get me no money 'til you dig me my hole. So I'm just gonna whup you, boy. 'Cept this time I'm gonna whup you like a man so's you can see how you like that."

Billey had let Otis get behind him. He felt the big man pin his arms behind his back. Billey kicked at his daddy, but he couldn't land a good one. He felt the blood spray from his nose with the first blow.

The next ones all ran into each other until Billey found himself back on the ground, watching through a swollen eye as the pickup sprayed dirt and gravel.

Chapter 23

Pairs

Everything about Roscoe and Linda was so right that their romance seemed inevitable. He bought her fuzzy slippers, lavender sachets and a mother of pearl hair brush, not the kind of gifts you'd expect from a guy.

They were always laughing and making plans for dinner, for the weekend, for the matching peejays they would one day buy their grandchildren. They were so happy that sometimes Sandy forgot how much older Roscoe was.

Linda had dated a lot of guys—a lot more than Sandy—but she had never said "we" when she talked about them. It was always "I went to the movie with Joe," or, "Tom took me miniature golfing." Now she never talked about any experience, thought or plan that was not prefaced with "we."

"We spent Sunday catching up on our reading by the pool," Linda announced. "We love the brunch buffet at his complex."

Another time, she said, "We really like those new Japanese cars. We might trade in the Cutlass on one."

"What? One of those little Toyotas?" Sandy raised an eyebrow.

"I guess so. We saw a real nice green convertible at the stoplight yesterday."

Sandy didn't know what to make of the new Linda. She couldn't recall a boyfriend of Linda's who had evolved much past the point of shedding fins and sprouting feet. Linda poked fun at the way they walked, how often they changed underwear, even what *they* thought was fun.

By contrast, she accepted Roscoe's most casual remarks as gospel truth. She figured the whole world wanted to know what her new love thought about Congress or spark plug gaps or how to slice an avocado without killing the stone. It even embarrassed Roscoe to hear these things repeated, and that was his saving grace for Sandy.

"I was just thinking out loud," he protested when Linda repeated his theory about why tomatoes, chocolate and cheese should be purchased in small quantities and stored at room temperature.

"Maybe so, but you've got to admit you're right," she countered. "Isn't he, Sandy?"

"I never really thought about it."

"Neither did I," Roscoe chipped in. "I was just running on."

"See?" Linda arched an eyebrow and nodded. "He doesn't even have to work at being smart."

But Sandy couldn't hold that against him. She found it refreshing in contrast to Stephen X who wanted so badly to be smart.

"You look a little like Stephen X, and he's always talking about you," Sandy told Roscoe once, "but you two are so different."

"Knock on wood. Don't you have any brothers or sisters?"

"I'm an only child," she said, then added after the briefest pause, "now."

"The younger kid always resents the older one," Roscoe said, and Sandy felt he'd thought this through before. "They think their genes have been used up already. They never get to discover anything because the older kid already did it a year or ten years before them.

"And the older one is jealous when the baby gets away with murder because the parents are worn out by then. Sometimes I wish I could be an only child."

"I wouldn't wish it on you." Sandy wanted to tell him how awful it was, but she saw that he was smiling and she didn't want to spoil that. Then Linda came back and the subject drifted away. Even the air in the room seemed to shift directions.

Sandy felt happy for her. Until now, Linda's love life was patterned after a Las Vegas tourist looking for the slot machine with her name on it. And as she came to know Roscoe better, Sandy felt happy for him, too. They deserved everything they gave each other. She felt more empty than envious.

Driving home along Westmore Avenue, she saw a one-armed man at the Delancey stoplight. The breeze pinned back the sleeve of his tee shirt as he talked to a one-legged woman who leaned on a rough, old crutch. They laughed about something Sandy couldn't even guess at while she waited for the light to change. Everybody had found someone and there was nothing and no one left for her.

In a way, it reminded her of high school when the brainy girls scorned her for being too pretty and the pretty ones for being too smart. Everyone else in the world seemed to fit in somewhere.

Meanwhile, Stephen X dedicated himself to monopolizing Sandy's life. When they got out of the matinee, he confirmed his plans for dinner. After dinner would come the network news, followed by some black and white monster classic with shoddy special effects. In between, she had to sneak a little time for classes, work, a few hours of sleep.

The relentless activity trampled the nagging feeling that she had been denied some very basic component of life, without actually correcting the situation. It was like the rest of the world enjoyed clean air, but the Stephen X Express only helped her adapt to pollution.

They planned to make a foursome to see a matinee of *The Hatchling*. But Roscoe and Linda weren't at Roscoe's apartment when Stephen X and Sandy showed up.

"I've got a key," Stephen X announced, sorting through the collection on his two-inch D-ring. "We can wait inside."

Sandy rose from the sofa when the phone rang, but Stephen X pulled her back down. "It's not for you," he said. "Nobody knows you're here."

"But someone's calling Roscoe."

"He's not here either."

She sank back into the cushion, but the phone kept ringing, eight times, ten.

"Cheese," she breathed, picking up the receiver. "Hello?"

Linda was on the line. "Wouldn't let you answer the phone, huh?"

"Who?"

"Stephen X. Is someone else there?"

"No—"

"Look, we're going to be a few minutes late, but make yourselves comfortable."

"How'd you know we were here?" Sandy rubbed her forehead.

"Aren't you?" Linda laughed but she sounded far away, like an old person's idea of a long distance call.

"Yes, but—"

"Roscoe said Stephen X has a key. See you in a bit."

After she heard the click, Sandy said, "Okay." She put the phone back in the cradle and looked at Stephen X, who was watching her expectantly.

"Where are they?"

"Who?"

"Roscoe X and Linda."

She looked back at the phone, feeling distracted. "I don't know. They'll be here in a few minutes. How did you know it was them?"

"I told you I have my ways." He patted the spot on the sofa where she'd been sitting.

She plopped back down and stared out the window, feeling foolish. Everybody knew things about her. They shared her secrets so casually they didn't even care if she found out.

"What are we going to do?" she asked after a moment.

"The movie. Remember?"

"No, I mean after that. After all of this."

"We can do whatever you like."

She looked at him and he pretended not to notice the crease in her brow. "I mean after we've seen every movie that ever starred a bug-eyed monster," she said. "After we've eaten at every restaurant in the world and hit all the bars on Westmore, then what are we going to do?"

"We'll never make it through *all* the bars on Westmore." Stephen X laughed and rested a hand above her knee. "It would be an interesting exercise, though."

"Oh, be quiet." She stood and walked to the window, maybe thinking that if he couldn't see the tears, she wouldn't cry. It didn't work.

Over the catches in her breath, Sandy didn't hear him come up behind her. She gasped when he pulled her close to him.

"Come on. Tell me about it." He rested his head against hers and swayed slowly back and forth.

"Is that all there is? A bunch of stupid movies? A hundred kinds of hamburgers?" She pulled away to look at him. "Doesn't anybody have any more?"

"It's just a good time, Sandy. What's wrong with that?" He pulled her head back against his shoulder so that her mascara stained his shirt. Then he pushed her out to arm's length, with a palm on each shoulder. "What do you want to do? Look, tell me what you want and we'll do it."

She looked at him with a stranger's eyes. He already had a little too much skin for his face, and his belly had lost the flatness of youth, but his hair was a perfect, razor-cut helmet, his nails might have been beauty college templates. People could be so fastidious about easy things, so slack about things that took commitment.

She twisted away from him, but knew he was all she had,

all she would ever get.

"I don't want to do anything." She tried not to sob. "That's the whole point."

Stephen X opened his mouth but before he could say anything, they heard Roscoe's key in the door.

"We found the neatest little antique shop just off Delancey," Linda said. "I'm going to get a spinning wheel for my birthday."

"Where did you learn to spin?" Stephen X asked quickly, as if he were suddenly afraid of silence.

"I haven't yet, but there's a class at the library that Sandy and I can take." She noticed the blush and smeared make-up on Sandy's face. She scowled at Stephen X. "We hardly get to do anything anymore, Sandy. We should learn to spin together."

Chapter 24

The Man in the Moon

Billey slept late the day after Elwood whupped him like a man. Nobody came around with a shovel at dawn to make sure he was ready to dig. By the time he crawled out of the camper, he didn't cast much more shadow than a bowl of beans.

He rubbed his eyes to clean out the sleep grit, but he winced and pulled his hands away. Instead of sand, he found blood crumbs on his knuckles. His tongue tasted salt as it touched the inside of his lip through a new gap in his teeth. Dark purple lumps—as big as fists and boots—spread over his body.

Digging the hole always made Billey ache, but the whupping pain that shot through his body this morning turned him into a crooked old man. This kind of hurt didn't make him stronger. It only made him hobble as he went around the shack to the faucet. He clutched his belly and tried hard not to puke his guts out.

Once when his daddy drove him to some old warehouse in the pickup, they'd seen a ghost-white man in a long coat clutching a brown bag, steadying himself against a dirty brick wall. After they passed him, Elwood stabbed the brakes and ground the gears into reverse. "Damn if that ain't Acer," he said. He honked the horn and shouted, "Hey, Acer, you son of a bitch! What the hell you doin' out here?"

The man's stubbly face started to turn toward them, but suddenly his body shook and squeezed out a stream of pungent liquid. "Gah dam," Elwood had said as he threw the truck back into gear. "That was Acer."

Billey felt like that ghost man today. The hot water gushed brown from the spout, but Billey cupped his hands and drank. He straightened himself, groping for the wall. No matter how hard he tried, he couldn't help it: he puked his guts out. The stuff on his feet was thin, yellow and filmy, nothing like the puke he used to make when he was a kid.

Billey knew what it was like to be a man. He limped back to the camper and curled up, trying to find a position that moved the pressure off his bruises. And somewhere in the day or night, he dreamt of his daddy's voice, booming like a whirlwind across the rocky field. "You never brung me a nickel," the thunder roared, over and over. "You never brung me a nickel."

It was dark when Billey heard Otis's bugmobile sputter to life. He breathed softly and waited a few minutes after Otis pulled away before peeking outside the camper. He felt hungry now and thought his side teeth could chew some beans well enough while his gums were scabbing up in front.

In the moonlight, he moved around to the front of the shack, but stumbled to a standstill and lost his air when he saw Elwood leaning back with his feet on the spool, snoring like a heat bug in August. The smell of beans in the bowl between his daddy's boots drew Billey one cautious, quiet step at a time. He eased himself onto the porch's creaky boards, holding his own breath against the slightest change in Elwood's breathing.

Billey eased the bowl up from the spooltop and edged backwards down the step. He nearly spilled his prize in the dust when Elwood snorted at something in a dream.

When Billey got to the corner of the shack, he turned and jogged around the back where he sat on a flat rock and savored each bean's soft explosion of flavor. He wondered where Black Wolf might be and if the dog felt any better than he did. Maybe Billey didn't dig fast enough, but Black Wolf sure never did anything bad; nothing to get his tail all shot off for.

Billey leaned back and stared at the man in the moon.

That big old face looked as white and lonely as Acer's, with its mouth wide open and ready to puke down on the world. It made Billey shiver even though the air felt warm on his blotchy skin.

It wasn't fair that the moon never had to break a sweat as it moved across the sky. It wasn't fair that Otis got to sit on his fat butt and Elwood got to cuss and shoot while Billey and Black Wolf dug a hole clean through the earth. Black Wolf had helped him every day by pawing out craters in the floor of the hole and by softening the dirt with his pee. How could Elwood shoot at him if he really wanted his hole finished? How would Otis like it if somebody shot his peter in two? How would the man in the moon like it if somebody puked up in his mouth?

Billey wanted to run away, but he didn't know which way to go. Every place in the world might be just like this, with some people digging, and some people cussing and shooting.

He thought back to Tommy Lagocki's house and how maybe that was different. Tommy had lived in a playground, with his mother carrying in trays of cookies and milk even before he felt hungry. Mrs. Lagocki's hands were clean and smooth as creek rocks, her voice as soothing as the birds. But then he remembered how she'd cast him out. She didn't use the same words as Elwood, but her tone, her eyes and the pinch of her nails on his shoulder could have all been borrowed from him.

Billey struggled to his feet again and patted the dust from his jeans. He walked, very slowly at first, and then a little more freely as he worked the stiffness out of his muscles. He went to the tank which glowed like some monster lightning bug in the wash of the moon. He wanted to dig the hole so deep he could bury the damn thing forever—and his daddy and Otis with it.

He called softly to Black Wolf, but he was afraid to raise his voice much, even though he was far enough away that a death shriek wouldn't have pulled his daddy out of his drunken stupor. Black Wolf didn't come a'galloping with his floppy, pink and black tongue wagging in time to the staccato stride of his stumpy legs. Maybe he didn't hear. Or maybe he watched from the shadows, wondering why Billey had let his tail get shot off.

Billey knew he'd see his daddy again, and Otis and the bugmobile. But he wondered if Black Wolf was gone for good. It wasn't fair and it made his chest turn sour.

He slid down to the creek and walked its bank a long, long way. When the scrub thickened, or a tree limb blocked his path, he usually didn't mind getting his feet wet. But tonight he picked his steps with care. He was in no hurry because he had nowhere to go.

He came to the train trestle, about as far up the creek as he ever went. He felt tired, but had walked the pain out of his body, at least for awhile.

He slumped against the heavy, dark beam—so old it didn't even have splinters anymore—and called out to Black Wolf, louder now than he had before. "Black Wolf!" he screamed. "Where did you go, Black Wolf?"

When his throat hurt, he became quiet and leaned his head back to look through the railroad ties at the moon. It seemed smaller now than it had earlier in the night.

Billey realized he had soaked his shirt with sweat. He ran a hand through his wet, untidy hair and shook the drops off at his side. He listened to the bugs and the stillness and felt a million miles away from everything he knew.

Maybe the sweat stopped up his ears more than usual, but Billey didn't notice a thing until the voice rang out right behind his shoulder.

"I'm Uly Bondarbon," the voice said. "So, what's your name, big guy?"

Chapter 25

America Thinks, Inc.

By the end of her third lesson, Sandy knew she would never learn to spin.

It was nice to get away with Linda for a little while on Thursday nights. The act of spinning soothed her when she managed to fall into its rhythm.

But she felt queasy the whole time, almost guilty, although she couldn't have said why. Maybe guilt and dread had jumbled her life together. They were the only constants she had, but they lashed her to things that had happened years or moments ago—even things that had not yet come to pass—anything bad that still carried some blame.

Now it was like she was stealing the time from more important things—her studies, her work, Stephen X. She imagined him pacing his apartment, frowning at his wristwatch every twenty seconds, wondering what kept her.

So many urgent things pressed in on Sandy that she couldn't imagine taking six months to make a sweater.

Neither could Stephen X.

"Let's see what you've done," he said the night after her first lesson.

"There's nothing to see yet," she said.

"Come on. I won't laugh."

"I mean there's *nothing* to see. We haven't done anything yet."

"You were gone all night and you didn't do *any*thing?"

She realized what an indulgence this spinning was. "We'll be on the wheel next week," she said half-heartedly.

"How much are they charging for these lessons?" He clicked his tongue and moved his head through an exaggerated arc.

The calmness of the other women in the class unsettled her. Their constant chatter made her nervous. They were obsessed with television characters. At first, Sandy couldn't tell whether they were talking about the story lines of the shows or the private lives of the actors. Then she saw that the two threads were as tangled as those that wobbled off her wheel.

Most of the women were older than Sandy, but she wanted to scold them the way a mother would. How much precious time had they wasted studying these fantasy lives so that now they could discuss them hour after hour?

It was just as well when Stephen X found her the second-shift job with America Thinks, Inc. "You'll pull down twice the money you're making now and the work is pure gravy," he said. "They need number crunchers, so you'll be running the place in no time."

What they really needed was someone to tabulate endless survey results on every subject from gun control to the ideal shade of blue for soap wrappers.

Mountains of information—most of it useless except as camouflage for the real questions—rose from Sandy's in tray each night. She extracted the tiny valuable part and discarded the rest, like a strip miner working over a nation's soul.

She pictured Americans everywhere, in the malls, on the phone, answering intimate questions from strangers. Nobody ever asked ordinary people what they thought about anything. So when the chance to speak out came along, they were all too eager to spill their guts on any subject, no matter how trivial or profound. In the flush of release, they never realized that their most cherished feelings were being snared to be changed or sold.

After factoring in time for the computer, the pollster and Sandy, the cost to ATI worked out to something like two cents per opinion. Not much of a bargain, as far as she could see.

She started work at the bottom, which was all she

deserved. And with Stephen X as her sponsor, she figured she would probably stay there forever.

Wally Conner was Sandy's SDU—Supervisor of Data Uploading—when she signed on with ATI. When Wally turned sideways, only his huge nose and Adam's apple broke the thin line of his profile. A sweep of hair strayed down his forehead like a blond awning for his sad, sunken eyes.

Wally looked like a starving refugee, but acted like a gracious host, eager to make the work shift as comfortable as possible for everyone. He seemed thoughtful in a job that didn't require much thought. His consideration might as well have been a fringe benefit, like sick pay.

Wally got along fine with everyone, so Sandy never expected any special treatment. But as he rose through the ranks to VPI— Vice President of Information—he pulled her along in his tailstream. Nearly as old as Roscoe, he projected a different kind of authority than Jack Gore or Stephen X, or even the ATI patriarchy.

For all its glossy brochures and high-powered presentations, America Thinks, Inc. played to its backroom employees like a low-budget cross between *I Love Lucy* and *The Wizard of Oz*. A single, windowless corridor separated the slapstick in-basket struggles of Caroline, Cindy, Marion and Sandy from the grandstanding that came out of the front office.

"We keep a finger on America's pulse," stated the company motto. The employees added, "And a hand in America's pocket." Depending on their mood, they might also say, "And a thumb up our butts."

There was something unseemly about prying into a person's heart, then selling what you found for a penny or two. Sonny Nix, the company's founder and many-titled figurehead, didn't do much to help Sandy feel comfortable with her work.

Her first day on the job, even before Sandy knew what she would be doing, Nix burst through the door. A huge, blustery man, Nix could have made a killing in used cars, except that his bearing would have scattered the customers.

In three or four commanding strides, he crossed the room where the tabulators moved papers from one pile to the next. "Good evening, ladies!" he boomed, bouncing his voice off the walls and low ceiling. "Keep up the good work. We're counting on your counting today."

When he left, Sandy looked around and asked, "Who was that?"

"The CEO," said Caroline.

"The COO," said Cindy.

"The CFO," said Marion.

"The B-O-S-S," said Wally.

The next day, Nix's broad smile and bottomless voice made Sandy feel welcome, as if he were letting her in on some corporate joke so early in her tenure.

Wednesday at five-thirty on the dot, the door flew open and Nix bellowed, "Good evening, ladies! Keep up the good work. We're counting on your counting today."

The scene repeated itself Thursday and Friday, and on into the next week and the next. Sandy realized that Nix himself was the joke, a strutting robot with a limited vocabulary. Every afternoon, the women shook their heads and rolled their eyes when he blew back out the door.

By contrast, bone thin Wally Conner always seemed to be hovering nearby, eager to solve any problem that a Data Input Technician might come up against. For a week or so, it put her on edge to see his sad face reflected in her computer monitor. She thought he was squinting over her shoulder, looking for missed keystrokes or sluggish throughput. But often as not when she turned around he was gazing off somewhere else.

"Yes?" Wally said once when he realized she had twisted around to see what he was looking at. "Have you got it under control?"

"I thought that's what you were going to tell me."

"No, no, you're doing fine." She caught a whiff of his breath mint when he leaned over and lowered his voice. "You're already the fastest DIT we have. You've been processing sixteen point five two percent more forms than Marion each night. It's like doing an extra night's work every five and a half days—"

"Closer to five days, one hour, eleven minutes, forty-one seconds," Sandy said without thinking. She turned a little red while he blinked as if his mind had drifted far away.

"Forty one seconds, huh?" At last he chuckled, like someone not quite sure of the punchline, and straightened up. "Have you got all the supplies you need?" he asked. "Pens? Paper? Calculator?"

When Wally ducked out to get everyone coffee, Caroline hooked an arm around the back of her chair and snapped her gum. "Did you see the look on his face?" she asked. "What the heck did you say to him?"

"Nothing." Sandy couldn't think for a moment. "I told him a number."

"Must have been your phone number. He already knows everything else." Caroline laughed. "You just better hope he don't give it to Mr. Nix."

Sandy felt confusion color her cheeks. Caroline laughed even harder and said, "Don't worry. When it comes to the battle of the sexes, our SDU is MIA."

One night six months after she started her new job, Sandy was the last DIT out of the building. Nothing happened when she turned the key in the ignition. Thinking maybe she hadn't turned the key far enough, she tried again, but with no luck. She turned the knob for the radio and listened hard to the silence, hoping maybe she was only going deaf or crazy and her car actually worked just fine.

The shapes she saw in the shadows up and down Westmore Avenue scared her. She pushed down the lock button and held the steering wheel in both hands—if she squeezed hard enough the car would give up the foolishness and start.

Wally hadn't left yet, but the building was locked and she didn't have a key. She slumped in the seat, kept her breathing as shallow as possible and waited for him to come out.

The wind that had brought the cold change ripped the straggling leaves from the trees. Before long, she thought, this place would be as barren and unforgiving as the moon. Sandy pictured the trash men finding her frozen body locked in the car on Monday morning. They would smear the windshield with their gloves as they tried to see through the icy film that had crystallized out of her last breath. She imagined the red and blue lights of emergency vehicles washing over her poor, dented car. The cops would clap their hands against the cold. Her death would cause a brief flurry of paramedics and paperwork, and that would be the end of it. She pitied the person who got stuck with breaking the news to Stephen X.

A sudden chill which had nothing to do with the temperature ran down Sandy's spine. She scootched up to see over the dashboard and judged the distance to the building. She compared that to how far the threatening shadows were from her path. At least she would have a chance.

She spilled out of the car and ran for the door, losing the cold in her rush. She tugged the handle until the door rattled in its frame. She hammered her car keys on the glass.

"Wally!" she shouted. "Can you hear me, Wally?"

The frozen grass crunched beneath her feet as she circled the building to Wally's second-floor office window. At first she feared the sound would give her away if someone lurked in the shadows. Then she felt relieved that the crunching would alert her if anyone sprang from the hedges.

She saw Wally standing by his desk, talking on the phone. She called his name, but not too loudly—it was probably an important call so late at night. Sandy shivered and hugged herself to hold in her scant warmth.

She wanted to scream his name until the cold, crystal stars shook in the sky. But she knew she had to bargain with the thing that thrashed her heart against the walls of her chest. If she conceded a scream now, she would never be able to contain the demands of her terror again.

She tossed pebbles against the glass, playing the balance between making enough noise to get Wally's attention and shattering the window.

At last, he put down the phone and stared in her direction. "Wally," she said as if he were standing next to her. "I need your help."

He disappeared deeper into the building and she ran back to the door. She pressed her forehead to the glass, straining to see him down the hallway, fogging her view. "Come on," she whispered. "Come on. Come on. Come on."

The air felt so cold it seemed to freeze time in a chunk that she could step back and study. She could see intricate chains of events that had dragged her up to this doorway and then abandoned her. So many threads of her life had been drawn together to tie her to this awful, lonely moment.

As she waited for Wally, she became so lost in her thoughts that she never heard the footsteps behind her.

So when Wally spoke her name she screamed to shake the stars.

Chapter 26

Uly Bondarbon

Billey's heel crunched the gravel as he spun to see who was behind him. Instinct sent his hands flying up to protect his face, but he saw right away that Uly Bondarbon wouldn't whup him.

Perching on a thick, black cross beam of the trestle, Uly couldn't have weighed half as much as Billey. He didn't carry any more meat than the old cow bone Black Wolf licked on when he wasn't doing anything else.

Even in the moonlight, Billey could see that Uly Bondarbon's tiny, sharp features might have been stolen from a bird. He was older than Billey, but he looked like the kids Billey remembered from school. The little guy's shoulders and knees propped up his clothes the way tent poles shape canvas.

Billey knew that in a whup-or-be-whupped world, Uly posed no threat. Besides, all the whupping had worn him out. And he could see without asking that Uly had never dug a hole in his life. Billey figured maybe he could learn a few things from a guy like that.

"Since I like you so much, you can just call me Uly," the little bird man said, pulling a cigarette from behind his ear and holding it at eye level between them. "Smoke?"

The rush of words and gestures confused Billey. Nobody had ever told him they liked him; there was never much reason why anyone would. Maybe this stranger had been lurking behind trees and rocks, studying Billey for a long time, finding out good things about him. Billey dutifully took the cigarette because he thought Uly wanted him to hold it for a moment.

"Light?" Uly leaned back and fished in his pocket with

two fingers. He dragged a match along the scratchy side of the little wood box, then cupped his hand around the flame, although the air hung dead still.

Billey held the cigarette in the same patch of air where Uly had left it. The two of them stared at it a moment in the match's yellow light.

"Hell fire!" The stranger laughed and shook his head. "If you don't want to smoke that, I ain't too proud to take it back." He slipped it out of Billey's fingers and caved in his cheeks. The end of the cigarette glowed a fierce orange, like the sun rising over the scooped-out hill back in Billey's world.

Billey watched for a moment and admitted, "I don't smoke."

"Neither do I." Uly leaned back against the black post and let a thin cloud escape from his narrow head. "But I thank the lord ever' day for a cigarette that does.

"You oughta least sit down a bit. Men like you and me don't get to sit down enough. Always got 'portant things to do."

Billey studied the gravel around his feet and found a hollow without any sharp rocks. He eased himself down into it, feeling his knees stiffen up from the whupping and the long walk.

"Don't believe you told me your name," the stranger said as he let out another puff. "Like I say, I'm Uly Bondarbon IV, but I'd be more than happy to be called Uly by a man like yourself."

"I'm Billey Elwood."

"*You*'re Billey Elwood?" Uly shot up straight as the trestle's legs and stared at him with each eye wider than the moon that peeked through the tracks over their heads. "I'll be a vinegar pickle! That sure does explain a lot of things to me."

Billey waited a moment, but he realized Uly was done talking. "What do you mean?" he finally asked.

"Now, Billey Elwood, you're a sly one." Uly pulled his knees up and held them to his chest with his pencil arms. "You're not going to make me tell you how you came to be here and where you'll be tomorrow. You know better than that."

Billey's ears tingled with a new concept. "Where will I be tomorrow?" he wondered.

Uly just about spit the cigarette right out of his mouth. Instead, he grabbed it in his left hand and waved both arms high in the air. "Yes!" he cried so loudly that Billey thought he was calling to someone on the railroad tracks. Billey craned his neck to see who was up there.

"I knew it would be like this when I met Billey Elwood!" Uly went on, parking the cigarette back in his mouth. "No, I take that back. I never could have known it would be *this* good.

"You try, you try and you try," he shook his head, "but you just can't be ready for everything."

Uly struck another match and held it up close to Billey, dipping it to feed the flame. "Fr'instance, one thing I can't figure is what happened to your face?"

Billey looked at his hands as if they held the answer. "What do you mean?"

Uly threw the match down an instant before it singed his fingers. "I mean you look like you lost an argument with a freight train, Billey Elwood."

Billey didn't know what that meant, but he remembered how Tommy Lagocki's mother had scolded him once for having a booger on his cheek. He brushed his hands over his face—gently on the sore parts—and asked, "Is that better?"

"Better'n bein' dead, I reckon, but not by much." Uly shook his head. "I sure don't want to meet the man who can work over a big guy like you."

"My daddy says my mama made me look this way," Billey said.

"Your *mama* did that to you?" Uly didn't even try to catch the cigarette when it dropped off his lower lip.

"Did what?" Billey felt like he was listening in on somebody else's conversation.

"Did what? Did your face up like World War III. You telling me your mama gave you them cuts? Your mama made your cheekbones turn purple? She mashed your nose all outta whack?" Uly shook his head. "Your mama must have a kick like a horse."

Billey brightened up. "My daddy says she was a horse. A five-buck horse." That sounded mighty expensive, saying it out loud.

"Now, Billey Elwood, don't you go lyin' to your friend." Uly dipped his head and looked at Billey out of the tops of his eyes. "You can't tell me no woman did those things to you. A good woman brings you into this world, raises you up big and strong, and you go tellin' lies about her. Now what am I supposed to think about that?"

"I dunno."

"I'll tell you what I think. I think a man smashed you up like that. Fact is, I think your daddy did it."

Billey's mouth dropped open, giving Uly a good look at the spaces where his teeth used to hang. Suddenly everything fell into place like the way Billey settled into the deep spot in the mattress in his camper at night. "My daddy whupped me," he said. "He whupped me something good."

"Something bad, you mean." Uly reached out and ran a finger gently over the gash above Billey's eyebrow. "Looks like you been done wronger than a hungry dog. You sure he's your daddy?"

Billey shook his head like he had a drop of water in his ear. "Sure he's my daddy," he said. "Fact, he's my whole family, just like he told me. Ain't nobody else ever give me a can of beans. 'Cept Otis once when the pigs took my daddy."

"That's all mighty fine, but I gotta tell you, I have my

doubts, Billey Elwood. I don't know how a man could do that and be your daddy, too."

"Do what?"

Uly clucked his tongue and looked over the ground. "You see where that butt went?"

"I dunno."

Uly squinted and poked his head around like he was trying to see into the cracks in the moonlight. "It musta gone somewheres around here."

"Do what, Uly?"

"What?" He kept peering at the light spots in the gravel like one of them would turn out to be a gold nugget.

"Uly!" Billey shouted to get his attention. "What did you mean that my daddy couldn't do?"

He finally looked up. His eyes glinted in the faint light and he said, "I just figure a man that messes up his own son ain't got no respect—not for you, not for hisself, not for nothin'. You know as well as I do that's no real man. That's a false daddy now, ain't it, Billey?"

"He's my real daddy," Billey protested. "He says he can do any damn thing he please."

"Now, Billey, people been tellin' me what a brain scientist you are and then I hear this trash from your own mouth." Uly scratched his ear. "Let me tell you about this false daddy of yours."

He hopped to the ground and squatted in front of Billey. "Number one, he's gotta be one big mother to make you look like that, and if he's a mother he can't be nobody's daddy. That's just common sense."

Billey opened his mouth but he didn't have time to say anything.

"Number bee, why's he treat you so mean if he's your own blood? I ain't your blood—fact I could be your enemy on earth just pretendin' to be your friend—but you don't see me treatin' you all mean like."

"You said you like me," Billey insisted.

"And I do on a bible. But your blood should like you more than the world."

Uly held his hand in Billey's face and counted off to his third finger. "Three, why'd you come all the way out here in the middle of the night if you ain't got a false daddy?"

Billey felt his lip quiver. His jaw moved without forming words. Hot tears rimmed his eyes.

"Now don't get all emotioned up on me, Billey. See, you don't need no daddy at all anymore and you 'specially don't need no false daddy."

Billey thought a moment and said, "What about my beans? How am I going to eat without my daddy?"

"Billey, Billey, Billey," Uly stepped back and sighed. "Someday, I'm gonna show you how you can eat sirloin steak and get all the respect in the world." He turned and started walking down the trail.

"Where are you going, Uly?" Billey tried to get up, but his knees and hamstrings made him move like an old man. "Can I come?"

Uly looked over his shoulder and said, "I've got some 'portant things to do. You might as well just go back to that false daddy of yours."

Arguing or pleading had never done Billey much good, so he just watched as Uly threaded his way down the path beyond the train tracks. He lifted his hand and heard himself make a little grunting noise, but Uly never did look back.

Chapter 27

Wally Conner

Wally jumped back and said, "Ahhhh," like someone tottering for balance. He spun around to see what Sandy had screamed at.

Sandy spun in the opposite direction so they came face to face in an odd dance like two figures on a Swiss clock.

"What is it?" Wally was shaking more than Sandy.

"I thought—" Sandy's mind went blank as the fear drained away. "I'm sorry. It's nothing."

"I thought you went home."

"The car wouldn't start. The radio, the lights, everything went dead."

Wally carried jumper cables in his trunk, along with enough tools, hardware and spare fluids to open a garage. Just to be safe, he followed her home, his headlights reassuring her in the mirror.

As she drove down her street, she thought she glimpsed a familiar car idling at the crossroad, its exhaust rising in ghostly clouds on the frosty night. Wally pulled up to the curb while she fiddled with her keys on her parents' porch. He flashed his brights twice and waved in the dashboard light when she cracked open the door.

Six years passed before Stephen X mentioned that night. By then they were married and Sandy knew that nothing he focused on could be insignificant.

She was surprised to find his car in the drive when she came home from Thrift Aisles with Saury on a Tuesday afternoon. Economizing on sacks helped Thrift Aisles keep their prices down. So Sandy clutched a bag bursting with produce in each arm while Saury skipped in circles around her and she tried to open the back door without spilling the groceries.

She clenched her teeth and held her breath as she twisted the door knob a finger's width at a time, too tired and proud to put anything down.

"Holy garbanzo beans!" Saury shouted, showing off the word he'd learned half an hour earlier. His chest swelled. "Ho-ho-holy garbanzo beans!"

Just as Sandy won the wrestling match and burst through the door, the left bag lost its bottom. She twisted her right arm to hold back the green, leafy tide, but that made her spill the potato chips, eggs—and ultimately the apples—from the right bag onto the carpet she'd vacuumed that morning.

"Human beans and garbanzo beans!" Saury yelled in a voice beyond his years. "Beans, beans, beans."

Sandy cursed and threw the rest of the groceries in a heap in front of her. "Please be quiet for just one minute, Saury," she said.

She looked at the pile a moment, then knelt and tried to scoop the eggs back into their shells. It wasn't going to work. But as she rose to get paper towels from the kitchen, she stopped and gasped.

Stephen X was standing dead still in the middle of the room, staring at her.

"What?" she asked, too surprised to manage more than a syllable.

"For God's sake, Sandy, look what you've done." His face hid behind a mask as pink as flesh, as hard as steel. "I work my butt to the bone to give you a decent place and this is how you treat it."

"I'm sorry." Sandy appeared to curtsy, not knowing whether she should get something to clean the mess or save time by kneeling down and doing what she could as quickly as possible. "Is something wrong?"

"Of course something's wrong. There's fifty pounds of vegetables rotting into the new carpet."

"I know. I know. I meant, you're home early."

"Ah ha! Giant garbanzo beans!" Saury shouted, jumping through the door into the midst of the potatoes.

"Saury," Stephen X snarled, "get outside and play, god-dam it." Saury froze an instant and then ran out, pumping his arms wildly.

Stephen X watched until his son disappeared around the corner of the house, then he turned back to Sandy.

"Have you got a problem if I come home early? Have you got something else planned?"

"No. I meant—"

"Don't look at me like that. Are you afraid I'll catch you with your boyfriend?"

"What boyfriend?"

"You mean which one? How about Wally? Long, thin Wally?"

"What are you talking about?"

"You think I'm stupid?"

"No," She said quickly.

"I've known about Wally since the first time he followed you home, back when you were living with Jack and your mother."

Sandy had no idea what he was talking about.

"I'll bet he's just like a hot needle on those cold nights, isn't he, Sandy?"

"Oh, please." She shook her head and crouched to clean up the mess.

Stephen X grabbed a fistful of hair and snapped her head back. "Don't you look away from me when I'm talking to you." He yanked her to her feet and showed her the devil in his eyes before the first blow cracked against her jaw.

•

Some of the women at ATI thought Sandy was putting on airs when she wore tinted glasses and turned up the brightness on her VDT. "Miss Hollywood," they called her behind her back.

Others figured she was hiding hangovers. They could relate to that, except Sandy never joined them when they closed the bars after the Friday night shift.

One night, Sandy stopped at the mirror in the rest room. She took off the glasses and studied the dark bruise around her left eye, gently testing its tenderness with her fingertips.

Suddenly, the door swung open and before she could put the glasses back on, Carla came in. Each of them gave a little start to see the other, then Carla's eyes locked on Sandy's reflection in the mirror.

"Did you get rid of him yet?" she asked.

Sandy felt the hot wash of embarrassment match the tone of her face to the bruise. Her mind raced and the world seemed to shift into slow motion. People made so many assumptions. They could never begin to understand. They just wanted to ridicule her, to set her apart so that none of her uncleanness would come off on them. "Who?" she said at last, but she had to squeeze the word out of her throat.

"Who? Your husband—you did marry him, didn't you?" Carla, a new DIT, was a dark-haired, blunt-chinned woman. She spoke like a teacher who already knew the answer and just wanted to get you to say it.

Sandy turned the water on too hard so it sprayed up from the bottom of the sink. Before she adjusted it, she waved at her face. "I had an accident," she stammered.

Carla burst into laughter, but Sandy didn't feel threatened so much as curious. When the older woman calmed down, she said, "Get rid of him. That's all there is to it. And the sooner, the better."

Sandy slipped her tinted glasses back on and finished washing her hands when Carla locked herself in the nearest stall. She looked around at the spotless tile, then hurried back to her desk, worrying that she'd been gone a long time.

She'd been at ATI long enough that most of her co-workers had given up trying to include her in their plans for coffee breaks and off hours. Lucinda always came by when the gang made its quarterly trek to The Bun Shop after work, but everyone knew Sandy would politely decline the invitation.

"What would you do if I said yes?" She asked Lucinda one April evening.

"I'd say it's about time, mama! Let's go."

Sandy rolled her chair back snug to the desk. "I didn't *say* yes," she protested. "I just wondered what would happen if I did."

They were nice enough, but she didn't feel close to any of the women at the office. Now she wondered if Carla had divined something they could use as gossip fodder. She wanted to hang around as if she were someone else, so she could hear what they really thought of her. She planned long monologues, how she would explain everything to someone who could never begin to understand.

They might have been from another planet for all she knew of them. The closest she came to social interaction with them was when Wally called everyone on the shift together for his monthly GIGO Gatherings.

To computer nerds, GIGO - Garbage In, Garbage Out - is a law of the universe more dependable than gravity or the speed of light. It holds that the system will produce the correct answer if it is fed the proper questions and data. Only the human element corrupts the search for truth.

Wally twisted the acronym into Goodies In Garbage Out. On the third Wednesday of each month, cookies, cakes, pies and ice cream filled the office. He figured if he loosened the tongue with sweets, problems in the work place could be hashed out before they became serious.

"I just don't see how some people can keep their data straight if they're taking personal phone calls at the keyboard," Shelly whined with a sideways glance at Caroline.

That gave Wally a chance to explain the company's intricate telephone policy, based on a three-dimensional Phone

Usage Matrix Sonny Nix had constructed. The PUM allowed a certain length for any given call based on the frequency, duration and shift positioning of an employee's calls for the week.

"How come DataBasics gives its DITs three weeks vacation and a buck an hour more than we get, and they're still working three full shifts?" asked Maureen, the pear-shaped woman who always looked like she'd put her mascara on while standing on her head.

"I think we should have parking spaces assigned by seniority," she went on before Wally could open his mouth. "All the real companies do that.

"There's never any good stuff in the vending machines.

"Do we have to listen to Sonny Nix *every* night?

"Why don't the janitors come after our shift? That hunchback guy looks up my skirt every time he picks up my wastebasket.

"A hundred times a night, I key all the way down to the bottom of a survey before I see it's been invalidated with a double response. Why the hell doesn't someone sort those out before the DITs ever see them?

"Trouble with this place is, the bosses don't know what's going on. One thing after another."

Wally waved both hands when Maureen finally paused for breath. "Improvements are part of the process, Maureen—"

"Pretty damn small part, if you ask me."

Wally leaned against the frame of the window that looked out over a brightly lit courtyard.

"Reminds me of when I was in QC at TimeTek," he said. "We worked up the best Stress Test they'd ever seen. We pulled watches off the line at random and put them through it to see how long they kept running. We squashed 'em and dunked 'em and twisted 'em and poked and pounded 'em until their guts flew across the lab.

"We made it so tough the engineers started competing

with each other. They built watches by hand in their spare time just to see if they could beat the Stress Test. They might spend weeks honing the tolerances down until they were tighter'n a wino on Westmore.

"Then they'd turn it over to us and make bets about whose watch would last the longest—but the only way to find out was to destroy them. When a guy broke the record, we handed him a little plastic bag with whatever was left and he'd tape it to his door until someone built a watch that could last a couple minutes longer."

"What's that got to do with this place?" Maureen asked.

Wally laughed and unfolded his arms. "You're the best, Maureen." He walked back to the table of pies and cakes. "You must be the best to keep going no matter how hard we try to make it for you."

"Anhhhh!" Maureen waved her hand as if she'd seen a bug on it.

The other women enjoyed a laugh, but Sandy's mind had wandered before the punch line. She realized she was staring at a tray of ginger snaps, but she felt no hunger.

Chapter 28

Driving

Billey hobbled home well before daybreak, but he didn't go back to the camper. Instead, he hunched down between the tank and the hole and watched the sky turn red as a stinging ant.

Sunrise added one stroke at a time to its sketches of the shack, the camper and the dead catalpa. Those shapes looked almost pretty in the dim light, like they belonged to someone else. Billey imagined a warm fire, like in Tommy Lagocki's house, the crackle and smell of bacon, the catalpa swelling with buds and blossoms.

Those pictures came from a different world than his, a place where you could sleep without a gun waking you, where a dog might walk right up to the spool and beg for scraps of sirloin steak without getting himself kicked.

When the sun broke free of the landscape and washed out the sky, everything looked ugly again and Billey's thoughts came back home. The shovel's handle found its place in his hands. The hard wood, worn smooth by his own sweat and callouses, gave him comfort. It anchored Billey's life against the pain and uncertainty which buffeted him day after endless day.

He jabbed the shovel into the flinty earth and pressed its blade down hard with his foot. He rocked back to loosen a handful of dirt and tossed it high over his shoulder.

The familiar motions worked the stiffness out of his muscles and deadened the hurt that burned inside him like a swig of sour milk. As he loosened up, he moved more quickly, throwing each scoop of dirt and rocks farther than the last. The shovel and the hole belonged to him and there was no way Elwood or Otis or even Uly Bondarbon could take them away.

Billey lost himself in the heave and grunt of his work so he couldn't say exactly when the noise started. It may have been going a long time, off in the distance, before he noticed.

Billey froze in the middle of his swing so the dirt flew up from the blade, then fell back against it to make a little cloud of dust. He strained his ears until it felt like they would turn themselves inside out.

Then he heard it again - more distinctly now - a dog's excited bark, coming closer with each yelp.

Billey jammed his shovel in the loose dirt that collected at the side of the hole. He used the handle for balance as he stood on his tiptoes to peer over the edge.

"BLACK WOLF!" he cried in a voice he'd never heard before. He'd always been too afraid to use this raw voice that had been bottled up deep in his guts for so long. "Over here, Black Wolf!"   With each wild stride, the dog's legs - short and thick as cans of beans - flew out, then caught his weight at the last possible instant before his belly scraped the barren earth. His long, pink and black tongue flopped in time to his steps, flinging gobs of saliva to either side.

Billey waved his arms and scrambled to get over the edge of the hole. Black Wolf ran faster than ever, his enormous feet drumming out a muted, staccato rhythm. Just as Billey's head poked over the rim, Black Wolf skidded in to lick his master.

Billey took dog, dirt and slobber gobs square in the face and keeled back into the hole. The impact didn't even hurt his bruises because seeing Black Wolf took away so much pain.

"I thought you was dead," Billey whispered, pulling him tight against his chest.

Black Wolf panted like a freight train going home. He slopped his tongue across Billey's face and neck, his hands and ear. Billey ran his fingers through the dog's thick, knotted hair and looked at the gratitude and understanding that shone out from deep within those brown-rimmed eyes. Billey stroked Black Wolf's forehead and all along the squat body.

But Black Wolf yelped and stiffened when Billey's hand reached his butt. A short black stump, its end crusted with blood, stuck straight up where the plume of Black Wolf's tail used to be.

Billey lifted the dog over the rim of the hole and climbed out. He studied the rocky field, trying to remember where the tail had landed. If they found it, maybe they could get someone to sew it back on. It had gotten shot off so bad it might never grow back by itself. A dog needs his tail to wag when he's happy, else how's anyone going to know what he likes?

Black Wolf lapped at Billey's heel, never holding still. If you didn't know Black Wolf, you'd never know he'd had a tail. But Billey knew.

Billey shuffled his feet to draw a giant box in the dirt. He figured the tail had to be somewhere inside those lines, so he paced up and back, studying the area inch by inch.

Billey and Black Wolf lifted their heads and cocked their ears at the same noise. The pickup was bouncing and veering across the field in their direction. Billey looked down at Black Wolf and Black Wolf looked up at Billey.

"Go on," he said in a hoarse, urgent whisper although the truck was still a quarter-mile away. He waved his hands like he was treading water. "You'd better go away for awhile."

Black Wolf dashed twenty feet away, then turned and whined and began to slink back, dragging his belly on the ground.

"I mean it." Billey felt his voice rise out of control again. He kicked a cloud of dirt in the dog's direction. "Get outta here!"

Black Wolf darted and turned, darted and turned until he found cover in the bushes that ran along the creek.

Billey jumped out of the way as Elwood hit the brakes, locking up the up the wheels and missing his son by inches. Before Billey found his balance, Elwood and Otis were both tumbling out of the truck. Otis tried to slam his door but he slipped and spun around twice, waving his arms in giant circles to keep his nose out of the dirt.

"Thought we'd find you down here," Elwood said.

"You can't hide from Mr. Peter," Otis said, stroking his rusty zipper and trying to look composed.

"Get in the truck, Billey. We're gonna go for a little ride."

Otis prodded Billey onto the seat and the two men squeezed in on either side of him.

Elwood let the truck find its own jolting way across the field while he fished for a smoke and a light. He took such a deep drag that his head lolled back to get it all in. With one hand playing on the outside mirror and the other resting on Billey's knee, he let the great cloud of smoke roll over his son.

"You look like shit, boy," he said, rubbernecking between Billey and the narrow spot they would have to go through to get out on the road. "Anybody ever tell you that?"

"Nobody I remember," Billey said, looking straight ahead.

Otis clapped his hand down on Billey's other knee. "Didn't I tell you that once, Billey?"

"Maybe you did, Otis." Billey looked at the big man with an expression as empty as Otis' eyes, "I bet that's why I couldn't recall."

Otis spit out the window, but the glob blew back in and landed on the glass just behind his shoulder.

When Elwood pulled onto the road that ran along the highway, he steered by draping his wrist over the wheel. Most of the traffic was on the big road, so he didn't have to worry much about smashing into anyone else.

"It's about time you learned to drive, Billey." Elwood patted his son's knee. "Boy's old enough to grow whiskers, he's old enough to drive, ain't that so, Otis?"

"'Sright." Otis grinned at Billey. "I been drivin' since first time Mr. Peter needed a haircut. You don't want people to think you're backwards, do you Billey?"

They stopped and Billey changed seats with Elwood.

"You're a real smart kid, so you just do all the things I done, Billey."

Billey reached out stiffly and searched for first gear. The pickup bucked twice and died.

"What the hell you doin', tryin' to bust my clutch?" Elwood squeezed Billey's shoulder with both hands and shook him. "Give it some gas, boy."

Billey revved the engine to a high whine and left a short arc of rubber on the pavement. Otis braced himself against the dash board. "You're gonna be a drivin' fool, Billey, just like your daddy."

"You learn to drive and you can start earning your keep," Elwood said. "You don't think I can afford to feed you if all you can do is dig holes, do you?"

Billey shook his head, but kept his eyes locked on the center line of the road. His knuckles turned white on the steering wheel.

"Man's gotta take charge of his life," Elwood went on, rubbing his fingers to signal Otis that he needed another cigarette. "Man that don't do nothin's no better than that ugly little dog of yours, Billey. Just make a lot of noise and stink the place up."

Elwood ran Billey up and down the gears a hundred times. He drilled him on hard turns and sudden stops. He showed him how to kill the engine and glide to a standstill.

"Keep your goddam foot off the brake," he shouted. "They can hear them brakes halfway 'cross the county. You gotta learn to do your business without ever'one starin' at you."

Except for being jammed up against the door, Billey was starting to like driving. At least he didn't have to sit next to Otis. With no more effort than it took to squash a bug, he could make the big old pickup lurch, bellow and skid. In the back of Billey's mind a picture began to take shape of slipping into the truck with Black Wolf sometime and putting a million miles on his daddy and Otis and the spool and the hole.

"Slow down, goddamit." Elwood slapped the dash. "There's more pigs on this road than the backyard of the wiener plant."

Otis broke off his snore and blinked. "Where you want me to plant my wiener?"

"Goddamit, Billey, don't you know where the goddam brake pedal is yet?" Elwood scootched forward and scanned for pigs.

For the first time, Billey felt like he was in control. He saw a tanker coming at them in the distance so he pressed down hard on the gas as if the floorboard could yield more speed. The wind whipped around his head so he couldn't make out what Elwood was yelling. It peppered them with bits of glass that had fallen inside the pickup when Elwood shot the window out. The speedometer's needle lost its place and flew all over the dial.

The tanker rushed toward them and Billey strained against the gas pedal. He let the pickup drift over the center line. He could drive smack dab into that tanker. Elwood and Otis would wind up looking like bean juice that dribbled out of the can and got all fried up on the Coleman. They could all just go to hell together. That would show them.

Billey steered into the tanker's path. Through the wind and Elwood's shouting, he could hear the blast of its air horn as it began to swerve for the shoulder.

Elwood grabbed the wheel and tried to pry Billey's hands off. Billey stole a glance to his right and saw the same wide-eyed, drop-jawed look on his daddy's face as the time the tornado ripped past the shack when Billey was a kid.

The tanker couldn't fit on the shoulder and the momentum of its cargo sent it whipping back and forth across the road. Billey could count the bugs splayed across the truck's radiator. Then he pictured Elwood surviving the crash, dusting himself off and cussing his dead, shit-brained son.

He slammed on the brakes and let Elwood tug the wheel. The pickup spun a full circle and began to tilt on two wheels before it wound up with its engine stalled, pointing at a tree. Billey watched a hubcap roll down the road and crash into a mail box. Otis cracked his door and puked.

"You're right, daddy," Billey said without looking at Elwood. "You can hear those brakes halfway 'cross the county."

Elwood was so mad he couldn't even cuss. He shook and made fists in his lap. Then he saw the trucker, a huge, red-faced man in a sweaty tee shirt, jogging after them.

"This bastard's gonna do you in time for Christmas, Billey," Elwood said.

Billey started the engine and drove hard until the man disappeared in the mirror. He leaned forward to look around his daddy. "Hey, Otis!" he laughed. "You ever drive like that?"

Chapter 29

Masks

Stephen X towered over Sandy. His hands clenched and relaxed. The veins in his forehead swelled to make him look like a Hollywood monster. In her daze, Sandy wondered if that might be why he loved those shoddy horror flicks so much—they showed him new ways to contort his features.

"Get up!" he screamed, bending at the waist for maximum volume. Sandy heard him, but she couldn't move. "Don't give me that. You're not hurt."

She tried to think of what she had done or failed to do, but her mind wobbled in loops that kept coming back to the pain which pulsed down from her face through her whole body. She wanted desperately to get up because she knew her stillness fueled his rage. The irony of it flitted past the fringe of her consciousness—how she couldn't even meet his requirements for a punching bag.

"Quit that bullshit and get up." Stephen X prodded her hip with his foot. Her hair seemed to make the tiniest crackling noise, like a distant fire, as her head turned against the linoleum. She strained to remember where Jennifer was; where Saury was.

Stephen X reached down and grabbed her hair, but he stopped before he jerked her off the floor. He stared at the blood that painted his hand as if he hadn't noticed it before, as if he hadn't seen the pool that spread beneath Sandy's swollen nose and mouth.

"Look what you've done!" Disgust replaced the more dangerous fury in his voice. "Why do you make it like this?"

•

Sandy used to tell her mother when things happened, but that only made her feel worse.

159

"He hit me in the face with the cutting board," she said into the phone.

"Hard?" asked Mrs. Gore's thin voice.

"Hard enough to knock me down . . . but I wasn't expecting it. Maybe I could have stayed on my feet if I'd known." Sandy heard her voice come out flat, like she was telling her mother that Thrift Aisles had slashed ten cents a pound off the price of ground beef.

None of it seemed to surprise Mrs. Gore. "You'll never learn, will you, Sandy?" she said.

"What do you mean?"

"I mean, what on earth did you do to make him hit you?"

"My God, mother! Just what do you think would make someone do that?"

"Well, he's your husband, isn't he?" Mrs. Gore became easily irritated when her daughter played simple-head. "You should know better than anyone."

"So what makes dad hit you?"

"Your father has never raised a hand to me," Mrs. Gore spoke rapidly.

The phone turned into a cold, scientific instrument in Sandy's hand. It sucked all the life—the emotions and perspective—out of her mother's voice. It left only the words, like desiccated lab specimens.

"Even when you were a little girl you used to make your father so mad," the words went on. "You get so caught up in yourself, you forget there are other people in the world. You know, you can be very selfish sometimes."

Maybe her mother's implications were right. Mrs. Gore didn't get knocked around, therefore she was a better wife, a better mother, a better person. None of the girls Sandy knew from school, or their mothers or sisters or aunts or girlfriends, had ever told her about being beaten or raped. In all her world, only Sandy was a bad enough person to provoke an innocent man to violence.

160

Poor, star-crossed Stephen X. Marrying Sandy had ruined his life. She had forced him into these brutish patterns, so foreign to his nature.

The real Stephen X was the one who sent flowers even before she'd finished dabbing antiseptic on her wounds.

The pimpled, gawky boy who rang the bell almost gasped when Sandy opened the door. His gaze darted around the porch, searching for a safe place to land.

"I'm sorry," he stammered. "They must have gotten the cards crossed up at the shop. Just a minute."

He pushed the vase of roses and baby's breath into her arms and jogged to the van. He came back with a blank "Get Well" card.

"Do you want me to copy the message onto this one?" he asked, looking at her as if he thought she might strike him at any moment. When she shook her head, he began backing up, mumbling, "Sorry. I'm sorry." When he'd put a safe distance between them, he turned and jogged the rest of the way to the van. He pushed down the door lock before starting the engine.

"My darling," read the ornate inscription on the card that came with the flowers. She opened the flap to see where someone at the florist shop had written, "I just wanted to let you know that I'm thinking about you. Love, Stephen X."

She studied the neat, flowing curves of the stranger's handwriting. It bore no resemblance to her husband's pointy, constricted letters. She wondered if someone had helped him with the wording, too.

The next bouquet didn't need a card because Stephen X brought it himself.

Sandy had gobbled aspirin and slept fitfully through the middle of the day. She hoped that if she got some rest, she would feel well enough to pick up Saury at Kid'n'Kaboodle before it closed.

But at three o'clock, Stephen X tiptoed into the bedroom

holding a spray of mums in front of his face, shushing Saury and herding the child in before him.

"Let's surprise mommy," Stephen X said in a stage whisper. "One . . . two . . . three . . ."

"Surprise!" they shouted in unison as Stephen X flipped on the lights. Saury jumped on the bed and crawled up to hug Sandy, but he stopped when he saw her face. He reached out to touch her swollen lip ever so gently.

Stephen X was so attentive to her that it seemed strange he couldn't see the bruises.

"I missed you and I wrapped up the Johanson business ahead of schedule, so I thought I'd pick up Saury and come home early," he said. "We can go to Mama M's for dinner. Maybe catch a movie, too."

Stephen X never acknowledged what happened. After each attack, he became the ideal husband, considerate of her every need. It was as if Sandy's blood washed away the evil that had used him. Then he brought her gifts. He burnt pancakes, sliced away the blackest parts, and carried them in to her on a tray. He smoothed the creases in his maps and planned weekend trips that he could write off on his expense account.

Once when they were dating, Sandy remarked on the cuteness of some salt and pepper shakers they saw on a back shelf at Derringer's. The salt shaker was a white cat, the pepper a black one. Two years or more passed before the first time Stephen X hit her. The next day, she found those shakers on the kitchen counter. She smashed them with a rolling pin, ground the china into dust and left the mess where he couldn't miss it.

Weeks went by with Stephen X on his best behavior. Then she asked him what time it was while he was reading the paper, or she left the fridge open while unpacking groceries, or she spent his money on a new blouse, and she suffered the consequences. The next day a new set of salt shakers appeared in the kitchen. This happened so many times, she began to wonder if he had ordered them in bulk. Maybe there was a storage shed somewhere on Westmore Avenue full of black and white china cats.

Stephen X paid no more attention to the battered gifts than he did to Sandy's battered features. He could shape reality simply by choosing not to recognize some brutal fact. His conviction that the sky was green, the grass was blue, and their marriage was upscale and serene began to make Sandy wonder if she were losing her mind. By forcing an appearance of normalcy in the most bizarre situations, Stephen X could even suck others into his world.

Sandy gathered that Stephen X planned to use Gene Watkins, a man he worked with, in some quasi-legal maneuver at the office. To begin gaining his confidence, Stephen X invited Gene and his wife, Lawanda, over for dinner on a Saturday night.

A few minutes before they were due, Stephen X discovered that Sandy had bought the wrong wine.

"I specifically told you cabernet sauvignon," he said. "This is sauvignon blanc. Do I have to draw a picture of the label?"

"The man at the liquor store said this is very nice." Sandy picked up the bottle and began reading the description on the back label.

"You think some minimum-wage moron is a wine connoisseur because he's wearing a clean shirt?"

"He was nice. He was trying—"

"My God, Sandy, wake up. This is a white wine! Red meat, red wine. Everybody knows that. And it's room temperature besides. Don't you even know enough to chill a white wine? Watkins will think we're complete idiots."

"I can put it in the freezer—" Sandy started.

"Don't you—" Stephen X lost his last shred of rationality in mid-sentence. He shoved her against the counter.

Rage transformed his face. When these things were over, Sandy sometimes wished she had before and after photos of her husband. His features broke up in sharp angles and furrows so you could not recognize this as the same person you were looking at an instant earlier. The only thing the two faces held in common was the eyes—she could see hints of hatred and disgust in his eyes even when Stephen X was at his calmest.

The twisted face *looked* like a mask, but she knew that the other was the real disguise.

He locked his fingers around her chin and smashed her head back against the cupboard over and over. He only stopped when the doorbell rang. He looked at Sandy coldly. "Make yourself decent," he said.

As he went to the door, she heard him clear his throat the way he always did, with two short hacks followed by a longer, harsher one. "Gene!" he said in the deep voice he saved for company. "And this must be Lawanda. Come in, come in."

Stephen X had served cocktails and was in the middle of a complicated story about his car phone by the time Sandy came in, twisting her fingers at her waist.

"This is my lovely wife, Sandy," Stephen X said, hugging her close to him around the shoulder. Gene and Lawanda nodded and grinned as Stephen X went on, "Anyway, the guy in the Lincoln picks up his phone and starts making hand signs at me . . ."

After he finished and they'd laughed as much as they were going to, Sandy excused herself to bring the hors d'oeuvres. On her way to the kitchen, she overheard Stephen X say, "She's been sick, but she's very brave. She wants everyone to think everything's fine."

When they sat down for dinner, Stephen X poured three glasses of wine. "Some of the better restaurants in New York have started serving warm whites with beef," he announced.

"You'll be seeing it everywhere next season."

Lawanda reached over when Sandy lifted her empty glass. Their hands touched, forcing Sandy to look her guest in the eye.

"You don't need that, dear," Lawanda said softly. "We're here for you."

Nobody could begin to understand any of it, least of all Sandy. The world laughed with Stephen X and at Sandy. He was confident, well-spoken, respected. She was awkward and ridiculed; she always had been. Even in junior high, when friends had talked of shopping or boys, Sandy's mind had drifted off toward higher math, things that made the girls roll their eyes and elbow each other. So whose version of reality was right—Sandy's or Stephen X's?

She had to hold it all inside, like the deep breath that turns to poison when you swim underwater.

Linda and Roscoe seemed so happy together that Sandy couldn't tell her what was going on. Even though Linda detested Stephen X, Sandy felt she had to protect her from the whole story. Knowing about her brother-in-law's violent habits would have been a terrible strain on Linda's relationship with Roscoe.

And what about Roscoe himself? He projected the image of a warm, caring person, but such strange things went on within families that she couldn't say what he would do if confronted with Stephen X's behavior. Maybe he would side with his brother. Maybe he could find sympathy for a man thrust into such a situation.

After all, Stephen X cloaked himself in human form, just like that green jelly thing in *It Came from Zone X*. Maybe all men disguised themselves that way. Maybe that was something coded into the Y chromosome, like the urge to brush their hair over a bald spot.

Chapter 30

Dynamite

Billey pulled the pickup into the Shell station next to Thrift Aisles.

"Gas it up, Otis," Elwood said. "May be the last time we ever have to get gas here."

Elwood stomped his feet on the floor as if they'd gone to sleep. He slid over to the passenger's side when Otis climbed out to work the pump. He flicked his ashes out the window and said, "I sure do hate the hump. Cramps my legs all up."

Otis splashed gas on the side of the truck. "Me, I love to hump." He grinned. "I could just hump until the sun goes down."

"Then you can set your fancy ass in the middle on the way back." Elwood scowled. "I swear, Otis. You're the only man I ever knowed that likes to set his butt on a hump."

"You's just jealous 'cause the ladies like me more than you," Otis said. "Looky that one over there." He pointed to a slim woman with a child on her hip in the grocery store's parking lot. She waited for a small, thin man to finish loading groceries in the trunk of an ancient Impala.

"Honk that horn, Billey. Get her to look over here." Otis rattled the nozzle in the fuel pipe. "What I wouldn't do to turn into a dog right about now," he said.

"Why's that, Otis?" Elwood made an OK sign and shot his cigarette butt out the window.

"If I's a dog, I could go right up to her and have me a sniff between them legs," he said with his eyes locked on the woman. "Have me a good, long, juicy lick, too. Them dogs can get away with anything.

"Billey, didn't I tell you to honk that horn good and loud? That poor lady don't know what she's missin' if she don't take notice of Otis. Honey," he raised his voice. "I'm over here with Mr. Peter."

Billey had slouched down behind the steering wheel so nobody would see him with his daddy and Otis. He lifted his head to peek over Elwood's shoulder and see if the woman had heard Otis. He was relieved to see she had her back to them. But he gasped when he saw that the bag boy looked like Uly Bondarbon.

"What's the matter with you?" Elwood snapped. "You ain't comin' down with Otis Fever on me are you? One goddam Otis is about more than I can stand."

Before Billey shouted to his friend, he realized that Uly would see him with his false daddy. Billey didn't think he could bear that much shame all at once. He slumped down and pressed the back of his head into the deep slash where the stuffing spilled out of the vinyl.

It seemed like forever, but Otis finally quit playing with the pump. "Looky here," he said, but nobody looked. "This thing's just like my peter—gotta shake it real good to get that last drop off." He thought a moment and added, "Course it's not as big as my peter."

Elwood stepped out and let Otis wallow over to the middle of the seat. "You see that lady, Billey?" Otis breathed. "I'd give an inch off my peter to turn into a dog right now."

Elwood slammed the door and said, "Let's see how fast you can get outta here, Billey."

Otis looked at him. "Ain't you gonna pay for the gas?"

"Otis, if you had as much money as bullshit, I'd pay double. You ain't got none. I ain't got none. I know Billey ain't got none 'cause he never brung me a nickel. 'Sides, I'm tired of always payin' for stuff. It's time people started payin' me.

"Now you get us outta here real quick like, Billey."

Billey glanced past his daddy to the parking lot, but Uly had gone and he knew better than to argue.

•

Billey didn't know if Elwood was spending less time whupping him because he figured he'd whupped him enough, or because he had other things on his mind. Elwood always made like he had big things to do, things he couldn't bother with telling Billey about. As far as Billey could see, they mostly involved sitting next to the spool with a flat bottle, mumbling and stroking his gun until deep into the night.

Billey didn't much care why Elwood left him alone as long as he did. And he felt that if he thought about it too much, somehow that might hex it and the old man would start coming around again with knuckles as hard as creek rocks.

As long as Billey kept chipping away at the bottom of the hole, he seemed to stay out of trouble these days.

Black Wolf didn't come around either. Billey mopped his forehead on his sleeve and thought of how Black Wolf used to flop out that big old tongue of his and lick the salt off Billey's skin when the sweat dried. He wondered if he'd let his friend down, or if the dog might just be too scared to show himself, knowing that the pickup could come bouncing across the way any minute.

And Billey felt too ashamed to look for Black Wolf because he never did find the end of his tail. Probably some old stray cat came by and took it home with him.

A couple of weeks after the big whupping, Elwood and Otis drove up at sunset. "Get on outta there and fetch me the biggest rock you can carry," Elwood said, looking down into the hole. "We can't wait forever for you to dig this thing."

Billey staggered back from the creek bank with a rock that he could barely wrap his arms around. He dropped it over the side of the hole and it hit the bottom with a deep thud.

The two men were down there chipping away a little depression in the floor of the hole.

Once in Billey's school days, Dankowski showed him a pack of two-inch firecrackers at recess. "Hold onto these,

Billey Elwood," he said, striking a match.

The sparking, sputtering fuse surprised Billey, so he held the package at arm's length. But the kids who ringed around him were yelling so much, telling him not to let go, that he knew something was up. At the last possible instant, he threw the pack back to Dankowski who peed in his pants but was otherwise unhurt. Now Billey saw something that looked like the mother of all firecrackers poking out of Elwood's hip pocket. Elwood set it in the slot they'd carved out and told Otis to bring the big rock over.

Even from ground level, Billey could smell the sharp fumes that rose from Otis. The man stumbled as he picked up the rock and nearly fell onto the firecracker as he tried to set it in place.

Elwood struck a match on the seam of his pants and lit the fuse. He hustled over the rim by Billey. Together, they looked down at Otis wobbling over to the side of the hole.

"Get your virgin ass outta there, Otis," Elwood laughed.

Otis looked over his shoulder at the shrinking fuse. He clawed the wall of dirt, but he looked like he was trying to bury himself for all the good it was doing him. He finally got his elbows over the rim and rested his head on the ground, panting.

"Better hurry, Otis," Elwood said.

Otis tried to pull himself out, but Elwood pressed his boot down against his head. "Ain't got much time now, Otis," he taunted. "Look at that fuse burn, Billey. How long you s'pose it's gonna take to blow up?"

"I dunno."

Otis tried to say something, but he just made the most pitiful noises Billey could imagine. Elwood kept stepping down on Otis' tangled hair every time Otis tried to lift his head.

"Billey," Otis said through the whimpering. "Billey!"

Billey hated Otis plenty, but he didn't want to see his butt get blown off. He kicked his father's boot off the big man's head. "Quit it," he said.

Elwood swept Billey up in a bear hug and held him over the edge of the hole while Otis wobbled to his feet. "Quit it!" Elwood whined through his nose. "Baby Billey says to quit it."

Otis lunged into Elwood so that all three of them tumbled to the ground just as the dynamite exploded, showering them with debris.

Elwood wiped the dirt from his face and rolled over on his back. He kicked his heel into the ground and laughed. "Thought for sure you was gonna piss your britches, Otis."

They all stood up and clapped clouds of dust out of their pants. "You son of a bitch - " Otis started.

"Aw, don't be a such a pussy." Elwood spat a black, muddy goober at his feet. He looked at Otis a second, then reached over and squeezed a handful of dirt that had collected in Otis' shirt pocket. "Just take a look at these knockers, Billey."

Billey was more interested in looking at the hole. The dynamite had saved him six months on the shovel. All he had to do now was scoop out the loose stuff and the tank would fit down there real good.

If Billey didn't know better, he might have thought his troubles were over.

But he did know better.

Chapter 31

Shopping

One way Thrift Aisles kept prices so low was by letting customers bag and carry their own groceries. Sandy didn't necessarily enjoy that—especially when she had Saury on her hip, but she could scarcely afford to shop anywhere else with the household budget Stephen X had allowed.

One night Stephen X got up during a commercial and jabbed a cigarette into the ashtray he kept by the fridge. "Did you ever look at this, Sandy?" he called out, sounding distracted.

"What is it?" She came in from the laundry room.

"In here." He held the cupboard open and waved her over. "Check it out."

She looked in the cupboard and brushed a loose wisp of hair behind her ear. "I don't understand."

"Potato chips," he said with authority. "A seven-ounce bag of potato chips."

"Do you want me to fix you some? Do you need a bowl?"

"I never eat potato chips." He sighed. "Sandy, I thought you agreed to work with me on this."

"I don't know what you mean."

"You've forgotten last week when we talked about the budget? You said you understood then. If you have any questions, I'll be glad to explain it to you. I try to save you from worrying about all this shit, but if you want, I'll tell you how taxes are shooting through the roof. Do you want to hear how inflation is eating our lunch? Do you want to know how hard it is for me just to keep my head above water when there are spies in my own office? Do you need a detailed explanation of why we can't afford to keep these goddam potato chips around here all the time?"

He threw the bag on the floor so hard it popped. He stomped on it and sent crumbs shooting in every direction. Reflex pulled Sandy back beyond arm's length. She winced and judged the distance to the door. But Stephen X calmed down as abruptly as he'd flared.

"We just have to cut back to the essentials now, Sandy. When we turn things around, we can have chips and soda pop. We can get Saury more of those plastic dinosaurs he likes. But right now, we have to pull in the belt."

Shopping at Thrift Aisles didn't seem so bad when Sandy thought about countries where a baby could still starve at its mother's breast.

And one good thing about a tight budget was that she could seldom afford more than two sacks of groceries. That was about all she could manage at Thrift Aisles in any case, because another way the store held costs down was by scrimping on shopping cart maintenance.

The wheels twisted and jammed and screeched over the scarred linoleum in a bent-metal ballet. Sandy couldn't tell from the carts' mad circles whether they needed an engineer or an exorcist. After half an hour of veering into shelves and plowing through produce, she preferred to carry her groceries through the parking lot, rather than tempt disaster.

Sandy didn't see the little guy come up the first time he offered to carry her bags. She was too busy keeping an eye on the new girl at the register. There was always a new girl at the register at Thrift Aisles. The store paid as little as it could and squeezed its employees until they became numb or quit.

Today's girl had a face as round and pale as a mushroom. She pinched Sandy's ginger root and held it up between two fingers. "Eeewww!" she gasped. "Look what I found in your basket."

"I like to fix Chinese some nights when my husband won't be home," Sandy explained.

"Yuck!" The girl tossed the ginger into the trash basket

beneath the register. "They just never clean those carts," she said.

Sandy was too surprised to say anything. She watched the girl pick up a cucumber and begin flipping through the laminated price sheets, squinting at sketches of fruit and vegetables. Finally, the cashier crinkled her nose and looked up at Sandy. "Is this a zoo-chinny?"

"Pardon me?" Sandy leaned closer to hear better.

"Did you see how much this cost?"

"They were three for a dollar."

The girl looked at the items that remained on the conveyor belt. "But you only got one." She whipped a calculator out of her apron and punched a long sequence of keys. "It doesn't work out," she announced at last.

"Let's call it thirty-four cents."

The girl glanced over her shoulder for the manager and then rang it up. "You won't tell, will you?" she asked, smoothing her apron. "Arnie would kill me for this.

"I owe you one," Sandy sighed. Maybe this was some sort of honesty test, with someone taking notes behind one-way glass. That's the kind of thing that could happen at ATI. She looked around and saw the little man standing at the end of the counter, not two feet away.

"Paper or plastic?" he asked in a reedy voice and waited eagerly for her answer.

Sandy was confused. "I've always had to sack my own," she said.

"That's the exact difference between yesterday and today. You won't have to do that again for as long as Uly Bondarbon IV is here to help," he said with something that wasn't really a smile. "And that'll be for the rest of your days on this earth. That's a dead-set guarantee, ma'am."

"Okay. Plastic."

Sandy didn't want to discourage any primitive customer-service overtures from Thrift Aisles. Maybe they would even include greasing the shopping cart wheels in their next five-year plan. But it occurred to her that she could handle the bags better than this frail kid.

Uly Bondarbon couldn't have measured out to more than five feet and ninety pounds between thick soles and his swirl of hair. At first glance, Sandy thought he was maybe fourteen years old. Then she noticed his face had the flat, dry skin that the sharpest razors leave.

He took a couple of bags in each hand, shrugged and leaned back to get clear of the checkout stand. "Which way's the car, ma'am?" he asked.

"That's okay," she said, reaching out. "I'll take them from here."

"Oh, ma'am! You do my heart damage." Uly took a step back, as if reeling from the blow, but he almost toppled over backwards as the bags swung away with his balance.

Sandy felt the stares of the mushroom-faced girl and the large, severe woman who waited for her to clear the line. She realized that none of the other registers had bag boys.

"Really, it's okay." She wanted to sound convincing so she could get out of there. "I've carried them myself my whole life."

"And this is how a whole new life begins, ma'am," Uly said. "Looking for new ways to do things is what sets us apart from the apes in the trees. That's the only way we can get over the hurdles our parents laid out for us."

Sandy looked at Saury who eyed the candy rack behind them. "Look, I need the exercise," she said, feeling her foot begin to tap the ground.

Uly grew impatient, too. "Then catch me, ma'am!" He lurched, with the bags skimming the floor, and stumbled into a jog for the door.

Sandy ran two steps after him, then backed up to sweep Saury into her arms. She made chase, but broke her stride when the electric door hesitated before letting her out. She looked around the parking lot frantically and found Uly leaning against her car.

"What do you think you're doing?"

"Some folks just like to even the score a little," Uly said as he caught his breath. "You had your burden. I hadn't any. It all works out now, don't it?"

Sandy gave up and unlocked her trunk. "I didn't even know Thrift Aisles had bag boys," she said.

"Now that's one thing I never seen," Uly said. He took a deep breath and hoisted the bags into the car. "Like to put me out of business."

"What do you mean?" Sandy hitched Saury back up her hip. "What do you call yourself if you're not the bag boy?"

"Me?" Uly leaned against the car and surveyed the parking lot. "I'm an independent contractor. I see a need and fulfill it. I do whatever calls me to be done." He rocked forward on his toes. "That way I always know people 'preciate me, if you understand what I'm saying."

"You mean you don't work for Thrift Aisles?"

Uly shook his head and grinned. "No future in that, is there, ma'am?"

Sandy felt her face drop. "So—what? You want a tip now? Is that it?"

"Oh, ma'am, we've only just met and you've hurt me twice in the one day." Uly hid his hands in his hair. "The first time I help you, that's just for free.

"The second time I do something for you, that's when we can work something out." Uly nodded. "And I can do all kinds of different things for the right kind of person."

Sandy huddled Saury into the car and closed his door. She climbed in and fumbled with the seat belt. "Thanks," she said, praying that her fingers would work.

"Just remember me now, ma'am." He waved his matchstick arm. "Uly Bondarbon IV."

Sandy pulled up to the light at the corner before she won-

175

dered how he'd known which car was hers. She looked in the rear view mirror and saw him still waving his arm slowly over his head.

Chapter 32

The Hole

Billey and Otis put their weight into the two-by-fours that poked out from beneath the tank. Elwood stood behind them and shouted, "One . . . two . . . THREE! Come on, you muthahs. Roll it on down there."

Billey looked over and saw sweat pouring down Otis's nose just like he had a faucet in his head.

"One . . . two . . . *threeeee!*" Elwood took a running jump and landed a solid kick on the side of the tank just as the other two gained some leverage. The tank began to move in slow motion like a big old bug egg on the side of an ant hill.

"Don't let it get away," Elwood cried, as if he'd suddenly realized that gravity mighty defy his orders. "You gotta get it in there straight. Otis, you stop that thing 'fore we have us a royal mess."

Otis lumbered around and pushed against the tank with his shoulder. When he'd steadied it, he walked over to the short end. He spread his arms over the surface and leaned back, thrusting his pelvis forward as if the enormous tank had sprouted from his crotch.

"Hey, Billey," he shouted. "Know what this looks like?"

"Looks like a hot dog takin' a crap," said Elwood, beating the tank with a two-by-four like a giant drum. "Lordy, Otis, most folks gotta live to be a hundred to get as dumb as you."

It hadn't taken Billey long to clear the loose dirt from the bottom of the hole, but then the project stalled. Like most of Elwood's plans, the idea of burying the tank had been engineered by whiskey. Some of the details, like how to drop the tank into the hole without cracking it, or how to get it down there with its mouth pointing up, had been left to take care of themselves.

The thing didn't weigh all that much, but it was big and awkward. When the men strained against it, the smooth surface became slippery with their sweat.

"Gah-*dam*, I wish I had me a hel'copter." Elwood circled the tank for the hundredth time. "Just lift that bastard up and slip it in smoother than a five-buck horse on Sunday morning."

Otis offered plenty of other suggestions until Elwood threatened to stop passing him the flask.

Billey began sleeping late while the two men went down each morning to knock off a bottle while studying the puzzle of the tank and the hole. They drew pictures in the dirt. They hauled ropes, chains, pulleys and posts from the shack to the hole and back. They plotted the kidnapping of ten Billeys who could finish the job with brute strength.

Finally one morning, Billey heard Otis rattling the latch on the camper door. "Come on now, Billey," Otis yelled as if Billey were encased in three feet of concrete instead of a flimsy metal skin, pocked by years of Elwood's wake-up calls. "We got it all worked out now."

Billey expected them to drive back down to the tank, but the pickup and the bugmobile were both gone. Walking from down there to the shack must have been the most work Otis had done in his life. The big man had to light a cigarette before they headed off.

As they walked back together, Otis motioned Billey to wait every time he took a drag on the cigarette. Otis stood still and inhaled. He pretended to be interested in the rusty engine blocks or hubcaps or tangles of barb wire or whatever pile of crap they were closest to. He exhaled forcefully through his nose. Then they walked a few more strides before he stopped again.

"We gonna get there by night, Otis?" Billey asked.

Otis didn't say anything, but he sucked double and threw the last half of the smoke down like it was a cockroach that had sneaked into his hand.

They found Elwood sitting on the pickup's hood, sucking the juice out of a cigarette butt. He got up, straightened the cricks out of his knees and said, "See what we done. It's complicated for a shitbrain kid like yourself, but you gotta try to understand the situation."

The pickup stood next to the tank, but they'd parked Otis' bugmobile on the far side of the hole. They'd lashed the tank to each of the vehicles with heavy ropes.

"See, first we's gonna drive apart to stretch them ropes good and tight." Elwood showed Billey a crude diagram he'd drawn in the dirt. "Next, we's both gonna drive this a'way until we're holding the tank right where we want it over the center of the hole."

Billey glanced at Otis who nodded and moved his lips. Elwood punched Billey's shoulder. "Pay attention," he barked. "This is gonna take 'bout all the brain energy you can come up with, Billey.

"Now, you're gonna take this pole and climb on top of the tank. Otis and me are gonna go in reverse to slack up those ropes so the tank goes down into the hole." Elwood waved at the next drawing in the dirt.

"What's that?" Billey pointed to a broad smudge that had erased half the pickup.

"Aw, hell, Otis." Elwood spat. "You walked all over the plans. Don't you got no sense at all?

"Don't pay no mind to that part, Billey. See, now you're on the tank with the pole, and we're drivin' closer together to put some slack in them ropes. As the tank goes down there, you gotta push the pole against this side or that side to keep it from gettin' all smashed up. Understand?"

"I guess so," Billey nodded. "But I think I ought to drive Otis' car and Otis can get on the tank with the pole."

Elwood looked at Otis. "I dunno, Billey. You ain't never done much drivin' in reverse. There's a lot of stuff to it."

"Yeah, but Otis knows a lot more about handling a big pole than I do. Ain't that right, Otis?"

The doubt cleared from the big man's face. "That's right," he declared. "He's right about that for sure."

Billey revved the pickup as Elwood climbed into the bug-mobile. They drove away from each other until the ropes grew taut. Elwood poked his head out the window and shouted things Billey couldn't hear over the pickup's rough idle. Both vehicles moved slowly eastward with the tank jerking and scraping along between them. Otis stood by, grimacing each time the tank bounced off the gravel.

The tank finally hopped off the edge and swayed over the hole. Otis inched his way along the rope, then flattened himself against the round surface, trying to find his balance.

Billey feathered the clutch just enough to make Otis nervous. Maybe if Billey made him sweat a little more, he'd slip off by himself. Otis swatted the pole around, trying to keep from crashing into the sides of the hole, but not having any more luck than a beetle on its back.

Elwood climbed halfway out of the bugmobile to shout and wave, but Billey still couldn't make out a word of it.

"I dunno," Billey said under his breath. "What do you think, Otis?" He played with the pedals a little more.

When he saw Elwood get in the car, he let the truck back up slowly. Otis swore and threw the pole down. He held on for his life as the earth swallowed up the tank.

Billey couldn't tell if Elwood had the same idea, but together they gave Otis a good work out until the tank hit bottom. Elwood climbed out and put his hands on his hips.

"Look at the angle on the mouth," he said. "You put it in crooked, Otis. That's a hundred gallons less we'll be able to get in there."

Otis looked a little green beneath the sweat and mud. He wobbled to his feet and jumped from the top of the tank back to solid ground. "Looks straight as my peter on Saturday night," Otis said. "Not as big though."

The two men strutted around while Billey began shoveling dirt back in to fill the space around the tank.

"Now we're gonna do some business," Elwood said. "Now we're gonna get us some respect."

He paced around the perimeter of the hole, but stopped when he got down wind. He sniffed, tentatively at first, and then deeply. "Otis!" Elwood snapped. "You been peein' in my tank?"

Chapter 33

Predators

The worm has its bird, the bird its cat, the cat its dog. But a woman contends with the male of her own species.

The predators hunt alone and in packs. They enforce curfew at sunset, but they strike just as swiftly in broad daylight. They test their skills at an early age, then sharpen them throughout their lives.

Sometimes Sandy thought men were transformed by the idea that bleeding was nature's plan for women. As kids, boys teased girls with frogs and bugs, but that was no worse than the torments the boys inflicted on each other.

When a girl faced the scary metamorphosis of her body, the boys saw some of the changes, heard about others. Maybe the boys felt threatened by the way their own bodies seemed to have been left behind in childhood.

Maybe when their own hormones finally kicked in, the boys felt betrayed by the girls' conspiracy of silence. Maybe they felt cheated and inconsequential, that everyone knew how awful puberty's cruel mix of pimples and longing was about to make their lives, but nobody bothered to warn them.

When Sandy walked out to get the mail one Saturday morning, a Volkswagen full of teenagers slowed down. From the back seat, a boy who couldn't have been more than thirteen leaned forward and stuck his head out the window. "Nice tits!" he shouted just before the car sped away.

The scene left Sandy stunned for a moment. Then the absurdity of it struck her: a child barely weaned proving his manhood by screaming about breasts. She laughed as the car disappeared around the bend. It was too ridiculous.

She placed her hand on the mail box as she opened it. She chuckled again as she noticed the short skid marks the car had drawn across the asphalt. Then a sudden tiredness overwhelmed her. She rested her forehead against her outstretched arm and looked at how thick the lawn had come in this year. One more sound that could have passed for a laugh gurgled out of her throat before the sobs racked her body.

Even home offered no shelter in a world populated by Jack Gores and Stephen X Skinners. Men ruled their houses. They valued their property above all else, maybe because they found comfort in things which conformed to a balance sheet. Maybe if women could be priced and sold in more honest ways they would be worth something, too.

Her father once rebuked Sandy for letting Jennifer's diaper bleed through to the carpet. Tacking a calendar to the wall without permission sent Stephen X into a rage. "You just punched a hole in the residual value of my house," he yelled, growing even more furious when the thickness of the pages kept him from ripping through all twelve months in a single motion.

Only by the grace of men could you escape the rain, and only on their arbitrary, fluctuating terms. Why did they tell you they loved the way you laughed or dressed or cooked or screwed before they began peeling away every shred of your identity?

Why do they want women in their lives at all if they hate us so much? Maybe the urge to control and punish lurked in the darkest, stinking chambers of all men's hearts.

A week or so before her father and Uncle Josh killed Jennifer, Sandy heard an ungodly wail from behind the Airstream where Mama Gore had lived. She found Josh on his knees, leaning over a cat that struggled against his weight. He looked over his shoulder when Sandy yelled at him.

"I hate cats," he said in a voice all the more terrifying for its total lack of emotion.

"Let her go," Sandy shouted, pulling at his beefy shoulder.

"Aw, what's the matter?" Josh said. "They do it to mice."

Or maybe it came down to selfishness, hunching over a woman not to protect her, but to guard her for himself. Men knew what other men were like.

Even distant men found ways to wound her. Artie Sandoval, the teenager who had attached his fantasies to Sandy before taking a swan dive from the water tower, never had to face her. He never had to explain why he singled her out to carry his burden of guilt.

And Uly Bondarbon, who didn't look big enough to cause her physical harm, could still knot up her stomach with dread. She had no idea what he wanted from her; she had nothing left for anyone. It had all been snatched away from her years ago.

She couldn't stay home or shop or check her own mail box in peace. She tried to bury the gnawing fear that one day Saury would wake up transformed into a brat who shouted from car windows as he entered his apprenticeship of abuse.

From the first time she saw Saury's flushed face, Sandy thought her baby looked more like her sister, Jennifer, than Stephen X. It would be nice if all Saury's tickets in the gene lottery had been purchased on her side of the family. Then again, she thought of her own parents and her father's father. Maybe that wouldn't be such a bargain after all.

If they'd been together as infants, Stegosaurus X and Jennifer could have passed for twins. They shared blue eyes, a button nose that begged to be tickled, a wide, laughing mouth—even the way they waved their arms straight up and down and gurgled when something excited them.

Still, Stephen X hardly ever started a fight over whether or not he was Saury's biological father. He seemed to hold that subject in reserve for those rare occasions when he couldn't come up with a more immediate excuse.

And as Saury entered the Terrible Twos, Sandy began to fear that Stephen X had passed along things much worse than his unblinking stare or the pudgy bulge of his cheek. When

Saury missed a nap, he could unleash an all-consuming tantrum or a flood of self-pity.

Pound for pound, Saury's fits rivaled the intensity of his father's. They had similar provocation and they were followed by similar periods of calm as the child slept off his tears.

What if he stayed that way forever? Is that what had happened to Stephen X—he never evolved past being a two-year-old tyrant? But Saury mellowed in his third year, becoming as cherubic as his appearance.

Sandy tried not to dwell on the notion that her son might be absorbing awful secrets of manhood from his father. Maybe the lessons men passed on to boys seemed harmless at first, but they were as relentless and powerful as carcinogens. One day the child woke with a sickness that had been rotting his insides for years.

That was the bright side of Stephen X's recurring idea that someone else—Wally, the mail man, even Roscoe—had been Saury's father. He paid so little attention to the boy that he might not be able to twist his son's heart in his own image.

Of course, he didn't pay much attention to Sandy, either, which made life bearable. Stephen X spent long hours at the office or wrapping up business in the bars or on his car phone. But you never knew when he might show up in the middle of the day demanding sex, a snack or solitude.

He left his engine running one Thursday when he surprised her at noon. "Let's swing by Thrift Aisles and pick up a few things for lunch," he said. "We'll take my car."

Sandy stiffened. "I don't want to go there."

"Don't be silly. It's the closest place and they've got the best prices."

"If you know what you want, why don't you go? I'll stay and set the table."

"You know I hate shopping for groceries by myself."

Nestled just off Westmore, a block down from Rollingwood

Drive, Thrift Aisles attracted an odd mix of customers. Enormous young mothers pushed carts full of cookies and kids down the same aisles where Stephen X, in his three-piece suit, strolled ahead of Sandy.

Although Stephen X rarely ate anything that came from the ground or from trees, he loved the produce section. He held a foot-long cucumber between the palms of his hands and leered at Sandy. "Hey! What do you think?"

"What?"

He wiggled his eyebrows and held the cucumber higher.

Sandy glanced around to see if anyone were watching. "What are you doing?"

"Come on, Sandy. Is it me?" He slipped his thumb under his belt and stuffed the cucumber into his pants.

A large man wearing a white apron over his shirt and tie cleared his throat, startling Stephen X. "Can I help you?" the man asked.

Stephen X sized up the situation in an instant. He stroked the bulge behind his zipper. "It's not a banana, I'm just glad to see her." He closed the distance to Sandy and slipped his arm around her, moving his hand up to lift her breast. "What else can a guy do with a woman like this?"

Sandy felt her face redden. The man was not amused. "Do I have to call security?" he asked.

Stephen X pulled the cucumber out of his pants. He was going to place it back on the vegetable stand until he saw the man's frown. "I guess we'll buy this, won't we?" he said.

Sandy didn't break down until they made it outside. Now it was Stephen X's turn to see if anyone were watching. "What's the matter with you?"

"You're disgusting!" She didn't care if that made him strike her dead in the parking lot. She couldn't stand it anymore.

"Don't be such a prude," he commanded. "I was just having some fun."

186

"Get away from me." She kept walking past his car.

Stephen X grabbed her arm from behind and twisted it around like a pretzel. "You look at me when you're talking to me," he shouted, shaking her by the neck.

"Let me go."

She dug her nails into his cheek, but lost her balance when she tried to kick him. He took the advantage to shove her against a blue van. He cocked his arm for the first serious punch when the voice called out.

"You shouldn't be doin' that, mister."

They both turned their heads to see Uly Bondarbon calmly walking toward them.

Stephen X stepped back, allowing Sandy to slip around the van to safety. She pressed her cheek against the cool metal and tried to catch her breath.

"This is none of your business," Stephen X said.

"What kind of business is it, pickin' on a woman like that?" Uly asked. "A dog wouldn't do those things, so you must be less than a dog."

Sandy peeked around the van to see Uly standing with his hands on his hips, giving Stephen X a hard look.

"I don't appreciate that kind of talk," Stephen X said. "You don't understand the situation."

Uly never flinched. "Suppose you explain it to me then, Mr. Dog—or should I say Mr. Dogshit?"

Sandy couldn't see Stephen X, but she knew what he looked like during the long silence that followed. Her husband never felt comfortable when things drifted out of his control. His face could go blank for minutes at a time when confronted by anything unusual.

"You're more fun than a bucket of monkeys, aren't you?" Stephen X said at last. "I haven't got time for this." Then he raised his voice and said, "Come on, Sandy, let's go home."

Sandy held her breath and tried to shrink until she became invisible and safe. She heard Uly say, "You'd best leave this woman alone until you can treat her with the respect she deserves."

She wanted to tell him to stop, that every jab Stephen X took from Uly would be repaid a hundred times when he finally cornered Sandy. But she heard Stephen X say, "Real comedian," as his footsteps moved away.

"You watch yourself, Mr. Dirtydog," Uly called out. "I know a lot of things about you."

Stephen X stopped. "What do you mean by that? Are you threatening me? You can go to jail for that, buddy boy."

"You just watch yourself."

The footsteps began again. Sandy heard the car door slam and the tires squeal into the distance. She sniffed and smeared the tears across her face.

"Are you okay, ma'am?" Uly asked, holding out a tissue.

She didn't want to look at him but she took the tissue. "Yes." She shook her head. "Thank you."

"You know, I got ways to help you. Lots of ways to make things better."

"Please, just go away and leave me alone," she pleaded. She knew a lot more things about Stephen X than Uly ever dreamed of. "It's going to be worse than ever now," she said.

Chapter 34

Plans

There was no way of telling how long Elwood had been working on his plan. Probably since before Billey was born. Probably since the first time Elwood's own daddy whupped him.

So many nights, as Billey tried to sleep, he heard his daddy mumbling over a bottle by the spool. He never could make out the words, but the volume rose and fell like the sound of rain on the camper on a gusty night. Most nights, when the voice grew loudest, Billey would hear things crashing around on the porch. Sometimes the gun started and Billey knew he wouldn't sleep before day break.

Elwood never bothered to tell Billey much of anything important and Billey gave up trying to find out a long time ago.

"Why do I have to dig this hole?" Billey asked once.

"'Cause I said," Elwood snapped.

Another time he asked, "Why's Otis so stupid?"

"'Cause I said."

And, "How did the side of that hill get all scooped away like that?"

"'Cause I said."

Since everything Billey did carried equal weight in Elwood's world, it was hard for him to figure out how the pieces fit together. Fetching Elwood a drink or digging a hole big enough to swallow the tank—one thing was just as important as another. And they all carried the same penalties for failure. What it all meant remained a mystery to Billey.

Still, Billey could figure out a few things. Elwood seemed positively sweet-natured some days, so that meant whatever he was planning would give him a laugh on the pigs.

Elwood loved to tell people what to do and he hated to ask for favors. In fact, he hated to ask for anything. So he probably had some way to make people ask him for favors.

And whatever Elwood planned to do, it would have to happen at night, since he spent most of the day time passed out next to the spool.

Otis came over just before sunset and the two men shot tin cans off a rock. After it got too dark to see the cans, they just kept shooting for the fun and the noise of it. Billey thought it was a good thing nobody but the pigs ever paid them a visit. It was too dangerous to walk around with all those bullets zinging everywhere.

Most of the junk around the place had been there since before Billey was born, so he didn't pay too much attention to it. But one afternoon, he sat on a tree stump and studied one of the old engine blocks in back of the shack.

It could have been as old as a rock the way the dirt had pushed up around it. It looked like the earth had gagged when it tried to swallow the stupid thing. Weeds grew out of its holes.

Billey didn't know much about machines, but he could tell that someone had followed a plan to make this thing. The holes were evenly spaced. The ridges and bumps on the surface stood out in patterns so Billey, without ever seeing it, could guess what the buried part of the engine block looked like.

This wasn't like his daddy's plans where one thing got tacked on to another until everything was poking out in a hundred different directions all at once. Fact is, the engine block would have looked out of place within a mile of Elwood's things, except for the rust and weeds and the big crack through the top of it. Somebody had tried to use it too hard and busted it. Once something was busted, it fit into Elwood's world just fine.

But maybe people used to have real plans, good plans,

back before Billey was born. Maybe there was a time when everything kind of fit together right and you could figure one thing out from looking at another thing. Maybe somewhere somebody still made that kind of plans. It wasn't impossible. In fact, maybe that's the way it was everywhere in the whole world except this one little place around Elwood.

A sudden buzzing, like a bumblebee as big as the tank, startled Billey. He followed the sound to the porch where Elwood's arms were flopping around the spool top. Elwood opened his eyes just enough to see the clock that made the noise. He pounded it three times until it fell quiet, then he threw it at the road.

"What you lookin' at?" Elwood demanded.

"I dunno."

"Gotta get up," he said, more to himself than to Billey. He rubbed his hands down his chest. "Today is the day."

Otis didn't show until after dark. Billey drove Elwood in the pickup while Otis followed them in the bugmobile. Elwood made Billey stop at the crest of a long hill on a road that didn't have much traffic. Otis drove on down to the bottom and then they waited.

Billey sighed and looked out the window, but there was nothing to see. After an hour or so, he asked, "Why are we sittin' here?"

"'Cause I said. Quit your blabberin'. Gets on my nerves real bad."

It seemed like they were going to sit there until daylight. The only thing Billey could do without making his daddy mad was shift his butt every so often when it got sore. Billey, who didn't stay up every night like Elwood, dozed off.

He woke up with Elwood shaking him. "Flash the lights," Elwood whispered. "Flash the gah-*dam* headlights."

Billey flashed them a couple times just before a big tanker truck whizzed by them. The pickup rocked in the wind the big truck made.

"Now keep your lights off and drive on down there after that truck."

Billey looked at his daddy. Even in the dark he could tell this was not a time for asking questions.

He could see in the big truck's headlights that Otis had parked the bugmobile straight across the road at the bottom of the hill. The tanker braked hard and stopped just before it crushed the beat-up old car.

Elwood made Billey stop behind the truck. He slipped out of the pickup and walked around the far side of the truck. Billey could see Otis standing on the step of the truck's cab, waving his arms like a fool. After a minute, Otis trotted over and moved the bugmobile off the road. Then he climbed inside the big truck.

Elwood came around the other side of the tanker with a man who had his hands tied in front of him and a rag wrapped around his eyes. He jabbed his gun in the man's back and pushed him into the seat next to Billey. Elwood climbed in and slammed the door. "Let's go, Bobby," he said.

Billey eyed the man who was sweating and trembling next to him. He leaned forward to look at Elwood, but Elwood was already leaning forward to stare at Billey. "I said, 'Let's go, Bobby,'" Elwood said impatiently.

"My name's not Bobby," Billey protested.

"I know it ain't! Do you think I woulda called you Bobby if it was?" Elwood shook his head. "If I called you by your real name, this guy would know what your name is." Elwood tapped the passenger's chest with the gun. "If he knows what your name is, then we gotta kill him. If he knows what my name is, we gotta kill him. If he knows what Otis's name is, we gotta kill him. Understand?"

Billey opened his mouth to say one thing, but he thought a second and said, "yeah" instead.

"So you're gonna be Bobby until we kill this guy or get rid of him. Got that?"

Elwood made him drive down all kinds of roads Billey had never seen until they were out of town. He heard the man crying and saw that tears had soaked the rag over his eyes.

"What's your name?" Elwood said suddenly.

"Bobby," Billey shot back.

"Not you. You, mister. What's your name?"

The man stopped sniffing. "Me?"

"I got ten names to call everyone else in here." Elwood sounded irritated. "Yes, you."

"McKinney," he said. "Hank McKinney."

"Your cryin' sure do make me edgy, Hank." Elwood rubbed the gun up and down the man's arm. "It's 'bout enough to make me want to cram a bullet up your nose."

"Please," Hank said. "You've got the truck. I swear I couldn't tell them who you are. I wouldn't even if I could. My wife had a baby two weeks ago."

"You left your wife alone to raise up your little baby?" Elwood clicked his tongue and shook his head. "Man oughta 'least get his nose blown off for that. That's what Bobby thinks, too."

Billey turned this way and that on his daddy's orders until he was good and lost. Finally Elwood sent them down a dirt trail that wound away from the main road into the woods. The trail petered out and Billey drove through the mud, trying to dodge the bigger holes.

"Stop here, Bobby," Elwood said. He reached in front of Hank and tapped something on the dash board. "Gah-*dam*. We's about outta gas. That ain't never gonna happen again now, is it, Hank?"

Billey turned the engine off to wait. Elwood climbed out and tapped the gun barrel against Hank's knee. "Climb on down here, you big old crybaby. We're goin' for a little walk."

Hank felt his way along the seat and slid out. Elwood prodded him with the gun, but he kept stumbling on the uneven ground. Elwood kicked Hank when he went down to his knees.

"Do I have to carry you?"

"I can't see," Hank said.

"Shit fire," Elwood said. "I'll take that blindfold off, but you gotta promise to keep your eyes closed until you can't see the truck no more. Understand?"

"Yes," Hank said. "Please. I'll do anything."

Elwood pulled the rag off the man's head and poked him in the back. Billey watched them disappear behind a stand of trees.

Billey craned his neck out the door and looked up at the stars. There were more than he'd ever seen, and they seemed brighter here, so far from the city. The sky looked blacker, too, like maybe the night was better here than it was back at the camper.

Billey jerked up so fast he bruised his head on the window frame when he heard the gun shot. He stiffened in the seat and strained to hear the night's deepest messages.

After a long time, Elwood came slogging through the mud. He brushed himself off and climbed into the pickup.

Billey looked at his hands and saw they'd locked themselves onto the steering wheel. He squeezed it tight to keep them from shaking. "That man—" Billey stared straight ahead and coughed. "Did you kill him?"

"Sure I killed him, Billey," Elwood said. "Didn't you hear what a whinin' little crybaby he was? That's the only thing to do for bastards like that. Tell you what, he won't be cryin' no more.

"This is a pow'ful, pow'ful gun, Billey. You ever see a watermelon fall off the back of a truck? That's what his head looked like. I bet it flew a hundred yards 'til it hit that tree. Just a little stump and some bloody jawbone left on that man's shoulders."

Billey felt his daddy staring at him, but he was afraid to

turn his head.

"You got a problem with that, Billey?"

Billey felt the end of his daddy's gun press against the side of his neck. It was hot and it smelled like a box of matches that had been lit all at once. Billey tried to say "No," but the word turned out to be a wet booger stuck so low in his throat that he couldn't spit it out.

Elwood leaned forward to whisper in his ear, "You just nod your head if that's okay with you."

Billey closed his eyes and moved his head down about an inch and a half. He felt the gun leave his neck and he heard his daddy shift back in the seat.

"You gonna start that engine?"

Billey opened his eyes and felt the sweat bite into them. He moved his right hand along the steering wheel until it was as close to the key as he could get it. He caught his breath and shoved his hand out quickly to turn on the engine.

Elwood laughed and looked out the side window. He scratched his forehead with the gun barrel. "Naw, I didn't kill him, Billey. I just wanted to make him mess his britches so's he'd be too embarrassed to come lookin' for the highway soon as we get outta here.

"But you're right. I shoulda killed the muthah. You wait here while I go back and find that bastard."

Billey tromped on the gas and made the pickup fishtail through the mud back up to the road.

Chapter 35

Words

It drove Stephen X up the wall that his brother didn't care about things Stephen X would have traded his left nut for.

Roscoe acted embarrassed by the way his most casual remarks found a ready audience in Linda who amplified them for the benefit of mankind. Stephen X, on the other hand, took himself so seriously he didn't have a clue why the world ignored him.

Roscoe could tell you anything you wanted to know about spark plug gaps and oil viscosity, even though the subjects bored him. Kids who hadn't begun to shave could point out Stephen X's fallacies when he talked about anything mechanical.

Roscoe predicted which stocks would go through the roof based on what he read in the news and lifestyle pages. Stephen X went blind poring over market reports and still managed to lose money.

The only things Roscoe had that Stephen X apparently did not care about were the love and respect of those who knew him best. If Sandy had envied Linda anything, it would have been to have a man, a companion, worthy of those gifts.

The closer Roscoe and Linda became, the less need they had for language. Not long after they met, they began communicating in sentence fragments.

"Did you—?" Linda asked.

"Day before yesterday," Roscoe replied.

"The whole thing," Linda concluded.

Sandy felt excluded from their conversations although she knew that wasn't their intention. It was as if they had discussed every conceivable subject earlier in private. A few syllables of shorthand were all they needed to confirm their thoughts.

Their relationship gradually transcended the need for complete words.

"Uhm. Ah ha," Roscoe said, nodding.

"Mmm," Linda responded.

Finally, the tiniest flutter of an eyelid or a lift at the corner of the mouth signaled everything that needed to be told.

It was so different from Stephen X who locked Sandy in the bedroom and repeated his demands for hours until she cracked.

"Say that you love me." He knelt on her hand and pried against her nails. "Say that you love me. Say it."

He didn't always use violence to make her miserable. Sometimes he made her sit on the chair. He crossed his arms and stood between her and the door until she realized she would never leave the room until she mouthed some meaningless string of words.

"Say that you love me, God damn it."

She used to hold out, strictly on principle. But what was the point? She would be better off giving in with her fingers crossed. She could pretend she came from the planet Htrae, where everything was backwards. She could make the words drip with bile so they meant less than nothing. It didn't seem to matter.

It reminded her of Richard Kirkland and the multiplication tables. Richard was the only one who could keep up with Sandy when they studied math in elementary school. "Two times two is four. Two times three is six," he droned on until Miss Wagner waved and asked him the product of fourteen times eleven. Richard fidgeted beneath a giant multiplication sign which Miss Wagner did not yet notice had been transformed into a swastika during recess.

Richard turned red as a negative number even though he'd said the answer himself less than a minute earlier when he went past eleven times fourteen. Sandy cringed at his embarrassment and whispered, "A hundred fifty-four." But it scared her that learning the right words or numbers to say could be so important to someone who didn't understand them, who didn't know where they came from.

"Okay, I love you," she hissed once at three in the morning.

When Stephen X finally stepped out of her way, she said, "I lied. You make me sick."

His lips spread back from his gums in a horrible, mirthless grin. "I know," he said, cheating her out of even the satisfaction of telling him the truth. The next night, a week, a month later, they did it all over again.

Sometimes it seemed like the only escape she had was to go shopping with Linda. She didn't enjoy shopping, and that made her feel deficient, almost a traitor to her country. America's roots tapped into the deep, sweet waters of commerce, but she would just as soon have stayed home and ordered what she needed from a catalog. Besides, she couldn't spend more than five bucks without Stephen X's consent.

She liked Roscoe, but his presence deprived her of Linda's attention, so just the companionship of shopping made it attractive. And when she was away from it, the mall seemed at least to offer a haven from Stephen X. But shopping added up to less than the sum of its parts.

One Saturday when she was pregnant with Saury, she felt Linda's elbow prod her in front of the greeting card shop. "What's the matter, kiddo?"

"I don't know," Sandy said.

"Take the crowds . . . puhleeze!" Linda said. "I get it. You could be the Shopping Impulse Deficiency poster child. Don't worry. They're getting close to a cure."

Sandy felt petty. "No," she said. "I like to shop with you."

"But you don't like shopping." Linda knew her too well.

"If I were by myself, I'd just get what I needed and get out of here," Sandy admitted.

Linda clicked her tongue. "Poor Sandy," she said, sweeping her arm at the masses pushing past them. "You need some remedial work. Try shopping for someone else until you get the hang of it. Look at these people—are they having fun? Of course not. It's a battleground. The more blood they shed finding the right thing to buy, the more it's worth to them.

"If you spend all day looking for something that costs two bucks, you go home happy. You've invested something a lot more important than money. You've paid the price with your sanity. That's what makes the things you buy bargains."

"You're full of shit," Sandy laughed. Linda made her feel better, and the drudge of shopping was a reasonable price to pay for that.

•

Roscoe took many things with him when he died. As Sandy watched her friend's physical injuries heal after the wreck, she saw how Linda's spirits sagged. Once in a while Sandy wondered if that was how it all evened out—if the presence of a Stephen X didn't make you miserable, then the absence of a Roscoe would.

Before Linda went home from the hospital, Sandy spent an entire Saturday at Rollingwood Mall trying to find her a gift. She wandered through the department stores and specialty shops, past the food court and the arcade, looking for something to restore her friend, but unable to focus on the merchandise. Several times she turned away and then could not recall what she'd just looked at.

"Ma'am."

Sandy heard the voice and wondered who would call anyone "ma'am" these days; what kind of a person would be called "ma'am?" Then she felt the woman touch her sleeve.

"Ma'am, we're closing now. Is there anything I can help you with?"

Sandy saw a woman much older than herself watching

her with concern. They stood alone in one of the big stores, where the ceiling arched fifty feet above them. Plastic torsos in bras and panties surrounded them and Sandy couldn't remember what she thought she might buy there. She looked up at a mannequin that loomed over them with outstretched arms. The mannequin's nipples stood out through the satin which covered them. Sandy felt the floor begin to roll beneath them and she broke away and ran for the parking lot.

The pain and loneliness of Linda's loss engulfed Sandy as she stood in a moth-filled cone of light next to the only car left in the lot. She imagined what it would be like to lose Saury without warning in a cataclysm; how the metal would fold and he'd be gone. How could you go on and wake up the next morning, and the next, and the next . . .

For all his blindness, Stephen X could focus on your vulnerable spots easily enough. He played on Sandy's secret fears whenever she gave the smallest, unspoken hint that she might leave him.

"You know, you'd never see Saury again. You don't make enough money at ATI to support yourself, much less him," he said calmly. "No judge in the world would give you custody. You're too unstable."

It dawned on her much later that, despite her resistance, she had been swallowing Stephen X's pronouncements as uncritically as Linda used to accept Roscoe's. It didn't matter if Stephen X's words sounded ridiculous when repeated. If they carried the tiniest shred of truth, Sandy fell for them.

What was it about the Skinners that gave their words weight? Maybe families shared more things than Sandy ever imagined.

Sandy remembered how Mama Gore used to braid her hair as they sat outside the silver Airstream. Mama Gore leaned forward and held her own long, silver ponytail alongside Sandy's shorter braid.

"Your hair will be this long some day, but I won't be here

to braid it for you then," Mama Gore laughed.

Sandy pointed at a liver spot on her grandmother's hand. "Does that hurt?" she asked.

"Oh, no, sweet child. The things that hurt are never that easy to see." She pressed her cheek against Sandy's. "I was so lucky. At least I wasn't one of them. They were hard men."

"Who, grandma?"

"Gores," she said. "They were all Gores."

At that age Sandy had not yet realized what her grandmother meant about luck, about how just being related to a bad person could make you feel you were bad yourself. She was too young to see the distinction between marriage and blood.

And if the Gores passed on some gene for hardness, the Skinners shared the credibility chromosome. Roscoe used to tell about some family friend who drank himself into oblivion on New Year's Eve, wrapped his car around a telephone pole and sat through a night of sub-zero temperatures before rescue workers found him. If not for the alcohol in the man's bloodstream acting like anti-freeze, Roscoe's story went, the fool would have died of exposure.

The first time she heard that, Sandy laughed. Linda arched an eyebrow and asked, "What's so funny?"

Sandy looked at the nodding heads all around her and figured she had missed something. "Nothing," she mumbled.

They still did things together after Linda recovered from the accident, but something had changed in their relationship. Although she sometimes longed to, Sandy had never been able to tell Linda about Stephen X. Now it would be harder than ever to talk about it. She would have felt guilty about the way she had squandered her chance if she confided the secrets of her monstrous marriage.

Once in awhile, Sandy even went to the mall alone, not that she ever planned to buy anything. She thought of Linda's advice to learn how to shop by finding things for someone else. Saury was changing so fast she couldn't buy anything that would hold his interest for more than a few minutes. She couldn't afford the things she wanted to lavish upon him anyway. And there was no one else to put on her list.

That's why she was looking for something for herself at Action Lady when she met Marti.

Sandy found a light jacket she liked for a hundred bucks. Stephen X wouldn't want her to spend that kind of money on anything she couldn't wear to bed. That appealed to her more than the fabric or design. She didn't need or really even want a jacket. She wanted to treat herself to the forbidden pleasure of paying too much for something. That would be a nicer gift to herself than any material thing.

She wondered whether she would tell him the price when he asked. Maybe so, if he made a crack about its ugliness. And she knew he would. Sandy stood between two racks of clothes trying to decide what to do. Maybe she should find something even more expensive. But maybe her little fling wouldn't be worth the anguish after all. Or maybe she should just touch a match to a hundred-dollar bill and send Stephen X the ashes.

A small woman with long, straight brown hair—like Jennifer used to have—brushed past Sandy and busied herself with looking at the racks. The woman—just a girl, really—tugged sleeves out of the crush of hanging clothes, but she kept glancing over her shoulder.

The girl's nervousness as she moved down the cramped aisle distracted Sandy. The two girls who had been working in the store when Sandy came in seemed to have disappeared.

The girl took an expensive leather jacket to the dressing room and Sandy turned back to her decision.

A moment later, a muscular man in jeans and a tee shirt came in from the mall.

"Lou Anne," he shouted, waiting the barest instant for

response. He stormed to the dressing rooms, crouching in front of each one to see if someone hid in it. When he got to the door the girl had used, he slammed it open.

Sandy could see the girl in the new jacket pressing herself into the corner of the tiny room. The man grabbed the girl's shoulder and a handful of hair and threw her sprawling into the store. "Come out of there, you bitch," he yelled.

The girl tumbled into a display of accessories and the man lunged after her.

In one of those frantic moments where everything is clear only in the recollection, Sandy ran forward with the jacket she'd been looking at. As the man bent over the girl, Sandy came up behind him and wrapped the jacket around his head.

"Leave her alone, you bastard," she shouted, pulling hard on the sleeves. She kicked him in the small of the back just as the girl regained her balance and pushed up against his chest.

The man tumbled on his side and clawed for an opening in the jacket. Before he uncovered his face, Sandy grabbed a plastic hand covered with rings from the shelf and swung it through a giant arc which ended with a thud on the side of his head.

His body flattened out on the floor. As he began to push himself up, Sandy kicked him hard between the shoulder blades, sending his head into the tile with a loud crack.

When Sandy saw that the man would not get up, she looked around. The store's two clerks peeked out from behind the corner of the fitting rooms. The girl stood next to Sandy, struggling hard to catch her breath. They stared at each other until Sandy saw one of the clerks had slipped over to the check-out stand and was punching a number into the phone.

"We'd better get out of here," Sandy said, tugging the girl's sleeve.

Chapter 36

Over the Edge

By the time Billey and Elwood got home, Otis had already parked the big truck down by the tank. Otis sat high up in the cab with his feet propped against the open door like he thought he was the King of Trucks. When Billey parked the pickup alongside the truck, Otis flicked his cigarette butt and watched it trace a bright orange arc through the night.

"What the hell you sittin' on your ass for?" Elwood hollered, jumping out of the pickup.

As Otis climbed down, he muttered something Billey couldn't understand. His legs bowed and wobbled like a baby's when he touched the ground.

Elwood pounded the sides of the big truck with a wrench and cocked his head to listen to the deep, metallic tone. "Ain't that just music, Billey? Ain't that just the sweetest noise you ever heard?"

"I dunno," said Billey who was still sitting at the wheel of the pickup.

"What?" Elwood bellowed.

"I dunno."

Otis staggered nearby with a hose as big around as his leg. Billey saw him snorting like a pig in the darkness as he let the end of the hose swing down from beneath his belly. "Hey, Billey!" Otis called like a ghost with no one to haunt. "Hey, Billey. How's this for a peter?"

Elwood sneaked up from behind and planted a kick on Otis's butt that sent the big man stumbling forward, wheeling his arms for balance. "You get yourself busy or I'll make you piss your peter inside out."

"Yeah, yeah, yeah." Otis fastened the hose to the tank and fiddled at the side of the truck.

Billey stayed in the pickup and watched his daddy and Otis swap the flat bottle back and forth. They cussed and sang and weaved around in a slow, drunken dance while the tank filled. Billey's thoughts drifted to Black Wolf and to whether his daddy had lied when he said he shot the truck driver, or when he said he didn't.

He thought about what that man would look like, spread out in the spindly grass and mud with no more than a bloody jaw bone where his head ought to be. He wondered what that man must have felt like, driving down the road one minute in his big, shiny truck and the next minute having Otis and Elwood poking guns up his nose.

In a funny way, Billey felt lucky to have Elwood for his daddy. It made him feel safe the way burrowing under his dingy blanket in the camper used to make him feel. At least he knew that nothing could ever sneak up and make his life worse than it already was.

Billey sat like a statue in the pickup until Elwood pounded the door and scowled at him. "Get your butt up there with Otis right quick-smart now," he snapped. Then he began mumbling. "Things gonna be different from now on. You sonsabitches are gonna have to start living up to your 'spon-sibilities if you 'spect to stay around."

Billey climbed up the passenger side of the big truck and saw bleary-eyed Otis drumming his fingers on the steering wheel.

Otis nodded as Billey slid in the door, but he bolted upright when Elwood clanged his wrench against the truck's tank again, producing a deeper sound than before, like metal thunder. Otis wrestled the gear shift into place and rocked in his seat as the truck stuttered across the field.

When they wallowed onto the road, Otis worked his way up through the gears, cursing each clash of metal. He veered onto the shoulder and mowed down a speed limit sign.

"You see that?" Otis slapped the steering wheel and buried his shoulder blades deep in the back of the seat. He ran his right hand along the wheel's rim. "This is some pow'ful rig. Makes a man feel like his peter's got two hundred horsepower and not a pig in sight."

"That all you got anymore, Otis? Two-hundred horsepower?"

Otis gloated over the light coming up from the dash. "Power's smashin' up whatever you want, whenever you feel like it and nobody askin' why you did it." He swiveled his head back and forth. "I'm gonna get one of these myself. Gonna get me a lot of things now."

Otis sent gravel flying when they got to the place where they'd stolen the truck. Billey drove the bugmobile and followed him as they went along roads that became narrower and rougher with each mile. Otis slowed to a crawl as they wound along a dirt track that took them past burnt-out cars, abandoned refrigerators, heaps of trash.

When Otis climbed down from the cab, Billey killed the engine and walked up to see what was going on. Otis had pulled up near the edge of a vast quarry. It looked like the hole Billey had dug except its walls were solid rock. It would have taken a million Billeys a million years to dig it. In the starlight, Billey could see the skeletons of a few old cars that had fallen to the rocky floor a hundred feet below.

The darkness played tricks with Billey's balance. The bottom of the quarry tried to suck him down, along with Otis and the bugmobile and the big truck. That big old hole might just reach up, grab you by the ankles and pull you on down there before you ever knew what happened. Billey's stomach twisted in his belly and he felt like he was peering over the edge of hell.

"Last stop for Billey," Otis said, wrapping his arms around Billey's chest and lifting him off the ground.

Billey's legs pedaled high above the pit. His elbows beat against Otis like the wings of a bird knocked out of its nest.

Otis used to pull this shit all the time, but now that Billey weighed two hundred pounds, it wasn't so easy anymore. Billey caught a sickening whiff of the fumes from the flat bottle that still clung to Otis. He held his breath as the big man stumbled back and forth on the edge of the cliff. Everything seemed to slow down and get bigger so that each of Otis' misplaced steps took a thousand years, his boots dug into the gravel with the sound of mountains tumbling, his breath smelled like an ocean of puke.

Billey's heart drummed as loud as Elwood's wrench beating on the tank. He felt his insides turn sour and push up through his throat so that he couldn't even scream. He knew that Otis was too clumsy and drunk to keep his balance much longer, but he didn't know if Otis knew.

The two men lurched as one and the world spun beneath them. Billey kicked high, trying to push them back to safety. Otis wobbled and fell on his back. Billey landed on top and knocked the wind out of Otis in one big grunt.

Billey rolled off Otis and pressed his cheek against the sharp gravel, fighting his dizziness while Otis's chest heaved. Otis's head rolled toward Billey and they stared at each other for a long time, like each of them wondered if the other knew a secret. Billey heard the diesel churning behind them and realized that sound had been there the whole time, like frogs on a summer night.

"Aw, shit, Billey," Otis whispered at last. "I's just funnin' ya."

Otis turned onto his stomach, pushed himself up from the ground and studied the dimples the rocks had left on his palms. He patted little clouds of dust out of his jeans and spat over the edge of the quarry. "You're just as ornery as your daddy, Billey Elwood. Just as goddam crazy, too."

When he climbed into the cab, Otis goosed the throttle a couple times. Then he popped the clutch and sent the truck chugging toward Billey and the cliff. As the truck picked up speed, Billey dived out of the way. He saw Otis bail out of the cab just before it went over the edge.

Billey heard the awful crash and twist of metal a moment before the explosion. He scrambled to the edge of the quarry on his hand and knees, but shrank back from the ball of fire that rose from the floor. He heard Otis standing over him, breathing heavily.

"I'm gonna get me a rig like that, Billey. You wait and see."

Chapter 37

Snakes

Sandy drove three miles from the mall, checking her mirror every block for squad cars or the face of the man she'd wrapped in the jacket. The brown-haired girl never said a word until they stopped at a small park.

Sandy and the girl both stared out the windshield at a few kids and ducks that took turns chasing each other on the far side of the pond.

After a few moments, the girl cleared her throat softly and brushed a line of hair back behind her ear. She extended her hand and said, "I'm Marti."

Sandy looked at Marti as if she were afraid the girl might shatter in tiny pieces all over the Impala's cracked seat.

"I thought he said Lou Anne—" she started, then caught herself. "I'm sorry. I'm Sandy." She pressed the girl's hand between both of her own. "I thought he called you Lou Anne."

"Yeah. That was so we wouldn't get caught."

"Caught?" Sandy stared for a moment before she realized Marti was still wearing the leather jacket she'd tried on.

"Yeah." Marti ran her hands over her sleeves as if she were cold. Her voice trailed off. "You know . . ."

"Don't worry about that. We can go back when it's safe and pay—"

"When it's *safe*?" Marti shook her head and looked back across the pond. "How's it going to be safe? What's going to happen that makes it safe?" She slumped back in her seat. "I don't care. Do whatever you want with me. It doesn't matter."

Sandy felt confused by how quickly everything had happened. It had all seemed necessary and natural at the time, but she felt her stomach knot up now that she realized what she had done. All she knew about the law she had learned from television, but she counted off the charges they could slap on her: aggravated assault, shoplifting, fleeing the scene of a crime, aiding a fugitive, conspiracy—the list went on forever.

"I don't believe this," said Sandy, not even trying to control the rise in her voice. "You're telling me all that was just an act so you could steal a damned jacket?"

"Yeah." Marti folded her arms and burrowed into the seat. "No!" She shook her head. "I mean sometimes it is—"

"What is it? Yes or no?"

"I don't know." Marti raised her hands to her face as if she wanted to peel the skin away from her head. "I can't tell you."

"Why not?"

"Because I *can't*. Because nobody can understand."

Sandy put her arm around her and listened to the girl's story. The first time Dave attacked Marti in a store was because she had humiliated him in front of his buddies by forgetting to bring home the beer before she went shopping. He tracked her down and threw her into a hat display in the accessories department. The security cops held them in separate rooms until the real police arrived and that reinforced her vague feeling that she'd done something wrong. When Marti refused to press charges, they went home together. Hours passed before they realized she was still wearing the bracelet she'd been looking at in the store.

Dave was no fool. He figured the more brazen they were, the bigger their haul. The sales clerks and security cops—all the little people on the fringes of his life who might have kept him honest—were so distracted by the raw, senseless violence that they never noticed the goods that went out the door with the victim.

Marti said that sometimes he planned everything, choreographing the fight as carefully as a professional wrestling match. Other times, she was just as surprised as the people who formed a loose circle around her and stared in horror. It didn't make much difference to her whether his rage was calculated or spontaneous. The bruises felt the same either way.

Sandy shook her head. "How can you let him do those things to you?"

Marti waved her hand in frustration. "See? You don't understand at all," she said. "He's better than the other guys. Believe me, I've seen them. Dave treats me like I'm a princess. He's always buying presents for me . . ." Her voice drifted off for a moment before she added, "I get all kinds of nice stuff we could never afford to buy."

"So it's just a trade-off for you?" Sandy felt like she'd made a friend and been betrayed, all within an hour. "He gets to beat the crap out of you and you get a new jacket?"

"Everything's a trade-off, lady." Marti snapped. "I get a jacket and I don't get killed. What do you know about anything? It's easy for you."

"Then tell me. I want to understand." Sandy took the girl's hand again.

"It's like those religious people who sleep with the rattlesnakes," Marti said slowly, looking across the pond again. "My mother had a cousin who did that. If you don't get bitten, it means you're a good person, that your faith is right. If you're a bad person—or even if you just think you might get bitten—those snakes will take you just like that." She pulled away from Sandy's hand to snap her fingers.

"If I'm good and I make Dave happy the way I should, then everything's fine."

Sandy had never come closer to a snake handler than the newspaper. "What happened to your mother's cousin?" she asked.

"Got bit and died."

Sandy shivered. "You can't live like that. You don't need it and you sure as hell don't deserve it." The picture looked so clear to Sandy. "You have to get away from him."

"I've tried." Marti shrugged. "He'll find me. No matter where I go, he'll find me. He told me he'll kill me if I try to leave him again.

"Dave's just a mechanic down on Westmore, but sometimes I think if there's anyone in the world he doesn't know, then he knows their friend. He can ask questions so that people don't even know they're telling him things. There's no place on earth to hide from someone like that."

Trying to plan their next move paralyzed Sandy. Whatever they did would have a thousand repercussions which she had to sort through to be sure they were doing the right thing.

"Let's—" she started, then shook her head. "Maybe we should—no . . ."

When she realized it was time to pick up Saury at Kid'n'Kaboodle, everything else seemed to fall into place.

"Who's that?" Saury asked climbing in the back door and pointing at the woman hunkering down in the front seat.

As they drove down Westmore to Rollingwood Park, Marti tucked her head between her knees so no one could see her. Saury peered over the back of the seat and poked Sandy in the shoulder. "Mom, what's the matter with her?"

Sandy had to drive into the garage and lower the door before Marti would come out of the car.

Sandy put her keys on the kitchen counter and wondered what to do next. "Would you like to take a shower?" she asked, but she saw how foolish that was when Marti shook her head. "Can I get you anything? Coke? Coffee?"

"I'm just tired is all. Could I take a nap for a little while?"

Sandy showed her the guest bedroom, found a picture book to keep Saury occupied, then went and collapsed on her own bed. She didn't know how long she'd been sleeping when a noise nagged at her to wake up.

Her grogginess gave way to panic when she realized it was the sound of the garage door opening.

Chapter 38

False Daddies

The sun was rising and Elwood had passed out spread-eagled on the spool by the time Otis dropped Billey off in the bugmobile. Billey felt tired—more tired than he'd ever been—but all the things spinning inside his head wouldn't let him sleep. They wouldn't even let him close his eyes.

Instead, he walked past the tank which you couldn't even see anymore except for its mouth sticking up from a fresh mound of dirt. He followed the creek a long way, calling out for Black Wolf, but never getting an answer. He sure did miss the way that dog stood on his hind legs and waved his stubby paws when he saw Billey.

Billey had trudged nearly all the way to the railroad trestle when he heard someone shouting his name. It surprised him so much it took him a moment to recognize the voice as Uly Bondarbon's. He ran toward it, thrashing his way through the bushes, hollering, "Uly! I hear you now, Uly!"

"Billey Elwood, I swear I never thought I'd see you again," said Uly, who was swinging his legs from the same black cross beam he'd been on the first time Billey met him. "Thought you'd forgotten Uly, your best friend in this poor old world."

"How could I find you when I didn't know where you went?" Billey felt defensive. He listened carefully to his words to make sure he was thinking straight.

"You can bet yourself a dime to a donut you'll always find me right here." Uly patted the trestle like it was his favorite dog. "Trains come from ever' part of the world right to this track here. I have to signal them when they go by. Let the engineers know everything's okay on this end."

"You must keep awful busy." Billey had heard the trains in

the distance late into the night.

"Sure do, but I'm never too busy to see my friend Billey." Uly winked. "Even if you have been spending all your time with that false daddy of yours."

Billey lost his smile. "My daddy's been doin' some bad things, Uly. Real bad things."

"That's what *I* told *you*. Don't you remember that anymore?"

"I mean *new* bad things. Not just to me and Black Wolf. And Otis."

"Like I say, he's a false daddy, but he's not the only false daddy in the world, Billey. Lots of people try all their lives to get rid of one false daddy and when they finally do, they turn around and ring-a-ding-ding, here's a new false daddy waitin' on the doorstep.

"Some folks even got two, three false daddies fightin' each other for a chance to be mean to them."

Billey liked the way Uly knew about so many different things, even if he didn't always understand what he was saying. "One daddy's plenty for me," Billey pointed out.

Uly hopped off the beam and looked up, shading his eyes from the sun. "You see them cross ties up there?"

Billey nodded.

"You see them, Billey?" Uly raised his voice and Billey nodded harder. Uly glanced over to his friend. "Oh, you know I can't hear that head of yours goin' up and down, Billey."

"I see them, Uly."

Uly looked up again and pointed. "You're like one of them ties, Billey. "You're just as strong as a hardwood tree, but things run you over ever' live-long day of your life. Folks think a train's big enough, 'portant enough to go any damn where it pleases. But it ain't so. What lots of folks don't understand is that a train can't go nowhere without them cross ties."

Billey's head stopped moving. "What do you mean?" he asked.

Uly jumped back up and stood on the beam so he looked down at Billey. "I mean your daddy done you bad. A lot of folks' daddies done them bad. Everywhere I go in the world I see folks been done real bad. It like to break my heart into eleven pieces.

"Fact is, Billey, I know where your mama is today. And I know right where the man is who's doin' her badder than you ever seen."

"My mama?" Billey's ears pricked so high they nearly lifted him off the ground. "Where is she? Who's been doin' her bad?"

"She lives in a fine, fine house, Billey. It's a house to make you proud. You could pop your brain clean out of its socket tryin' to think of some item a person might want that she don't have, but she gets done bad just the same.

"I tell you what the truth is, Billy. I see her close to ever' day on the calendar and ever' day I see the bad things that eat away at her like ants a'crawlin' all over a lump of sugar. Somebody sure ought to do somethin' for your mama, Billey."

"What can I do, Uly?"

Uly patted his shirt for a smoke. He checked to see if he'd parked one behind his ear. "You got a cigarette, Billey?"

"No. How can I help my mama?"

"That's right, you don't smoke." Uly nodded slowly. "Reckon that's how you got to be such a big old critter. Never stunted up your growth with cigarettes."

"Tell me, Uly!"

"What?"

"About my mama."

"Tell you, hell! I could show you the house she lives in if I had a car. I could show you right where to find the man that does her so bad ever' day."

"Show me where."

"Oh, Billey, you know I gotta wait for this next train comin' along here by and by. They'll be lookin' for my signal."

"I've got a car," Billey blurted, surprising himself as much as Uly. "It's my daddy's pickup truck, but he won't wake up until dark."

Billey could hardly keep from running as he led Uly back home. He had to keep remembering that his friend's legs weren't as long or as strong as his own.

The sun hadn't even reached the top of the sky by the time they got to the shack. Uly turned his head slowly to take in the whole landscape—the shack, the camper, the dead catalpa, the trash that rose up from the dirt. He whistled and said, "So this is the place where Billey Elwood lives!"

Billey shushed him. "You don't want to wake my daddy," he whispered. "You won't be callin' him a false daddy anymore if you do. Ain't nothin' false about the way he can whup you."

Elwood never bothered to take the keys out of the pickup. Nobody would steal the thing and he never in a million years imagined that Billey would take it for a hell ride on his own.

Billey saw his daddy's arm twitch at the sound of the engine, but the man never lifted his head off the spool as they backed out onto the road.

Billey drove right past the railroad trestle where he met Uly. Then Uly showed him the way to a place where the streets all wound around in circles. Billey paid close attention so that he could find it by himself next time.

They stopped across the street from the house and Billey studied it for awhile. Its front yard was as big as the playground at Billey's old school, but it was smoother and it had grass instead of weeds and sand.

There were no cars in the driveway and the garage door was open to show it was empty.

"Looks like nobody's home right now, Billey," Uly said. "But I tell you what. The man that lives here—the man that does things to your mama that would break your heart into eleven pieces just like mine—he drives a white convertible. He's not fat, but he's got a soft, chubby face and eyes like a pig. That's how you can tell him, by those piggy little eyes of his.

"Ain't no price in this world a man could pay to make up for things like he's been doin'. Fact is, that's the whole reason Satan keeps his flames stoked up in hell. He's the only one who knows how to make them false daddies pay what they owe."

Uly rubbed his chin. "You ever been to church, Billey?"

"I dunno."

"Well, you'd know it if you had, so I guess not. Church is where they teach you all about God," Uly held his left hand out flat, "and Satan." He curled his right hand in a fist. "Them two never agree on anything except for one, single thing. You know what that is, Billey?"

"I dunno."

"God and Satan agree that Satan gets to put all the false daddies in his hot old furnace. They're *both* gonna reward anyone who helps him do that. You just ask any preacher man in the world if that ain't so, Billey."

Uly talked so funny that Billey couldn't always understand him. But this time Billey thought he knew what Uly meant.

•

Disbelief and terror churned together in Billey's guts when he got home and saw that Elwood wasn't asleep on the spool anymore. He wheeled the pickup around the camper and saw Elwood and Otis with the bugmobile out yonder by the tank. He figured he might as well take his whupping now as later, so he drove down to them, but he left the engine running, just in case.

But Elwood was too mad at Otis to whup Billey. "Where the hell you been with my truck, you little shit head?" was all he said.

"I dunno," Billey answered, but Elwood wasn't even listening.

Elwood pulled his big gun out of his jeans and shot it twice up into the sky. "Gah-*dam*, Otis, I can't believe you. I thought I knew every stupid dick-brained thing you could ever think up and then you pull this on me."

He tucked the gun back into his waist. Otis's hand had been fidgeting around the butt of the little gun sticking out of his pants. When he moved his hand back, he bumped the gun so that it fell down his baggy pants leg to the ground.

Elwood took two quick strides and scooped the gun up. He waved it in Otis's face. "You're so fuckin' stupid you're gonna blow your foot off instead of blowin' your brains out like you oughta." He handed the gun to Billey and said, "Put this in the pickup until I'm ready for it."

Billey jogged to the truck, but he stopped when his daddy began yelling again.

"Even Billey's smarter than you, Otis," Elwood said. "I got me a million gallons of gasoline, enough gasoline to set me up for the rest of my natural-born life and you don't even have the pea-brained sense to get a pump!"

Elwood rose up on his toes and breathed fire right into Otis's face. "'Spose you tell me just how in hell's name we're gonna get that gasoline outta the ground? We gonna scoop it out one cup at a time? We gonna cram your mother-fuckin' head down there so you can suck it out with your faggot lips? Huh, Otis? How we gonna do that?"

Billey had never seen his daddy get this mad at Otis before, and he'd never seen Otis look quite this sick. Billey slipped into the driver's seat and let his foot hover over the gas pedal as he watched Otis fumble in his pocket for a smoke. The cigarette wobbled in the big man's fingers as he lit it. Otis took a deep drag and turned his head to exhale. Then he offered the pack to Elwood who slapped it to the ground.

"You better think of somethin' real smart now," Elwood snarled. "'Cause when I blow your brains out you won't be able to think of nothin' at all."

Otis squatted down and fiddled with the mouth of the tank while Elwood paced and muttered like he did when he was fixing to whup Billey real bad. Billey slipped the pickup into gear and began moving at walking speed across the field. He looked in the rear view mirror to make sure Elwood hadn't noticed him leaving.

That's when he saw Black Wolf's nose poking through the scrub that ran along the creek. When Black Wolf saw Billey, he barked and left his cover. His stubby legs beat like wings, but Elwood and Otis blocked his path to Billey.

Billey gunned the engine and swung the pickup in a big circle to draw the dog away to safety. "Black Wolf!" he cried through the shot-out window. "Get over here, Black Wolf!"

Elwood turned and saw the dog sprinting for the truck that bumped over the field. Otis looked up from the cap he'd screwed off the tank.

"I ain't got no time for your shit today, Billey," Elwood yelled, pulling the big gun out of his pants again.

Billey saw the wisp of smoke rise out of the gun barrel before he heard the deep report. The bullet slammed into Black Wolf and sent him skidding across the rocky ground.

The sound startled Otis who said, "Oh!" The cigarette dropped off his lower lip. It never even entered the tank before it touched off the fumes and sent the earth, Elwood, Otis and the bugmobile flying into the sky in a stinking ball of fire.

It seemed like Billey watched the fire forever, but maybe it wasn't very long at all. He couldn't tell that the sun had moved in the sky. A couple of old crows looked down at him from the tree by the creek, just like they always did.

He got out of the truck and picked his way through the flames to the black twisted thing that used to be his daddy. The thing looked like an old tree branch that had burned up, but it smelled a lot worse than that.

Billey held out the little gun and fired into the thing. It didn't move or cry out in pain, so he shot it again and again.

As he drove back to the road, Billey thought about all the mean, hateful things his daddy had done to him in twenty years. And this was the meanest, most hateful of all—not even living long enough for Billey to kill him.

Chapter 39

Trouble

When the sound of the garage door woke Sandy, she shook her head to clear it and ran to the living room. She pulled back the drapes just in time to see the Impala disappear around the bend in Rollingwood Drive.

She slumped onto the sofa. How could Marti steal her car after Sandy had tried to help her? How could anyone just take something that big that wasn't theirs? How could anyone think they would get away with that? Why would anyone want the Impala anyway? She never bought more than half a tank of gas, figuring the car probably wouldn't last long enough to use it.

Sandy looked for a more comfortable answer. Maybe Marti just needed to get something from Thrift Aisles. No. She didn't know the neighborhood well enough to find the store. In fact, she didn't even know what neighborhood they were in. She'd kept her head down all the way from the park.

Marti's face and hair reminded her of Jennifer, but Jennifer would never have grown up like that. Maybe some people were just born to be good and some were born to be dirty double-crossers. The only trouble was you couldn't pick them by looking at them.

Stephen X got right to the point when he came home. "Where's your car?" he demanded before he'd even put down his brief case.

Sandy felt strangely calm as she told him, "I let a friend borrow it."

"A friend? You let a friend borrow it?" Stephen X tried to decide which angle would give him the greatest advantage. "Who?"

"Marti—"

"Who the hell is he?" Stephen X moved closer to her. "What? Are you screwing him? You must be to go around giving him your car."

"He's a she." Sandy folded her arms and came forward a step. "And I didn't give it to her. I let her borrow it."

Stephen X looked confused because Sandy had not backed up. "Who is this Marti? I've never heard of her. Does she have car insurance?"

Sandy just looked at him, which gave him the moment he needed to gather his thoughts. "Your insurance policy doesn't cover her, you know. She kills somebody in that car and you're responsible for every penny of damages. You should know better than that with those crappy brakes you've got on that Impala." He wagged his finger at her. "You know what the trouble with you is, Sandy?"

"I guess I do." Suddenly, everything fell into place and she almost felt like smiling.

All her life, the Jack Gores, the Stephen X Skinners and men like Marti's boyfriend had been committing atrocities against her and her world. Some piece—maybe just a very tiny piece of their heart or soul—was missing or broken. Maybe that precious flicker of conscience is what defines the human being. It's much more important than opposable thumbs or the ability to reason.

They had even absolved poor, sweet-natured Roscoe by blaming his death on a dark conspiracy of government and police instead of his fatal pig-headedness.

The Sandys and Martis of the world, on the other hand, saw terrible things unfolding around them. When guilt bounced off the guilty, they stood by, ready to pick it up.

Sandy had seen in an instant that Marti had to take every necessary step to escape from her boyfriend. It had taken a little longer to recognize herself in the same situation. That awareness calmed and strengthened her.

Stephen X raised his finger higher. "The trouble with you

is you just don't think, Sandy."

She brushed his finger aside with the back of her hand. "Oh, but I do," she said. "I think I'm sick to death of you. I'm sick of puny, little, frustrated cowards. Sick of being treated like a slave and a whore."

She stepped forward, pressing her hand against his chest until he moved back. "I'm sick of your drinking and your hangovers and your tantrums. Sick of praying that Saury won't wake you up when you pass out on Saturday afternoons. Sick of hearing your voice when I pick up the phone. Sick of wondering what we ever did to deserve a sorry bastard like you.

"That's why I called a lawyer this morning," she lied, pushing him back another step so that he flopped over the arm of the easy chair. "I'm filing for divorce."

Stephen X struggled to his feet and straightened the knot of his tie. "You better get a reality check before you start shooting off your mouth, sister. There's no way you can divorce me. It would take your whole damn paycheck just to keep the lights on in this house. You can't even afford a good enough lawyer to keep the judge from giving me the house and Saury, too. I'll see you pushing a shopping cart full of rags down Westmore Avenue."

"Fine, fine, fine." Sandy exaggerated the nod of her head. "Now get the hell out of here."

Stephen X looked so surprised that for the first time in Sandy's life she was not afraid to turn her back on him. She went to the phone and felt free of all those terrible weights that had dragged her down for so many years. Her chest felt clean and the air tasted sweet.

For the first time, she knew there was nothing he could do to her.

As she dialed Linda's number, she heard Stephen X open the front door. She was used to hearing him speak nonsense, but she cocked an ear when he said, "Whoever you are, you've got the wrong house."

She looked over her shoulder and saw Stephen X standing in the doorway. He cleared his throat with two short hacks followed by a longer, harsher one. "Look, I haven't got time for this," he said.

Sandy heard Linda's voice on the line just as the first bullet exploded from Stephen X's back and buried itself in the wall. He shrugged and coughed before the second bullet slammed him against the hardwood door.

Stephen X's head turned towards Sandy with his eyes bulging and his jaw twitching. His legs sagged and he slid down the door until he was sitting in a pool of blood.

The third bullet hit the side of his head. It sprayed a fan of blood over the dark, splintered wood and left him still.

•

Billey Elwood leaned against the black post of the railroad trestle and panted without taking in any air. Sweat collected like dew drops on the patchy, fine stubble that covered his jaw. He peered into the darkness up and down the creek and wondered where Uly had gone.

His right hand still tingled, as if he'd slept on his arm, cutting off the blood. It didn't hurt, but the feeling made him want to cry.

Seeing his daddy shoot rats and snakes, or even shooting his daddy's charred body could not prepare Billey for this.

Billey had been standing on his mama's porch trying to decide what to do next when the door opened. The man had squinty little pig eyes, just like Uly said, and he looked like he'd never smiled in his life.

Billey felt like he was shooting his daddy with the first bullet. It twisted the man up like a slug crawling through salt. Billey fired twice more. But it didn't make him feel good like he thought it would. It made him feel sick, the way seeing Black Wolf get shot did.

He ran without even seeing his mama. He had to puke in

the lawn a little bit before he could get into the pickup.

When Uly finally met him at the trestle, he told him everything that happened.

"You did a good thing, Billey," he said.

"Then why do I feel so bad?"

"Sometimes it hurts to make things right." Uly patted his shoulder. "But don't you worry, you'll get plenty of rewards now.

"Only thing is, Billey, Satan don't always pay up on his debts right away."

"What do you mean?"

"It's real complicated stuff, but some folks might think you were just workin' for Satan, when you were actually doin' business for God and Satan both. What that means is some folks might think you done something bad.

"Best thing is, you grab a ladder on the next freight train that slows down for this here trestle. You ride a couple days and find a new place to live for awhile."

Billey rubbed his eyes with the palms of his hands. "Where does the train go?"

"They go ever' which where, but don't you worry. They all wind up back here sooner or later, ever' one of them."

•

The good cop/bad cop routine would never work with Sandy. The big detective chewed an unlit cigar and wore a baseball cap with shirt sleeves and suspenders. If his mission was to bully her, then that part went like clockwork. But the shorter detective, the one who was supposed to gain her confidence, wore an immaculate green three-piece suit that might have come out of Stephen X's closet. She wouldn't trust him with the time of day.

From their questions, Sandy realized that the whole world knew those awful things she thought were secrets. The detectives recited a thousand rumors of her alleged infidelities that had made the rounds at Stephen X's office. They quizzed her about reports from the women at ATI that she kept to herself and came to work with bruises. Miss Busse at Kid'n'Kaboodle had always thought Sandy was a little bit strange. The cops wondered where her car was.

It all seemed so stupid. She told them everything she knew about Stephen X's death in the first fifteen minutes. But they went over and over the same questions. It made her think of the way Stephen X used to lock her in the bedroom. "Say that you love me," he'd droned. "Say that you love me."

At one point, the big detective tipped the cap back on his head and took the cigar out of his mouth. "How much does it cost to get somebody bumped off in this town?"

"I don't know," Sandy said wearily. "You don't bother me that much." Then she became angry. "What is this? Am I a suspect? Some loony is out there with a gun. He knows where my son and I live. And you guys aren't giving me the feeling that you have any idea how to catch him."

"No, Mrs. Skinner, you're not a suspect," the short guy said softly. "We're just gathering information. It's just a routine part of the investigation."

"How do you know it was a man?" the tall guy asked.

"What?"

"You said we don't have any idea how to catch *him*. Did you see a man?"

Sandy shook her head and wondered what life was supposed to be like.

Chapter 40

Fear

Billey opened his eyes when the rhythm changed. He stretched the kinks out of his arms and legs. He'd slept all curled up like a dog to keep himself warm without a blanket. He smelled old wood and hot grease as he felt the pockmarks the rough floor had left in his cheek.

He crawled over to look out the door. The shadows of telephone poles and grain elevators rushed past. Billey could make out the shapes of billboards in the distance whenever a pair of headlights swept the ridge.

The rush and rumble of the train eased, and Billey watched the stars lose themselves—never fading—in the wash of the morning sky.

•

Every Friday, the short detective phoned to update Sandy on the investigation. It disturbed her that the cops didn't seem to be able to come up with any solid leads.

She had no trouble thinking of a thousand reasons for Stephen X to be killed. What scared her was the thought that a person could enter a quiet neighborhood, shoot someone to death in a brightly lit doorway and disappear into thin air.

It was like her car. Sandy still didn't understand how Marti could have just taken it like that. The police found it a few days later, stripped of its battery and radio, the only parts that were worth anything. Sandy sold it for scrap and began driving Stephen X's Mustang.

Of course, she never felt like grieving—or even pretending to grieve—for Stephen X. But the way it all happened left its scars. The bullets had transformed him like an effect from one of his sick horror movies. One moment he was his usual, disgusting self and the next he was something entirely different, a twist of meat in a six hundred dollar suit, as if he had been turned inside out to expose all the blood and ugliness.

So often, as she had looked at the insane mask he put on while brutalizing her, she had wondered if he would kill her this time. And later, when she had survived and he had reverted to that other mask—the one he put on for the rest of the world—Sandy doubted her own sanity. If not for the bruises, how could she know that the violence really happened? How could she know whether questions of life and death had been asked?

In a way, the murder vindicated Sandy by condensing the horror of Stephen X in a last burst of savagery. She thought of those stories where a person on the verge of death hovers near the ceiling, watching himself. Stephen X probably would have enjoyed the spectacle of his grand finale. The gore seemed like the kind of touch he would have engineered himself, but at least it sealed that chapter of her life.

Sandy toyed with the idea of going to Stephen X's funeral to let the sense of finality wash over her, but she decided she had already moved past the need for that. All she'd ever wanted was for him to be gone.

But she still had to wonder where the killer was and if he wanted anything more of her.

The day they buried Stephen X, Sandy took Saury to the park. It was the first day that hinted at autumn. It reminded her of the sense of promise and anticipation that a new school year used to bring. She saw the excitement ballooning in Saury as he sprinted for the slide, and she felt as if she were breathing pristine air that had been saved for her far above the earth.

While Saury climbed the ladder, Sandy noticed a man in a conservative, blue suit sitting on a bench not far away, staring at them. She didn't know if he were a pervert or a cop, and she didn't much care. She wondered if men believed they were invisible—like cats crouching behind tiny objects—and that invisibility licensed them to gawk.

Each time she caught Saury shooting off the end of the slide, she noticed the man fidgeting with a small brown bag that might have been left over from his lunch. He crumpled the paper into a tight ball, then spread it across his thigh and stroked out the wrinkles, never taking his eyes off Sandy.

Once she tried to stare him down, but it didn't work because she didn't *want* to look at him, at the way his suit hung in lumps and billows, at his dry, parted lips, at his rude, puffy eyes. She turned away and tried hard not to feel his eyes boring into her.

Saury launched himself from the top of the slide. He lifted his arms over his head and yelled "Look out below!" so that his voice trailed off as he rushed down the ramp. When he reached the bottom, he flew into Sandy's arms and gave her his usual hug. But this time, he didn't let go when Sandy straightened up. He stared at something behind her, but before she could look, she heard heavy breathing at her back.

Sandy gasped to see a massive, black dog, its jaws large enough to take Saury's head, staring into the child's eyes. Sandy spun around and saw that the dog had a slim woman in tow.

"Now, Samson," the woman said without as much confidence as Sandy wanted to hear, "let these good people be."

Samson strained against the leash and licked Saury's cheek, to the boy's enormous delight.

"Samson!" the woman said, as harshly as she could. "No!"

The dog's tongue rolled over teeth as sharp as ivory daggers. Saury moved his embrace from his mother's leg to the dark, silky fur of Samson's neck.

"He's big," Sandy said, "What is he?"

"Part Rottweiler," the woman said.

"And the rest horse, I guess," Sandy laughed, running her fingers along the dog's powerful neck. "I thought they were supposed to be mean."

"He can be a hundred forty pounds of hell," said the woman with awe that familiarity had not dulled. "But only when he needs to be."

"How does he know? Have you trained him to K-I-L-L on command?"

She eyed Sandy curiously. "Haven't you ever had a dog?"

"No." Sandy shrugged. "My friend has a useless, one-eyed beagle. It was her husband's, but he died."

"They're very sensitive creatures." The woman crouched down and guided Saury's hand along Samson's broad face. "It's all non-verbal. They're loyal and forgiving and attentive. They give you unconditional love."

"Sounds better than a husband." Sandy meant to be funny but she didn't hear any humor in her voice.

The woman stood up and announced, "I'm not afraid anymore."

They looked at each other for several moments and shared something too common to be called a secret, but too private and sad to be spoken out loud.

"Goodbye, Samson," Saury called. When he finished waving, he parked his arm on his forehead to shade his eyes.

"Did you like that dog?" asked Sandy.

"Uh huh." Saury nodded deliberately. Then he pointed. "Mom, look at Samson now!"

As the woman passed near the park bench, the dog stiffened. His growl came out so deep and loud, Sandy felt it through the soles of her feet. The man's pink face turned pale, accenting his blue suit. He edged away, pushing his palms against the air. He opened a little distance between himself and the dog and tried to run backwards, but he lost his balance and fell. The tumble stripped away the last shred of his facade of dignity. Samson bellowed in triumph with all the strength of his mighty lungs.

"What's wrong with that man, mom?" wondered Saury, who had never seen such a spectacle, even on the weekends when Stephen X had been falling-down drunk.

Sandy pulled him against her leg. "Nothing anymore," she said.

•

Sandy surprised herself the next morning by finding a ninety-pound Rottweiler in the classifieds. So much of her life had required approval that acting on an impulse left an exciting, clean feeling inside her chest.

She followed Westmore past the city limits where the billboards and pre-fab buildings gave way to trees and livestock. Sandy lifted her foot from the gas to watch two young horses race across a slope, inspired by the change of weather.

A chain-link fence surrounded the place she wanted, a small, white ranch house set back from the road in a stand of maples. A chorus of dogs announced her arrival so that the breeder, an old woman named Irene, came to the porch even before Sandy put the car in park.

Something in the way the wrinkles played around Irene's eyes and mouth reminded Sandy of Mama Gore. The woman had tucked her white hair beneath a cloth cap, but a few delicate, beautiful strands spilled out. Sandy thought of the Saturday afternoons when she and Mama Gore had sat by the Airstream and taken turns braiding each other's hair. That might have been the last time Sandy thought she understood the world.

Irene led her in back of the house. The dogs in their runs seemed to be charged with the sight of her. They adored Irene, pressing their cheeks and tongues against the cyclone fence, but never barking in her presence.

Sandy had never been allowed to own animals. Her mother had blamed her for the sudden death of a shimmering tankful of fish, and Stephen X set household standards too high even for humans. So Sandy had no idea how to pick a dog for herself. She wished she'd brought Saury along to help.

"This is Suvi. He's crazy about you," said Irene. "He's still just a pup. He hasn't even grown into his feet yet, so you can expect him to get a lot bigger. He'll be good protection."

"Suvi." Sandy nodded. "That's a pretty name."

"It's short for Vesuvius." Irene studied Sandy carefully for a reaction. "I named all of this litter for volcanoes."

"Oh! Why do you do that?"

"You don't know dogs, do you?"

"Well, no." Sandy felt like she'd forgotten to do her homework. "But I want to. How do I train him?"

"You don't need to teach a dog about protection anymore than a dog needs to tell you how to bake a potato," Irene said, shaking her head. She worked her hands between the dog's teeth and pried open its huge, threatening mouth while Sandy worried for the woman's fingers. "You think you know more about self defense than this?" She nodded at the gaping jaws.

"He'll watch you and learn all he needs to know. A dog wants to please its master. That's just the way they're born. You might think he loves you, but it's beyond love; it goes beyond life itself. Dogs are smart about a lot of things, but they don't understand strings attached to things like love and loyalty." The woman stood up and laughed at herself. "Just listen to me—as if people understand those things any better than a dog does!"

Her laugh sounded like Mama Gore and Sandy felt comfortable with her decision.

"A dog will do what you want whether you teach it or not." She shrugged. "It's because they have no self-image. They don't have a clue what they look like. A dog doesn't see itself in a mirror, it sees another dog. You can have a terrible struggle for dominance between the real dog and its reflection. That's one reason I don't allow dogs in the house. Anyway, since they don't know what they look like, they figure you're one of them. They make you the leader of the pack, even if the pack is just you and one dog. They don't know politics from garbanzo beans, so a dog will never disobey once it knows what you expect of it.

"The only thing you have to remember is to never take away a dog's dignity."

"Why not?" Sandy felt so ignorant. She imagined that violating this rule would cause the animal to turn on her with horrible results.

"Why?" The woman shook her head again. "Because then it won't have its dignity."

Chapter 41

A Dog's Dignity

Kids knew a lot more about the world than Sandy did in her day, so Saury had no trouble adapting to a fierce-looking dog twice his size. He hugged Suvi around the neck, bared his own teeth and pulled back the dog's gums for the camera. For the rest of the day, he paraded around with his upper lip tucked behind the bottom row of baby teeth, saying "Rrrrhhhh. Rrrrhhhh."

Because of his size and the keenness of his soft, brown eyes, bringing Suvi home was more like adding a new person than a pet to the household. Relaxing, he came to Sandy's waist, and he could easily rest his chin on the kitchen counter, the dining table or anywhere else something unusual might beckon.

Suvi's head was already larger than Sandy's. Teeth as big as finger tips crowded his mighty jaws. The teeth jutted out in six basic shapes, each shape playing a special role when the time came to turn flesh and bone into juice and gristle. His rawhide toys might as well have been cotton candy.

Loose jowls and a down-turned mouth made him appear serious and noble. His compact nose and short muzzle spared him from the clownish face so common in the dog world. He showed Sandy what Irene meant by a dog's dignity.

Black fur with feathery, tan accents underscored Suvi's seriousness and enhanced his impression of bulk and power. The sleek fur creased and bunched over the dog's broad, chiseled muscles.

Suvi's legs, on loan from a horse, ended in great tan wads of feet. They gave him an adult Rottweiler's height. The next forty or fifty pounds would be added to his breadth and depth.

It stretched Sandy's imagination to regard something as large as the ten-month-old Suvi as a puppy. The dog didn't weigh much less than she did, and his silhouette filled the door when he rose to his full height in protest at her departure.

On the other hand, she could hardly keep him in bones, but she dared not run out because his teeth could always find something else to satisfy them.

Not long after she brought Suvi home, the interest his nose took in the tiles of the front entryway alarmed her. At first, Sandy thought he was looking for a place to pee. But as soon as she let him back in after giving him a chance outside, he followed his nose to the front door. Much later, she realized that the scent of Stephen X's blood probably lingered there. "Oh, go ahead and pee, if that's what you want," she sighed.

Without Stephen X around, she never seemed to lose things anymore. He used to stuff things in odd places if the sight of it offended him. If Sandy were distracted while putting away the laundry, her underwear might turn up beneath the bathroom sink or crammed behind the dresser. It was like the old joke about the husband sweeping dust beneath the carpet until a mountain rose in the middle of the room.

But she spent a good part of Saturday looking for one of her favorite shoes. Sunday afternoon, she caught Suvi flossing with a shoelace behind the sofa.

"Bad dog!" she said, waving a few chunks of the sole in his face. "You're a bad, bad dog."

Suvi shrank into the carpet and did penance. His moist, brown eyes rolled up to see how much trouble he was in. Although he probably had no idea what he'd done, he looked too ashamed even to whimper.

Sandy tried to sit down and read a magazine. Within moments, she felt Suvi's hot, steady breath against her fingers. She tipped the magazine and saw him peering intently, as if he were trying to read the perfume ad on the back cover.

She couldn't stay mad at anyone so earnest. She stroked the fine, smooth fur between his ears. "Suvi, Suvi, Suvi," she sighed. "What are we going to do with you?"

When Suvi played, he seemed more like a cat on steroids than a dog. He pounced on an orange leaf that skittered down the street. He crossed the living room in two bounds. He stretched out motionless—six feet or more from paw tip to paw tip—and waited.

The part that Sandy had least expected was the way Suvi showed such an intense interest in everything she and Saury did. Having lived so long with Stephen X's oblivion, that was something that took some getting used to.

Sandy crouched to tie her shoe and there was Suvi's nose in the laces. She stood on tiptoes to reach a pan in the kitchen, and Suvi nuzzled her leg. Sandy switched on her computer and Suvi cocked his head as the numbers raced across the screen.

She had seen goofy dogs before. They had vacant, dilated eyes, slobbery tongues and brains that compelled them to play fetch at a frantic pace until they keeled over dead. But Suvi accepted his doghood as a serious calling. Even the way he shadowed Sandy, studying her every movement seemed to be part of a larger plan. He acted like he thought he might need to fill in for her with the household chores one day.

Not that she had done a very good job of understanding humans, but it was tough for Sandy to get inside a dog's mind. Why would he want to drink from the toilet like a horse at a water trough? Why did he follow her everywhere? Why did he home in on the most disgusting things he could find when she took him for a walk?

She came home from work in the middle of the night and found him sprawled as big as a man across the carpet, gnawing on a goat's hoof. He just tilted his head and rolled his eyes when she came in the door.

"How did you know I wasn't a burglar, you big galoot?"

Suvi spit out the hoof and ambled to her side. He licked the back of her hand.

Maybe Sandy had made a big mistake. She'd thought this guard dog business would be like getting Rin Tin Tin with an attitude. What kind of protection could a docile, teething puppy offer, even one as big as a small horse? She bought him a choke chain and a collar with chrome studs so that he would at least look more threatening. But how would an attacker be deterred by a lanky, ninety-pound dog that sauntered down the street with an old popsicle wrapper in its mouth?

For a few days she entertained Saury by trying to tutor Suvi in basic growling techniques. She crouched on all fours and scrunched her face up. "Grrrrr," she said. "Listen, Suvi! Grrrrr." Suvi cocked an ear and tried to understand his role in this new game.

Sandy finally quit worrying on the Saturday afternoon when the insurance salesman came. She had been making a grocery list in the kitchen when she heard Suvi at the front door. The growl started as soft and low as distant thunder. But it grew urgent and loud, like a menacing train, as the man came up the walk.

Sandy watched Suvi plant his feet behind the door, ready to spring for the throat at the first sight of the intruder. When the doorbell rang, Suvi unleashed a bark that could defend a fresh carcass, a bark that warned strangers they had strayed into the wrong neighborhood.

By the time Sandy cracked open the door, the man had already jumped back from the porch, spilling his briefcase on the lawn.

"Suvi! Down!" she shouted, halfway hoping he wouldn't pay any attention to her.

Suvi forced his head between Sandy's leg and the door. He bared his teeth and barked with a voice that knocked birds off the telephone lines. At last, Sandy understood why Irene borrowed names from volcanoes for her Rottweilers.

"Hush, Suvi," Sandy said, tugging back at his collar and feeling her feet skid across the porch. She shot a glance at the man who was scrambling to his feet. "Can I help you?"

"Bob Adamowski, Metro Insurance," he said, stuffing papers into his case and patting his hair. "I'll call you sometime when you're not busy."

Sandy closed the door and knelt in front of Suvi. "Good dog," she said, massaging his neck the way he liked. "What a good, good dog!"

Even without the theatrics, Sandy felt safe walking Suvi at any time of day or night. Always curious, Suvi's eyes followed any human or dog they encountered. His size and the intensity of his gaze were enough to make some men cross to the other side of the street. Sandy came to realize that only men took detours at the sight of Suvi. Women felt no threat and children could hardly keep their hands off the calm, noble dog. Maybe the men feared that Suvi could read their unwholesome thoughts.

Maybe that was how Suvi could tell whether Sandy or an insurance salesman stood on the other side of a door.

Chapter 42

The Telephone

Death had a lot in common with the surveys Sandy worked with at ATI. Both caught people off guard and gave a slender moment an importance it would have lacked without the intrusion. ATI extracted opinions from thousands of people and then peddled the results as if they held an eternal truth.

Sandy knew that the survey itself altered the sample because ATI quizzed people about so many things they'd never considered and didn't really care about. So as not to look stupid, the respondent said the first thing that flashed into his head, then changed his mind moments later. The interviewers came back to the office and traded horror stories of people who pestered them for days, trying to amend their original answers.

In the same way, death preserved a particular stage in a person's life regardless of how that person might have wanted to be remembered.

Jennifer died young, with all her sweetness intact, so now Sandy couldn't imagine what she would have been beyond childhood. In all probability, she would have looked and acted a lot like Sandy. But she would have been a new, improved version of Sandy, able to see certain warnings more clearly.

On the other hand, Stephen X's death left him with neither a future nor a past in Sandy's mind.

Roscoe had told Sandy all sorts of stories about Stephen X's childhood, but she could never pull the image of the boy into focus. It was too hard to imagine someone like Stephen X ever spooning up strained carrots or having his diaper changed. How could he have wound up where he did if he'd started at the same place as everybody else?

Saury was so young—and he would always be her baby—yet she had no trouble imagining how he would look, how his voice would sound, at every coming stage of his life. At least now he would be safe to grow up and lead a normal life.

Sandy wasn't exactly sure what normal life was supposed to be like for herself, but she settled into a comfortable routine in the weeks following Stephen X's death. She went back to work. She dropped Saury at Kid'n'Kaboodle. She bought groceries and ate and slept a fitful sleep.

She felt a little bit better each day, as if she were coming out of a long, bad dream. The fact that none of the things that happened bothered Saury helped her. He never mentioned Stephen X and he began to laugh more often. She only wished she could get him some kind of blood transfusion to wash away the last traces of the boy's father.

A month went by before the first phone call.

"How have you been?"

Sandy frowned and looked at the ceiling, trying to place the voice. "Fine," she said. "Who is this?"

"Don't you remember me, your good friend?"

"I'm sorry. I'm sure I will when you tell me your name." She felt her finger tapping the receiver. Suvi rose and walked to her side.

"We should get together sometime soon."

Sandy grew impatient. "Okay. Anytime you like." She hung up.

•

The reporters usually called on Friday afternoons, never more than an hour after the short detective had told her how the police were running down some promising leads. By the time it became clear that the cops had run out of suspects, the incident had lost its news value.

Both the newspaper and television station reassigned women to the story and began mining it for human interest.

The reporters asked Sandy how she was coping with the stagnant investigation. Did her husband's death give her a feeling of independence? What steps had she taken to protect her son and herself? How had she told Saury that his father would not be coming home again?

It all reminded her of ATI's surveys where page upon page of pointless questions were designed to catch people off guard so they'd answer truthfully when the *real* question sneaked in. The reporters' probing made so little sense that Sandy couldn't even tell whether she'd been misquoted when the stories finally came out.

She still felt the lack of news was somehow her fault. She wanted to help them get their stories so they would leave her alone, but she had nothing to tell them. One of the reporters, Dorothy Something, seemed nice enough. She was just doing her job. But the questions left Sandy with a queasy stomach and a sense of impending doom that never quite lifted.

Sandy dreamt of walking down a crowded, endless hallway in some sort of institutional building—a school or a hospital. Vulgar light flickered over the scene as the fluorescent tubes crackled and sparked. She touched each person on the shoulder and asked, "What's wrong? What's wrong?"

The people just looked at her like there was nothing wrong with *them*. She wanted a mirror, not out of vanity, but to confirm her fear that some terrible message had been scrawled across her face—something that everyone in the world but her could see.

Each time she reached out, she expected the person who turned toward her to be a skeleton shedding rotten, maggot-ridden chunks of flesh on the floor. But that never happened. They were all clean, wholesome people.

"What's wrong?" Sandy demanded as she tapped an old woman's shoulder.

Mama Gore turned to face her. "Nothing, dear," she said, shaking her head slowly. "Nothing is wrong." Sandy woke with a start to find she'd knocked the pillows onto the floor. Suvi had sprawled over them, snoring in utter peace.

Every time Sandy's name splashed into the news, another volley of phone calls came from the shooting instructors and insurance salesmen, the fringe lunatics and heavy breathers. The mail brought letters from groups like POLICE—People Offended by Lax Investigations of Criminal Elements. Talk radio courted her.

When Sandy took Saury to Kid'n'Kaboodle's field day, she tried to cope with the burden of being a local celebrity.

"I saw you on TV the other day," confided a plump woman in a sweatshirt that matched the children's blue and orange Kid'n'Kaboodle t-shirts. Saury and the other kids ditched their parents for a noisy game of poison tag. "You looked terrific. The camera really agrees with you."

Sandy figured that was code for "you look like crap now." She smoothed her hair and wondered whether that meant that discussing Stephen X's demise brought out the best in her.

"Does your son know what happened?"

Sandy followed the woman's gaze to the soccer field where the kids darted back and forth. "*I* don't even know what happened," she said. "All I want is to forget about it."

"Oh, pardon me." The woman looked mortified. "I didn't mean anything."

"I'm sorry—" Sandy started, before she realized she'd done nothing to be sorry for. After an uncomfortable moment of silence, she pointed to the children and said, "Wouldn't it be nice to have so much energy?"

"If only we could harness it!" The woman shook her head. "Jason can run full tilt all day, but get him home and he's too worn out to pick up after himself."

"Really? Sometimes I think Saury is too neat for his age," Sandy had never thought such a thing before, but she knew at once it was true. "He should loosen up a little."

"Well, maybe we can work out a trade." The plump woman tugged her sleeves down over her hands and stamped her feet. "At least for evenings and weekends."

"His father was never a child."

The woman cocked her head in Sandy's direction. "You mean the guy who got shot?"

Sandy didn't seem to hear. "I guess he didn't hate children so much as he hated the child within people, the part that can still grow. He had real a real problem with that.

"But I don't think it's too late for Saury. He's just a little boy, isn't he?"

The puzzled look on the woman's face embarrassed Sandy. "It's been nice talking with you," Sandy said, "but we've got to go . . . to our next thing now." She tried without much success to smile at the woman as she edged away. After a few steps, she turned and called out, "Saury! Saury!"

The children sprinted and dodged each other in their identical Kid'n'Kaboodle t-shirts. Sandy had lost track of Saury and now she couldn't pick him out of the blue and orange swirl on the soccer field. Calling his name, she trotted into the jumble of children.

She thought she saw Saury, but when she touched him on the shoulder, it turned out to be another boy. "You can't tag me," he protested through a veil of freckles. "You're not it."

"Saury!" she shouted. Then she felt a tap on her butt. When she turned around, it wasn't Saury, but a girl she knew from his class. "Poison, Mrs. Skinner," the girl laughed. "You're poison. You've got to lie down."

She saw Saury spread-eagled on the ground. She knelt beside him and cradled his head in her hand. "Saury! Saury, what happened?"

His eyelids flipped open. "Shhh, mom. I'm playing poisoned."

Sandy's relief outweighed her embarrassment as they drove home. Why did she worry so much? Why did she always expect something terrible to happen?

"Couldn't you hear me calling you?" She frowned at her son.

"We were just playing, mom. Don't you ever just play?"

Having chided herself for her pessimism, Sandy couldn't quite believe what she saw when she opened the back door. Suvi whimpered and cast her a pitiful look from the middle of a heap of books, knick-knacks and planks. He'd apparently been bored, so when he ground his last goat's hoof into dust, he started gnawing on the bottom of the book shelves. With canine ingenuity, he'd managed to rock the shelves until they tumbled over on top of him.

The mess didn't bother Sandy as much as the way Suvi hobbled on three legs, dangling a paw in the air. He turned mournful eyes to her and licked her hand as if trying to show that he wanted her to lick his injury. The vet couldn't find any broken bones, but she wanted him to stay overnight so she could keep an eye on the swelling.

Suvi had come into their lives so easily that his absence made the house feel empty. Funny, Sandy hadn't felt anything like that when they let her come back after carting off Stephen X's body.

Sandy flinched when the phone rang at the usual time that night. The reedy voice said, "We should get together sometime."

"Do I know you?" Sandy snapped.

"You should know me after I helped you with that bad, bad man."

Sandy pressed the phone against her neck for a moment then slammed it in the cradle. She breathed deeply.

The murder had been in the papers and on television forever, making her fair game for every crackpot in the world. A chill played along her spine.

Faceless monsters crowded her life like the zombie hordes in Stephen X's precious tape of *Death of the Damned*. One replaced another after each was destroyed.

Sandy couldn't believe that other people's lives were like this. She felt singled out, like the watches that Wally Conner had put through his stress test. Maybe Sandy's tormentors were just pawns in a much bigger plan, like the destructive forces Wally had used. After all, when Stephen X lost his power over her, he was taken out of the game. So maybe one trial would come after the other until she finally went crazy or died or did whatever it was that all this led to.

She hadn't taken her hand from the phone when it rang again. She jumped back from the wall as the sound pierced the air. "Saury," she called. "Let's take the Mustang for a ride."

Saury came out of his room rubbing his eyes. "Why's the phone ringing, mom?"

"Because it's broken. We're going to go out for a little while so it won't bother us."

She drove around town with the top down for more than an hour, back-tracking and turning at random intersections until she felt safe and alone with Saury and the cool, starry night.

They were about to turn off Westmore onto Rollingwood Drive when the battered pickup came out of nowhere and hugged their bumper. It flashed its brights.

Sandy thought something was wrong with her car so she pulled over and twisted around in the seat. When she squinted to see past the pickup's headlights, she made out the delicate, bird-like features of Uly Bondarbon at the wheel. That's when she connected him with the voice on the phone.

As the door of the pickup began to swing open, Sandy jammed the Mustang into drive and tromped on the gas. The gaudy lights of Westmore flashed by as they never had in all those years she nursed the Impala down this street.

She lost sight of the pickup in her rear view mirror and turned down the dark road that ran along the railroad tracks.

She killed the lights and leaned back against the headrest, listening to the distant rumble of a train.

"What are we doing, mom?" Saury asked with the moonlight filling his wide eyes.

"We're just resting for a few minutes, honey. We'll go home pretty soon."

Sandy tried to blink the road dust out of her eyes. When she opened them, she watched the train's headlight roll across the trees and power lines that ran along the tracks. How could the engineer see where he was going, she wondered, when the light looped around like that?

The freight roared past, rocking the car with its wind. Then she felt the thud of the pickup truck against her rear bumper.

The reedy voice called out over the noise of the train. "You haven't forgotten your good friend, have you, Sandy?"

The Mustang fishtailed through the dirt as it picked up speed. When she straightened out, Sandy flipped on the lights again and drove as hard as the pounding in her chest.

She thought of Artie Sandoval who had even looked a little bit like Uly Bondarbon. He'd killed himself because he loved her, but he knew nothing about her. Nothing. Where did she fit into this creep's fantasies? Why couldn't they all just leave her alone?

When she pulled even with the engine of the train, she dared to glance in the rear view mirror. But with so many bumps jostling the car, she couldn't focus on anything behind her. If she turned her head, her hair whipped across her eyes. The pickup had doused its lights. For all she knew, it sat right on her bumper.

As she moved ahead of the train, she realized she didn't know this road. But there was nowhere else to go now. Sandy reached over and felt the coarse fabric of Saury's seat belt. She ran her hand along it down to the buckle and tugged to make sure it was secure.

The engineer pulled the horn for a crossing.

"Are we having a race?" Saury rocked in his seat.

"Yeah," she said. "Yes, honey." She was afraid to take her eyes off the road, but she didn't have to look to know that Saury sensed the truth in her voice.

The light from the train rolled over the road sign before her headlights picked it up. Just past the crossing, the dirt came to a dead end. She could go straight and be trapped, or she could try to make the crossing. When Sandy glanced over her shoulder to see how far ahead of the train they'd gotten, the corner of her eye caught the shadow of the truck.

The train blared again and its brakes began to wail as Sandy put both feet on the gas. She stole one more glance behind her and caught an impression of the engineer cursing and waving in the dim light of his instruments.

Sandy waited as long as she dared and promised herself not to look down the tracks. She slammed on the brakes and slid into the turn. The Mustang spewed out a great wall of dirt as it swerved up to the crossing. Sandy wrestled the wheel and the car swung past ninety degrees. Her heart shot up in her throat as she found herself facing the train head-on.

The car's back wheel slid off the planks that smoothed out the crossing for traffic. In a crazy, compressed sequence of events, the tire blew when it slammed into the rail. The impact flipped the Mustang into the air. Sandy and Saury rolled through the night sky in a lazy arc that ended with a jolt on the far side of the tracks.

The crash landing snapped Sandy's head back just in time to see the train crushing the pickup into an awkward slab of metal. Sparks exploded from clouds of steam. Then the pitiless force of the machine tossed what was left of the truck into the field.

Sandy lost track of time again as the awful wail of the train's brakes faded into cry of the ambulance.

•

Saury loved an adventure. The implications of the accident—the idea that the truck and train might have been driven by human beings—didn't sink in. He bragged to his friends about what a great driver his mom was.

Sandy envied the way each day could offer something fresh and new at that age.

When she held Saury close, she knew that things would be different for him. He would never have to know the Jack Gores and Stephen X Skinners of the world. Maybe that was Sandy's reward for surviving the stress test.

And it couldn't be too much to hope that the nightmare world she knew would disappear, like a scab that shrinks little by little until you can't tell exactly where the wound was. Already, time seemed to be straightening out for her, heading in one direction.

The police toyed with the idea that Uly Bondarbon had murdered Stephen X. With hindsight, they could have come up with an adequate, twisted motive for him. But there was a problem with the crime scene. Someone Uly's size could not have fired the bullets the forensics people dug out of the wall and the floor. The angles were all wrong.

"Bondarbon wasn't the shooter," the tall detective announced. "The real killer is still out there and we're not going to quit looking for him."

"How do you know it was a man?" Sandy asked.

"What?"

"You said you're still looking for *him*," she said, chalking up a point for herself. "Oh, never mind."

She didn't care if they ever solved the crime, except that maybe somebody ought to thank the guy. With Suvi back home, she didn't worry much anymore about the killer returning. Each day, the dog became a little bit bigger, a little bit more protective, a little more eager to prove his loyalty.

Like the woman with the part-Rottweiler she'd met in the park, Sandy lost her fear. The surprising part was how deeply that fear could weave itself into the fabric of a woman's life. She saw it now in the teenager who spent fifteen minutes fixing her make-up in the ladies room at Burger Castle. She saw it in the way women took their keys out of their purses before they walked into the parking lot at night. She saw it in the way women tried to ignore the rubbernecking men they passed.

Sandy got another promotion and went to work on the day shift. She found that Stephen X had squirreled away some decent assets. Apart from its usefulness, the money made her happy because he couldn't take it with him.

Sandy and Linda began making plans to do something fun on the long weekend. That was why she was expecting to hear Linda when she answered the phone on Tuesday evening.

"Hi!" Sandy said.

"Yeah," said the man's voice. "I'm looking for Marti."

Sandy opened her mouth, but didn't say anything. She lowered the phone from her ear and placed it gently in its cradle as Suvi watched, waiting for her caress.